BLOOD LINE

ANDREW VACHSS

Blood Line
Paperback Edition
Copyright © 2022 Andrew Vachss

Wolfpack Publishing
5130 S. Fort Apache Rd. 215-380
Las Vegas, NV 89148

wolfpackpublishing.com

Paperback ISBN 978-1-63977-246-4
eBook ISBN 978-1-63977-214-3
LCCN 2021950684

WOLFPACK
PUBLISHING
— EST 2013 —

Blood Line
Paperback Edition
© Copyright 2022 Andrew Vachss

Wolfpack Publishing
5130 S. Fort Apache Rd. 215-380
Las Vegas, NV 89148

wolfpackpublishing.com

Paperback ISBN 978-1-63977-241-4
eBook ISBN 978-1-63977-240-7
LCCN 2021953088

For
Steve "The Magician" Wiseman,
who crossed the Finish Line way too soon.

BLOOD LINE

ANYWHERE YOU GO, THERE'S ALWAYS SUCH PLACES. Marked by blacked-out glass or solid-faced fronts, with XXX signals blazing in neon. Some of them add an extra X or two, but they're all the same on the inside.

Usually the neon is stable, but sometimes it strobes softly, most often in shades of red and blue. Sometimes there's a splattering of DVD titles in the windows, but not as often as there was years ago. Always present is the word "Adult," as if it was some gang's sidewalk chalk mark that only those in the know would understand.

They range in size, those places: from narrow slots of storefront all the way to huge free-standing emporiums. Space costs more in the bigger cities. Bigger in population, I mean, not square miles. "Density" it's called, and that varies widely. I've done work in good-sized cities that were pretty much deserted. Plants close down, money dries up, shops go vacant the whole town becomes a building with a hundred years' worth of termites that nobody noticed until it started to crumble. Those who are able to leave, that's what they do. And every one that does adds to the outgoing stampede.

But other cities are just the opposite: they keep adding people until every inch of commercial frontage costs a fortune, even in the parts where it's not smart to walk around after dark.

Different people want different things, and they want them at different times. So most of those XXX stores never close.

The larger ones are built outside the cities, alongside highways where the land's much cheaper than it is downtown. They get the trucker trade that way, and the local people too, especially because there's always plenty of anonymous parking space. Some of those are laid out like malls, only they don't have food courts or retail stores—they're built for different customers. They'll have a motel, a gas station with a lot of diesel pumps, some fast food, even a sit-down diner...All selling products and services you use and dispose of, so I guess the XXX stores fit right in.

In those off-highway locations, there are always hookers working the parking lots. When you see a car sitting in those spots, it's for business. Not just prostitution, other transactions, too. It's as if those pieces of land were zoned for outlaw behavior.

But no matter where they're located or how big they are, XXX shops have so much in common that they look like some branded franchise.

———

THERE'S plenty of other ways to buy the same product. The Internet for sealed downloads or "live participation," cable providers for certain channels, pay-for-view in the motels...even regular mail for people who think one of those box-rental places actually buys privacy. But no matter the competition, what they call the "brick-and-mortar" shops never seem to go out of business.

Maybe that's because some buyers didn't want to leave a trail. Walk in, pay cash, walk out. But for all I know, those places take credit cards now, or even some phone app...anything that could transfer cash instantly. One thing I'm confident of, they wouldn't be taking checks.

But paying cash doesn't make you invisible. There's always a camera over the door with a *Theft Prevention* sign. The XXX stores aren't worried about a stick-up...how much of a take could there be? No, shoplifting, that's what they guard against. That's why those huge round mirrors in the corners, for warnings. And they've also got cameras, buried deep enough so they don't make the customers nervous, the monitors stored somewhere below eye-level behind the register. Some of those registers are behind bulletproof glass like in bad-neighborhood liquor stores, others look just like any other retail shop.

They all pick up information. And all that information is for sale.

A few of the bigger places have live entertainment every so often. Like a nightclub, but it's just porn stars signing pictures, or putting on fetish shows, or modeling underwear that they sell once they take it off. Some places even have old-style peep booths, only with live girls instead of film loops.

The ones that put on shows are more upscale, with a heavy at the door to collect the cover charge. Some even have a "VIP" door with a canopy over it and a parking lot surrounded by chain-link, a guy in a security uniform to watch the cars.

NONE of that matters to me—I never work indoors. And no matter how fancy the front, there's another way out...usually just a fire exit that opens into an unlit alley.

If a customer wants to use that exit, it costs extra, no matter how much he spends inside. If you know what to ask for, the man who works the register will sell you a disc with a number on it. You hand that to another man who's in a chair by that exit door. He looks away while you push it open and walk out by yourself.

I've been outside those places plenty of times. In different cities, different states. Even though I never do inside surveillance, I know I lot about the interiors. I've seen plenty of photographs, and some floor plans, too. But mostly, I just get my information from the people who pay me for my work.

———

PATTERNS. My greatest ally. And my mortal enemy. I watch for patterns with a raptor's eyes. And I avoid falling into them as though they were pits of boiling venom. This work I do, you have to accept that any job might end bad. If it does, you're done. You can plan all you want, be as careful as you can be, but it's still a spin of the wheel every time.

I say spin of the wheel because the usual risks—betrayal, equipment failure, informants—those don't factor in to my work. But there's always the danger of pure random. What some call luck.

Worrying about luck changes the random. It can paralyze you to the point where you won't be able to work at all.

So I don't worry, I plan. Bad luck, that wouldn't be my fault. But falling into a pattern, that would.

———

THIS TARGET DIDN'T HAVE VERY strict habits. He didn't visit every night, never more than once or twice a week. Sometimes, he'd miss a week altogether. No pattern on the surface, but two things were certain: He always came after dark. And he wasn't going to stop coming. Always in early evening, as if he was stopping off for a book to read on the commuter train going home.

I never saw anyone go into one of those places

without wearing a coat of some kind. Even in really hot weather, they'd at least have a jacket. Or one of those vests with a lot of pockets. This target always wore a topcoat to the knees, carried one of those fancy leather messenger bags by the handle...never used the shoulder strap. He looked like he could be a lawyer or an accountant, but I didn't know what he did. Or what he'd done for me to be waiting for him.

None of that mattered. It never does.

I KNEW the target never stayed long, but I didn't want to wait at the back door. Even though I knew there were no cameras out there, I didn't want a body dropped so close. So I set up across the street.

The kind of place I like best for my work is a neighborhood where people work for a living. Not a lot of street activity after dark, and what there was would make an effort not to look at anyone else. Prowl cars doing dull sweeps. Doors shut. Blinds down. No restaurants, no movie theaters. No lounging on the corners, no domino games outside barbershops, no homeless setting up for the night. No bars, no poolrooms, no gangbangers claiming the block with their tags.

THE TARGET STEPPED out through the back door. From watching all those other nights, I knew he'd walk to the far corner, turn there, then head back to wherever he could find a taxi. Or maybe wherever he told the Uber to meet him...I'd never followed him that far.

I was moving in the target's flow, using the background as a container, angling to cut him off. He was looking straight ahead, head tilted down a bit. As we crossed paths, I shot him twice in the chest. His legs went away. I stepped close, saw he was already gone. Probably. I shot him in the forehead. Then I went back to walking, keeping to the same rhythm.

The shots had been loud. To my ears, anyway. But that was because I'd been so close. Nobody's ever sure they actually hear gunshots. Car backfires, some idiot setting off fireworks, TV turned up too loud...people always question themselves about sounds. The longer they hesitate, the less sure they are. Especially if no more sounds come.

I kept walking, sliding the black wool watch cap with the long red hair extensions off my head as I moved through a shadow, stuffing it into a side pocket in the same motion. As I turned a corner, I reached over my right shoulder and grabbed the tab on the vinyl square stuck to the back of my coat. I pulled the tab, circling my arm over my right shoulder, moving my hand under my left arm and inside my coat. The Japanese flag—a red circle on a white background—peeled off and vanished. I'd practiced that so many times I wasn't even conscious of doing it.

I didn't toss the pistol. I never do, even though it would have my prints on it [even though it wouldn't have prints?]. I never put on latex before I work—that's exactly the kind of thing people notice. Anyway, I was carrying two other pistols, so I wouldn't pass a pat-down if I got stopped.

I wouldn't stand for one, either.

"YOU CAN'T JUST WALK AWAY."

That pronouncement echoes everywhere, as though it came from some holy book. Pure truth, beyond any man's dispute.

It's gospel that those who employ men like me have contacts and connections everywhere. Tendrils reaching out to every last outpost on earth.

"You can run, but you can't hide."

You can see how such a belief gained momentum. Maybe it was different once, but now, nobody's ever really alone. Trackers and targets alike, we're all surrounded. CCTV never sleeping, everyone's cell phones permanently set to live-stream just in case something happens that could fulfill their dreams of going viral, the entire Internet mass-uploading to some pregnant cloud always ready to give birth.

All conversation is monitored, every keystroke recorded. Privacy voluntarily surrendered for free toys and lying promises; all just a mouse-click away from dark-web browsers, "private" messaging, podcasts instructing on everything from hiding from the government to stalking the ex-girlfriend that same government ordered you to stay away from.

The Internet is as science-pure as objectivity itself. It's all neutral...and all there to be used. Every movement displaces molecules, makes a sound, triggers a switch, leaves a trace. There's always a network, working.

Registering every trip of the wire, every tear of the fabric.

And none of that's new. It's always been that way. Whether high-tech or primitive doesn't matter...because there's no such thing as a secret.

Every sound flows into some grapevine, goes out on some version of tribal drums.

What's not for sale gets stolen...and sold. Information has always been the hardest currency, be it behind-hand whispered or block-chained. People who set out to mine bitcoins end up being mined for their data.

Rumors could be true. The whole idea of "truth" could be a rumor. But I know this much for sure: I do what was done before me. For me. Then by me. And I'm finally done with that part of the job. My retirement plan is in motion. Now all that's left is to make sure the line continues.

———

EVEN WHEN I'M not working, I have to be by myself most of the time. So when I'm not reading, I watch a lot of movies. Never pay-for-view, never rentals, nothing that leaves a trace—just whatever's on TV for free at any place I'm staying. I'm not picky—there's always something playing.

From watching so many, I know that a movie praised for its raw realism isn't real, it's a movie about real. Some of the movie's true—because some of everything always is—but the "You can't just walk away" part, that's just some screenwriter's line. You're only in that movie if you buy the ticket.

———

I KNOW this because I did just that—walked away. And that was years ago. By now, anyone I did work for knows I never spoke a word about that work. Not to anyone, ever. They know because no one ever came to them about any job I did. Not the law looking to take them in, not some maybe-traitor looking for a payday, not someone on the other side looking to even the score.

They know. Nobody else matters.

————

AFTER THE FIRST few years of silence—their reach-out calls to the middleman never returned, dead-drop messages never picked up, coded online ads never answered—they would have assumed some job I'd done had turned out bad. And each of them would figure that as a job I'd done for someone else.

Me they'd figure for dismantled. Not just dead: taken apart, ground into powder, acid-dipped, dispersed beyond DNA.

Anything less than that, they would have heard. About me, or even from me, if I got desperate enough. If I'd been taken down by law, even if I was supermaxed, I could still get a message to at least one of them. But if I did that, no matter what words I used, they'd take the message as a threat.

They didn't know me, so they didn't know if I was a genius or a moron, a person thinking for myself or someone's robot. But that wouldn't matter.

They wouldn't expect me to make contact, because smart or stupid, I'd still know their next move: they only had the one. The minute they had me located, I'd be a staked-out goat.

But even if I had stayed silent as a scorpion, I'd still be carrying the poison. So they would have wanted to know if I was alive. Wanted to know badly.

"Dead men don't talk."

Another movie. Because the people who made them dead, people like me, they could talk. And anyone they hired to make me quiet, they could talk, too. Those old sayings only survived because they held some truth to them. I remember a character in one of those movies, saying: "If there's a thread hanging loose, takes only a little pull to turn it into a noose." So those employers, they would have checked as carefully as they could. Gone as deep as their own pockets.

But looking isn't the same as finding. Police records aren't perfect, even though they're shared a lot more than they were years ago. Computers make it easy. Easier, anyway. But that wouldn't help them—none of the linkages would work without a name. All the other stuff—date of birth, social security, race, skin color, height, weight, scars/marks/tattoos—that was as keyed to arrests as the mug shots. So no matter how good their connections, they'd still need a name, one that would match prints in records.

And, for me, they don't have any of that. I'd never been arrested. I couldn't ever be—that was part of my job, never to be taken as I worked. No one who ever hired me had ever met me—everything went through the middleman. And even if someone had gotten to him, he couldn't have told them much—he'd never seen me himself. The most he could have given up would have been some worthless recordings. Worthless because even if the middleman had kept safety tapes and turned them over for voiceprinting, the clip-on harmonizer I always spoke into would turn those into garble.

Individually, the employers might have little bits and pieces of info, but the people who hired men like me never share information. No matter what the movies call "commissions" or "combines," the people who hire me never really work together. The truth is just the opposite —otherwise, I wouldn't always have had work to do.

If life was a movie, one of those who hired me might have wanted to know who I was bad enough to put some of their own men on the same target. Not for a killing, just to watch. That way, they'd see me doing the work...maybe even take pictures of it. Then they'd have a hold on me. And they could make sure I never worked for anyone else.

But that wasn't possible. I never took a job with a time limit on it. And I passed up plenty of jobs that people wanted to hire me for without them ever knowing why. The way we worked it, the middleman would tell whoever wanted the work done that he'd have to ask around, see if anyone was available. While he was doing that—pretending to do that, really—I'd be looking over the job myself.

That was one of the tricks we used. The middleman didn't have a whole stable of killers on call, just me. As soon as I told the middleman I could do the work, he'd tell them, and the deal would be made. By then, I'd already know I could do it, because I would have been in place for long enough to be sure.

The middleman would tell whoever contacted him that I'd need some time to scope out the job. Two-three weeks, minimum. So if they were having the target watched, they probably wouldn't even get started before I was finished. And gone.

But I guess that didn't always work. In fact, I know one time for sure it didn't work, because the middleman told me later that a witness I'd had to kill had been working for whoever was paying me.

The target was locking up his store for the night, the same way he always did, pulling the solid metal gate down in front of his little pawn shop. He had two more workers inside, but they'd leave by the back door in a couple more hours. I guess, being the boss, he could go home early every night.

It wasn't as if you could set your watch by it, but the metal gate was sure to be down sometime between eleven and half-past. I already knew all the cameras were inside, and that the owner had to turn his back to the street when he locked the gate.

I had a furnished room only a block away. The kind of dump where you don't get fresh sheets—if you didn't keep the place clean, that was the next guy's problem.

Clean wasn't a problem for me—I had another room about a half-mile away, the room I slept in during the days.

Every night, I went out for a walk around ten. I didn't walk far, just to wherever I had parked the car I was using the night before. I'd take whatever I'd need for the work out of the car, and stroll around in a tight circle, keeping an eye on the pawn shop. I didn't even need to be that close—the metal gate made a racket every time he rolled it down to lock up and I'd have plenty of time to move in.

I needed the street clear to do the work. When I heard the gate start down, I moved over and got ready, the same way I had every night before. I thought I'd scanned the area close enough, but I was wrong. As I was moving away from the body, I caught a flash of light just past the corner. I had to make a quick choice, move toward it or go the other way. I was already in motion, so I closed the distance fast.

The man was just standing there. I never knew what caused the flash. Maybe his wristwatch, maybe his cell phone camera. He stood there like he was stuck to the ground—I guess he was surprised I was coming at him, and he didn't know exactly what to do. Maybe he even planned on following me, I thought much later.

I don't shoot random witnesses, but I was already way too close to that man. I guess I don't know exactly what I was thinking, but I had two shots into him quick. When I put the close-up round into his head, I saw his face, but it didn't mean anything to me.

I kept walking to my car, drove to the room I'd been living in, grabbed my stuff, and was gone in minutes. Since I was paid a week ahead, nobody would be curious enough to so much as knock on that door until the rent was due.

Weeks later, the middleman told me the papers had it down as a mob hit, because both victims were connected to the same organization. That's how I knew the people who hired me had sent someone to watch me work.

———

SO ANY SEARCH for me would come down to what it always does: not how much you have, how much of it you're willing to spend. Whether it's time or money, you can't play if you don't ante, and no one was going to empty their vault to find a ghost. Even a lock hand still comes down to how much patience you're holding.

I think about playing cards a lot. I believe I'd like to do that, but I never had any other people I could play with. I've watched horse racing on TV, but I never went to the track either, not even to work. Racetrack payrolls are huge, and all in cash, so there's always someone watching. And plenty of cameras to help them do that.

In the world I slipped through, those who got caught usually lacked the patience to go whatever distance was dropped on them. They find themselves looking at serious time and decide they can't do it. If you believe the movies, "He couldn't wait for the gate" is what they put on the tombstones of anyone who informs. But plenty haven't waited, and they're still walking around.

How do I know? Because I've seen them on TV, selling their books. And in all the years I worked, I was never hired to kill one of them.

I guess some of the employers would be extra careful, maybe use someone like me only once, then throw them away like one of those disposable cigarette lighters. But that only works if they know who they hired.

That's the equation our tribe works by: They don't know us, and we don't know them. I never knew why that one employer had sent someone to watch me, but it seemed just...wrong. Stupid, even. What could they hope to get...a quick look at me working, maybe some blurry camera snap?

Anything they could get from that, I could change.

The way I added it up, even if any of my past employers played it perfectly: spent the money, called in the favors, paid the bribes, waited for results and triple-checked whatever came back...they'd still be looking in an empty room. They'd never found any of those who came before me, and our line has been going on longer than any of those who ever hired us. Our tribe existed generations before any of their "families." No one can know us, because we don't even know each other.

MY BEST GUESS was they weren't looking. None of them. Not anymore.

The smarter ones would do the math. Even if I had been tapped on the shoulder, even if I had traded names

I knew for a new one of my own, who could I give up? Every contract I ever worked had been middle-manned, so I only had...what? Targets? And I'd already made sure those wouldn't be talking.

Did the middleman have employer's names? I wouldn't think so.

Probably just numbers to burners that had been burned—used once, and then only in places other than where they'd been purchased. Mail addresses that were either one-time use or public places for drops.

Oh, a smart middleman who was building ammunition for his future could make some good guesses, maybe put together who wanted some particular man dead. But the only middleman I'd ever used was in a place where they couldn't reach him. Left the business by one of the two roads such a life always ended at: aged out or taken out.

That was how we all did it. The fairest way. Even if I had wanted to talk, I didn't know any more about the people who hired me than they knew about me.

If names had been dropped, the ones who got named, they'd be the ones who dropped. Bosses aren't immune to what made them bosses. But not one of them was doing time because of anything I'd ever said.

How would they know that for sure? Easy. For me to have earned immunity from contract killings, I would have had to testify. If I did, even talking from behind a screen or with my face blanked out on some TV monitor wouldn't have shielded me—the testimony itself would have been a flaming arrow over my head. Pointing down.

That never happened. I did a lot of work for a lot of years, and the only sign blinking over all those jobs was "Open Investigation." The details were all buried in some police files, colder than a row of unmarked graves.

THERE'S no statute of limitations on the work I did, so the Law could be looking forever. Looking for the triggerman, looking for who hired the job done. But it had been a lot of years, and not one of those who paid me had ever been connected to what they'd paid me to do.

The truth is that there are plenty of unsolved homicides on the books in every jurisdiction. What matters isn't the bodies, it's the stats. That's why the cops have a label to slap on the cases where they've never made an arrest—"Exceptional Clearance." That means they know who did the crime, but either they don't have enough evidence to make an arrest or the DA nixed prosecution —the only stat prosecutors really care about is their conviction rate. That's what DAs run on when the machine says it's their turn. The only way to never lose a case is to always bet the chalk in a one-horse race.

But cold storage isn't always an option for law enforcement. If a case is media-churned enough, it can't be dumped in a dead file. Some cases have to be worked, because they never go away. Any unsolved homicide is a potential TV show, especially if websites spring up and those "true crime" fans get involved.

If the media stays on a case, the police can't do otherwise...especially if it becomes movie material. Serial killers get the most play—the game of "identifying" The Zodiac will always have players—but even a one-off killing will still get worked if the spotlight stays on. Whoever killed the Black Dahlia must be long dead himself by now, but new "leads" still get coverage. Cable TV is so starved for product that any headline-worthy crime will stay alive forever. Entertainment spurs investigation, so Jack The Ripper is immortal.

My work was never high-profile enough to matter like that. Some of it got covered, sure...with silly labels plastered all over the news. "Gangland" is always good for a headline. When the dead are "known to law enforcement," out come the charts and graphs for the press conferences.

Those make pretty visuals for those experts who pop up on an hour's notice when any TV shows calls. But coverage like that only fuels speculation, not solutions.

Even a "mob assassination" is a story without legs unless someone talks. Someone who actually knows, not some opinion-slinger. Eventually, all those stories turn into a stupid joke, like those about where Jimmy Hoffa isn't buried. Everybody has something to say, nobody listens.

Without media attention, there's no fires burning hot enough to thaw most cold cases. A teenage girl that disappears, that's the kind of story trash TV can feed off endlessly. Maybe she's a "sex slave" in some under-ground dungeon, maybe she was "trafficked"...Any story that could have one of those endings allows the same news outlets who crusade against porn to profit off it. For balance, they can always show clips of the grieving parents every "anniversary." And if the girl turns up dead, Internet pages will spring up to host virtual vigils and show pictures of street memorials with fresh flow-ers...usually attached to funding requests for proper funeral services and a nice coffin. But even those slimy TV shows they call "re-enactments" wouldn't bother unless the victim was juicy enough.

They wouldn't be calling in the FBI to look at the jobs I did, because the only thing they had in common was the pattern. The missing one. What did they have to connect me? I'd killed a number of people over the years.

Always with a firearm, and always at close range. But no profiler was going to add that up to the work of some serial killer. The only motive they could pull out was that the killer intended to make the targets dead.

Even if they somehow connected the faint dots, what did they have to work with? The targets were never young women. Never children, either. No bondage-abductions, no sex acts on the victims, no symbols painted on the bodies, no cryptic messages for the hobbyists to decode.

My work would never attract those twitchy freaks who get excited associating themselves with famous crimes, like that skin-crawling creature who held a press conference to claim he was in the basement when Jon-Benet Ramsey had been killed. All that "confession" got him was a free plane ride from Thailand to California. All it got the police was some overtime.

In my work, the "code of the underworld" is just another movie. Truth is, there's no rules about who to kill. Or how to get it done. Some organizations will machine-gun whole families just to send a message, some leave their messages with cut-out tongues or cut-off testicles. Some use bombs without a thought to the collaterals. Some like fire. Some torture before they finish the jobs. Some capture it all on their cell phones so they can watch it again and again. Or put in on the Internet.

But none of those organizations hire out their work, so I was never asked to do anything beyond making someone dead. I was never asked not to, either—all the employer ever wanted was a result.

You see how I said "asked", not "told?" The middleman would let me know what was on offer. If I didn't like it, he'd pass word that I was on another job. In another country. Could be months before I'd be back.

Passing up a job, that never caused a problem for me. I wasn't a prospect; I wasn't a guy looking for a way to prove himself. I was freelance, an outsider to outlaws. No affiliations, no ambition. I didn't want to join, so I wasn't a threat to move up. I didn't make anyone nervous.

Nobody wanted to see my face. I didn't want to see theirs, either. The idea that real gangsters never inform on the people they use, that's another movie.

So I never met the people who hired me. Never took any direct assistance from them, either. No fingers, no spotters, no cover fire, no drivers. The man who taught me to do the work also taught me that the people who paid you to make someone dead could pay someone else, too.

I always picked my jobs with great care. I didn't have rigid rules, but there was always work I wouldn't do. I wouldn't kill a man of a different race if just getting close enough to him would make me stand out. That's why I passed on a target who never left the back of a barbershop. How you look is important, so it's important that you don't look any special way. My father told me to always dress nicely—

I don't mean a suit and tie, son, what I'm saying, no matter the neighborhood, you can never look homeless. The cops might want to question you, some social worker could get nosy, some nasty kids might want to set you on fire...You never want to look like a victim. And you don't want to look like a hunter, either.

—but there are places where I couldn't blend no matter how I dressed, so I always passed on those jobs.

As for those who actually paid the money, they were never in my life.

Some bosses are smart. Some are stupid. Some crazy. Any of those might decide to cut any ties between themselves and what they paid to get done. I never met any of them, so I wouldn't know. But I know nobody cuts a cord they can't find.

If there was any information I needed—photos of the target, home/work, girlfriend's addresses, cars he drove, clubs he visited, stuff like that—the person doing the hiring could send it to where the middleman could find it. By the time I picked up a message to call, all that would be done. I didn't care how they worked it, so long as I was never in it. In all the years I worked, I never met a boss. No boss ever saw me.

I've got no contacts, no connections. If there was a price on me, I didn't know it.

And I didn't know any reason why there should be.

I WAS NEVER A MECHANIC. I don't know how to rig brakes to fail or packages to explode. I'm not a martial artist. I never worked with blades.

I was just a shooter. Usually very up-close. Never more than the width of an alley. And even when I first fired from a distance, I always finished right next to the target.

THERE'S nothing special about my work; no trick to it. No great skill either. Only the commitment: All or nothing. Once I started a job, it was the same as it being finished. Only two outcomes: fall into place or fall apart.

I can't be the only one doing this work. They're still looking for whoever walked up behind the Prime Minister of Sweden on a public street, gunned him down, and walked away. No cyanide-tipped bullets, no created diversions, no dropping some untraceable pistol on the ground. That killing happened thirty-some years ago, and nobody's been caught yet.

Dead bodies, dead trails. "Why?" only matters to cops who believe motive is always a trail-marker. Was the shooter some lunatic with a personal grievance? An assassin working for a cartel...or part of a cabal? Politics? Business? Revenge?

After all these years, it's just another movie script, still waiting on an ending.

I'm no sniper, no rifleman at all. Still, for what I did, patience was a weapon. Cutting down risk, there's more than one meaning to that. If a target had a bodyguard, that made two targets. I never left a target alive, never left forensics, never used the same weapon twice.

———

I WORKED AS ALONE as it gets. Having a whole network, that's more movie stuff: the gunsmith who custom-crafts the firearms; the inside-info guys who tell you where the target's going to be taking a walk alone some night; the safe houses for you to hole up afterwards. Oh sure, all that probably exists, especially if an organization wants to keep everything in-house, like the IRA. But every single individual link in that chain is a potential informant. Ask the IRA.

If an informant is a member of a crime organization,

the movies call them rats. If the organization is the government, the newspapers call them whistleblowers.

That's where patience played such a role in my work. I took money to make people dead, but I never accepted a deadline.

———

IT WAS NEVER hard to get firepower. I don't just mean easy for me; it's not hard for anyone. When guns are sold through what's called a "private sale," there's no background check required. Those outdoor gun shows always have plenty of private sellers looking for private buyers. But going that route would take you a long time to put together a deep supply. And those gun show sales expose you to the risk of personal contact. The seller could be someone keeping notes in case he ever needed a card to lay down on the table next to his plea deal. The whole show could even be an ATF operation, trolling for buyers already on their list.

So you look for a bundler. One of those guys who keeps track of all the coming shows. A smart bundler floods those shows with strawman buyers who take all the risks and get paid per transaction, like they were on commission. What the bundler wants is to build a whole warehouse full of untraceable firearms, to be sold off in bulk lots.

That's the word they put around, anyway. But those guns, most of them have a history. You buy from a no-paper dealer, you could be buying dirty merchandise. Not just used, but used in a murder too many agencies wanted to solve.

So I never dropped a gun at the scene. Any one I used, I'd leave in some other town. Nothing complicated

—I'd just wipe them down and drop them. In a commercial dumpster or a city recycling bin. Or more out in the open: a pass-through alley, under a freeway overpass. Once when I was really pressed for time, in a mailbox.

They'd be found...but probably never turned in to the law. By the time those guns ever reached a police lab—if they ever did—they wouldn't bounce back on me; they'd just confuse whatever database they went into.

Of course, if the government got the chance and put in the effort, it was always possible it could trace one of those guns back to the original private-sale guy. Who could he give up, some shill? Still, those kind always talk. And if they got to the bundler, he wouldn't be any more silent than the chain of people who'd given him up.

Not much chance of all that happening, but our work is based on trusting no one but ourselves. The window of risk is open only when we actually do the work. Other times, we keep those windows closed behind blackout curtains. And nail them shut.

That's why my father and I killed three of those bundlers. We always got them to meet with us by offering big-score money for a heavy package. But my father made it clear it had to be them in person, not some agent. My father trusted them, of course...but not some hired hand. That's what he would always tell them. Of course, if they wanted to have a bodyguard on hand, that was fine with him. Just business. Hell, he was bringing his own kid along, wasn't he?

That's how I did my first one. My father wanted to make sure I was ready, and he needed the test to be in a safe place, where he could watch over me. And be ready in case I failed. I knew that last part, but neither of us ever said it out loud.

"Do these things really work?" my father asked the

bundler, holding up the suppressor the seller wanted to add to the package.

"The top-quality ones," the bundler said, his voice muscled with confidence. He stood with his legs braced, handling one of the suppressors like it was a valuable work of art. He had a shaved head, costumed in red suspenders over a white shirt, black cargo pants, a heavy belt with a knife sheath attached, boots with red laces. "If the barrel's threaded correctly, and the device is built right, you won't hear much more than a loud pop. You can bring down the sound even more if you go sub-sonic on the loads, but you have to be real good to get a good result, if you know what I mean."

"Any way we could test one?" my father asked.

"Sure," the bundler said, screwing the suppressor into the barrel of what he said was "your basic ghetto piece" and giving it to my father. He raised his eyebrows when my father handed the little gun to me, twitched his lips a little, said "Down in the basement, we've got a—"

I shot him in the face.

He'd been exaggerating—even with the suppressor, the gunshot was louder than he'd boasted...maybe because we were indoors. I stepped closer, shot him twice more.

My father and I loaded all the guns and ammunition into the car we were using that day—a pickup with a camper-topped bed over a false bottom—and drove away.

Whenever the law got around to finding the bundler, the bullets in his head wouldn't help them—we took that pistol along with us. The suppressor, too.

———

BY THE THIRD ONE, word got around that gun-bundling wasn't such a safe business to be in, and the major players got anxious enough to pay for serious protection. So we just walked away from that tactic. Anyway, by then, I had enough firearms to work way past my whole term, however long that might last. My father was supposed to add to the supply whenever he got the chance while I was away, but I don't know if he ever did.

That didn't matter—I never came close to running out.

We couldn't keep those guns at our place. "We always stay search proof," my father told me. "If the police ever come around here, it won't be because of any of the work we did. It'll be an accident. Some mistake they made, some bad information they got fed, some suspicion they have. But it will never be because of the work."

"How do you know?" I'd asked him.

"If what we do ever gets to the law, they won't be coming with any search warrant," he told me. "And it wouldn't be locals, either."

"Federals?"

"A whole lot of federals," he told me. "And they won't be looking for guns. They'll be looking for me. Or for you, if I'm gone by then."

EVEN IF WE'D had a perfect hiding place for the guns on our property, it wouldn't have been of any use. Once I left, I couldn't come back until my father was gone, and I'd need to keep replenishing the stock after every job or two while I was out.

Storage units all come with problems. Some are better than others, but being better at keeping out thieves and vandals and homeless people looking for squatting space also made them better at security. Some used patrols, some used cameras. Some even used dogs. And they kept records, too. Bills had to be paid. On top of all that, there was no longevity guarantee—land is eventually worth money, no matter where it is. "Any time less than forever is too short," my father said. He said that all the time.

Finding some old house way out in the country wasn't any better an idea. Anything you don't protect gets used. Could be teens who want a party house, travelers who want out of the weather, crazies who get excited watching the flames of fires they set...

Safe deposit boxes have sign-in sheets. And even if we could get around that, we would have needed dozens and dozens of them...plus banks without metal detectors.

Junkyards get picked over. Every square inch. People looking for some rare part or something worth a lot more money than it looked like to whoever threw it away.

Not all trailer parks have cameras, but they all have people who spend a lot of their lives watching out their windows.

That had all been thought through before I came. My father told me the whole story on the day's drive over to our storage unit. He showed it to me way past closing, when the gates were locked. Access hours were 6:00 a.m. to midnight, posted all around the property.

We went in after my father de-activated the alarms and turned off the cameras. "You don't have to be skilled when you have the keys," he told me. He said things like that all the time, too.

We drove to the middle of three units he told me

would always be on the books as "rented," then parked our car in the empty one to the left.

Inside the middle one sat a rusted-out '57 Chevy Bel-Air two-door hardtop, neatly backed in. Someone's restoration project that they'd never gotten around to finishing, all kinds of parts scattered around as if the owner was coming back any day. Plenty of floor space behind the back bumper. My father rolled up the layers of plastic matting enough to work the lock that opened the path down to the cave that had been hand-dug and cross-braced like it was a diamond mine. Took years, he told me. His father had started it, and he himself had been working on it for years, even after I came.

That diamond mine was ours. A corporation owned the property, and my father was that corporation. The lawyer set it all up, and it turned a profit every year. Paid the taxes on that, too. Part of my inheritance.

That's where the firepower was stored, packed in white grease, waiting. I'm not one of those who love their guns, but I respect tools well enough to keep them clean, and I always test them before I use them. The diamond mine doesn't transmit sound above ground—we'd tested that ourselves.

ID is another thing. I never needed that to work, but I needed it for when I was finished working. Finished for good, I mean. There's plenty who traffic in that product, but those are techno-savvy people who keep records of everything—the opposite of the gun bundlers. So I never went near any of them. I had the best ID there is—a real one, my own. One only I knew.

"YOU CAN NEVER COME BACK HERE," the man who taught me said, just after I turned nineteen. "Not to stay. Not until it's time for you to continue the line on your own. I'll keep your ID active—renew your driver's license, buy things with your credit card every once in a while...you know. I'll do that for as long as I can. Same with taxes—I can generate a W-2 for you right out of this business, so you'll be good with IRS and Social Security. I'll pay by check, too—that's why you signed so many of them, with different pens. I'll fill the amounts and all in with a Pantograph. Adds another layer to the cover.

"You're not going to vote, but that doesn't mean anything—plenty around here don't bother."

"Why don't they?" I asked him.

"THIS IS A LOCKED-UP TOWN," my father told me. "Most of the people, they're honest enough, but they know part of this place—especially near the river that borders us off—there's houses where you can buy a woman's time. Or play any gambling game you want—big-stakes poker to casino stuff.

"Dope is around, too, but only the softer stuff. If you want to deal it, you need a license from the people in charge. Anything that's against the law, you can find it here, if you know where to look. And that's no secret. Not from anyone, including the police."

"If everybody knows, why don't they—"

"BECAUSE IT ALL WORKS," he told me. "There's almost no amateur crime around here, and what there is, the police handle just fine. Punk kids stealing cars, junkies breaking into places to steal whatever they can find, drunks who beat their wives...stuff that goes on everywhere.

"But here, where we are, this is a safe place to live. A quiet, safe place. And that's what folks want. Most don't want to gamble, or drink after-hours, or buy a woman's time...but they don't get worked up about those who do. What they don't want is street crime. They don't want home invaders; they don't want drive-by shootings, they don't want gang wars. And the worst crimes aren't the ones any of them see, anyway."

"The worst?"

"WHAT PEOPLE—SOME people—do to children inside their own houses.

The rest of the people know those things happen, but they comfort themselves with believing that they don't happen around here...as if we had the same protection from such things as the stores who pay off to keep their places from getting their windows busted or set on fire. They pay for that protection, and, for them, it's just the cost of doing business. What other people do—do to their own children, in their own houses—that's their own business, understand?"

"No," I told him. "What we do—"

"What we do is what we do, son," my father cut in. "We're not here to change the big things. We're not here to change the laws, or change the way people think. We're here to take from Them. And what we take, we make one of Us. That's why we're here, our whole tribe."

"So even if we knew—"

"We don't know," my father said. "We mind our own

business. We mind our own business so we can do our own business. That's all."

But I couldn't let it alone. "All the police here, they're crooked?" I asked.

"You mean, do they know this is a locked-up town? Sure. That's what I was explaining to you before, about a lot of folks around here not bothering with voting. There's really only one party. Whoever runs for DA, or to be a judge, or a Town Councilman or...It doesn't matter—there's only one real candidate, every time. What's the point of betting if you know the fight's fixed?

"But the police, just because they know how things work, doesn't mean they're all in on it. And if you look at our crime statistics, you'd see what I mean about this town being a safe place. The police here, they're holy hell on all kinds of crime. Not just tough with their hands and nightsticks, they're supposed to have some real good investigators, too."

"So those investigators, they just look the other way?"

"I guess you could put it like that. But don't be judging them for it. Remember, they grew up here, too. They solve crimes. They catch criminals. And when they do, those criminals get prosecuted. Convicted. Sent away.

"It's like a...balance. The people who really run this town, they're smart. Smart enough not to be greedy. Don't we have good roads, a fire department with the best equipment, a nice little hospital, good schools...all the things people really want? So some people want to...do illegal things, so what? There's illegal things that don't really hurt anyone.

"Take the dope, for example. You think anyone actually gives a damn about junkies shooting poison into their veins? No. What they care about is what those junkies have to do to get the money to buy that dope. And that word's been out a long, long time: Whatever those junkies have to do to get their money, they better not do it here.

"It's like there's a...truce of some kind. The people that run this town— actually run it, I mean—they don't do anything that would bother the people who live here. And the people who live here...well, they live in peace, see?"

I nodded that I did see. And my father went back to explaining more about the work I was to do.

"You travel a lot, but you always come back to visit," he said. "No one sees you doesn't mean you weren't here. And if someone thinks they did catch a glimpse of you, so much the better. You've got your own life, sure, but no reason why you couldn't come back for a visit, stay a while."

I didn't say anything, waiting for him to tell me the rest.

"We're done now, you and me. Things can't ever be the way they were before you left. That means you can't call, can't write letters, nothing like that. If you end up captured, you need help, you know how to get word to me. That doesn't happen—and it shouldn't, if you follow all I taught you—then you don't come in for good until you're called."

I knew my father was just saying "captured" to soften the truth.

Because that was a core lesson: We might get killed doing the work, but we never get captured. I just nodded, to let him know I understood. I didn't want to talk, not then.

"Once every few months—it doesn't have to be on a schedule or anything—you send a card. Doesn't matter what the card is, birthday or anniversary or holi-day...doesn't have to match anything. Don't sign it, and never send it from anyplace you worked. I just need to know you're...still working."

"If I'm not?"

"Then I have to find the next one. Me, I'll have to, because, that happens, it won't be you that does."

"Okay."

"Alright," he said, watching my face. "Now, that call, calling you back in, I mean, it'll only come once. You watch the local paper—you can do that from a distance, easy enough. What you'll be looking for is an obituary. I'm not important enough for them to publish one on their own, so I left the money with the lawyer—you know who I'm talking about, you met him a couple of times. The lawyer, he'll make sure my obit gets published, so you'll see it.

"Now when you see that, figure you've got six months or so to get back here. It could be quicker, you want; but it shouldn't be longer. I left you the shop—it won't be worth anything, 'specially because you never did get the hang of it—all you want is the house and the land. There'll be money in the will; I don't know how much, exactly. But the cash, you know where that's kept. So you come back here, slide right into the life. This life. However many years you've been gone, that won't matter. Understand?"

I nodded. He was right—I'd never learned how to build the custom birdhouses he sold all over the country, mail order. Or so people thought. He always kept a couple of dozen around, in case any of the locals wanted to buy. Or some tourist who saw the sign at the end of the property. When he ran short, he just ordered a bunch of them. Then he'd rough them up a bit, maybe hand-paint them, swap a few pieces, make some little changes. Put them up on the shelves in the shop for anyone who stopped by.

In all the years I was with him, I never asked a lot of questions. I remember I did once. Asked the one question that was always on my mind: "Why?"

"That's how I got here," he told me. "A man I didn't know got me as a foster kid. From that place where they were keeping me. He could have been...He could have been anything, for all the questions they asked him. When I got you it was from some people who had adopted you. And they never asked me anything. "When it was my time, I went to work. When my father died, I was finished working. Just like when I do, you'll be."

"There's still—"

"The rest of that 'Why?' is so that you carry it on. Things are different now, but not so much. You find a little child—a baby if that's all that's available—you bring him into the business—into our life—just like I did you. And after you're gone, that grown-up child, he'll keep it going. Might seem like it's not much, but, every time, that'll be one more they won't get. One more who won't make more of them."

I was young when I'd asked him the "Why?" But I already knew who "they" were. Knew what "them" meant.

———

COVER STORIES ARE JUST THAT. Stories. They won't stand up to bright light.

And they're never informant-proof. So when I left home to do my work, I needed other work. Actual work. "People don't like drifters," my father told me. "Never did, no matter where they passed through or what they were called. Tramps, hobos, bums, gypsies...always travelers. Nobody trusts them, either."

I kept quiet, knowing by his tone that more was coming.

"You've got ID. Real ID. That's like a trail marker, so you can't be dropping it where some tracker might stumble across. But there's such a thing as a false trail, too. So you never carry your ID while you're doing jobs. But when you're doing your cover, you're never without it."

"What would that cover be?"

"I've been thinking about that one a lot," my father said. "You can't be a painter, not any kind of an artist at all. At first, I thought that might work: You could just slap paint on canvas, tell people you do abstracts, something like that. But there's too much stuff to carry around, too many supplies that would dry up or wear out. Comes down to too many questions asked, and you wouldn't have the answers.

"A photographer, now that was good enough for me. Anyone who asked, I was putting together this book, showing the difference between places, showing how they were all the same, really. Just a line of nonsense. I didn't even need more than a roll of film—mailed the rest back home for processing, see? But that wouldn't work today. The serious camera people, they carry a lot of equipment...everyone else uses their cell phones."

"Couldn't I say that?"

"Cell phone camera? I don't think so. Those people, they all take those pictures just to show them off. Not to people they actually know, just...people. Most of the pictures they take are of themselves, I think. So someone might ask you where's your website or whatever those're called now. Worse, someone might see you using a phone for that and think you're part of their club. They'll want to look at your phone, see all your pictures, show you theirs. No, that's out. We've got to use something that could keep you on the road for years. A project, like."

"On the road?"

"Moving, like I said. Always moving. After you do the work, you leave. You never stay in any one place too long, and you never come back to any place you've been. You'll see the country—I saw a lot of it when I was out—but the only home you'll ever have is right here."

"What if I—"

"There's no 'if' for us, son," my father told me. "That's the hardest part of the job. You can't make a friend. You can't fall in love. You can't walk a different path from the one you start on. Not while you're out, anyway."

"So I never—"

"I can't say that." My father spoke that way: Flat, but not cold—the way you'd explain how to fix a carburetor or stack a load of lumber. "The way it comes out is like this: You get a childhood—and yours is well past, now—you give up being a young man—and then, when you're truly grown, you give a childhood to someone who wouldn't have one otherwise."

"Like you did me."

"Like I did you. We take from them, one at a time. But once that's done, we could...I don't know, anything at all. Make friends, get married...I'm...Hell, I'm no one to be telling you, son. Me, I never did any of that. Maybe because it took me a good while before I found you. But the thing is, I could have, understand?"

I just nodded, the way he did himself sometimes.

"Remember, no hitchhiking, no train-jumping," he

went on. "No favors, no obligations. You pay your own way. Always. So when you want to go someplace, you buy a ticket. A ticket where you don't make a reservation, don't need ID. Travel on cash. Plenty of places where you can buy a car for cash, too. Newspaper ads, stuff on the Internet...Stay away from the used car lots. They'll take cash, sure, but they'll want to see paper.

"You do the work, you move on. In a car if you have one at the time. If not, what I said. Bus or trains. This stuff about the cops covering all the depots after some gangster gets killed, that's the movies. You're not going to do any political work, so it's not like they're going to call out the FBI after any job you do."

"Okay."

"I've been thinking about this a lot. Thinking what you want to be is a writer. Writing a book, that could take years and years. All you need is a notebook and a pen. What you write in there, it doesn't have to make sense. Just...notes, like. For what you plan to write. Someday."

—————

I GUESS THAT WORKED. Nobody ever asked, except for one time. I was in a diner. It was near-empty—when I get a meal outside, I always go between the lunch and dinner crowds—so I had a booth to myself.

"You're a writer, huh?"

That was the waitress. I'd left my notebook open on the table so I could write some more meaningless words. I don't know why I was just staring at those words, but I must have been thinking about something...because I didn't know the waitress was standing next to me until she spoke.

"Just...trying," I said to her. Then I ordered a sand-wich and a glass of juice. She was a short girl just this side of stocky, with glossy black hair and a lot of lipstick.

"Me too, honey," she said. I watched her walk away, wondering what she was trying to be.

When I was finished, she brought the check, standing close enough for me to smell her perfume—lemons and honey, maybe?

I left a five-dollar bill under my plate and got up to leave.

As I passed the register, the waitress flashed a sweet smile, said, "Don't be a stranger."

I remember thinking: *That's what I'll always be*, as I walked out the door.

———

IT'S NOT hard to find places to rent that don't do credit checks. And cars are like guns—private sellers are looking for cash, not ID. Most of them offered to make the bill of sale out for a lower amount than I actually paid—save me money when I went to register the car. And, yes, I could keep their plates on for a few days, never a problem with that. A few days was all I ever needed. I always mailed the plates back, too.

It wasn't steady work, what I did. It wasn't supposed to be. I once went almost a year and a half between jobs. And I once did two jobs in a week, in different states.

I was never lonely. I knew I had a job to do. A mission to complete. My father wasn't a young man when he sent me out. Maybe a dozen years or so and I'd be done with this, finished when I was a lot younger than he'd been.

"There's things you're going to want," my father told

me. Not spelling it out, but, by then, we both knew what he was talking about. "You can never settle down. Not while you're working. After you're done, maybe you'll figure a way to carry our work on without your...girl-friend, or whatever...knowing what you're going to be teaching your son. I don't know. I know I never could pull that off. Neither could my father...although I don't know how hard he ever tried.

"But that's for down the road. Now, well...you remember what I told you about women?"

"They're not all alike."

"That's the purest truth you'll ever hear," my father said. "Never make that mistake. There's a saying, 'Better to do without than to do time.' That's one you always have to keep in mind."

"I will."

"Paying for it, that's the easiest. The way you buy a car or rent an apartment: Cash. You want a transaction, not a conversation."

"You mean like one of those—"

"Don't say 'massage parlors' like they've got down by the river here," he interrupted. "Those places, today, they've all got their own cameras. Whether they want to stop robberies or start a blackmail business, doesn't make any difference. Not to you."

"So...?"

"So here's the thing about prostitutes, any prostitute —I don't care if she's a thousand-dollar escort or a twenty-dollar street girl, it's all the same at the buyer's end of the deal. You know why they call people who buy sex 'tricks'? Because they're getting tricked...and they know it. They're paying for the illusion. Someone loves them for a couple of minutes. Or, for a couple of hours, if they can pay. They're...maybe, I don't know, powerful.

Or so sexy the girl should be paying them...only they're too generous a guy to allow that. The girl sells whatever they think the trick wants to buy.

"But you, you won't need the illusion. What you sure don't need is showing your ID at a VD clinic. Or coming up with all the insurance paperwork every doctor's office wants to see. So condoms, they're most important part of the transaction."

"I understand," I told him, trying to feel as cold as he sounded. I don't know if he knew I'd had...Well, not girl-friends, exactly. But sex, yes.

Somehow, I thought he did know, but it wasn't some-thing we'd ever talked about. My father had known a lot more about...things in the world than I ever had, so it was a good thing that my own son turned out to be a lot smarter than I'd ever been.

My father shifted position, but stayed standing. "Never order off the Internet. Or even the phone. That puts another person—at least one other person—in there with you. But even with street girls, there's this: The police know them all. Know them one way or the other, and neither's any good for you. Maybe they're paying the cops, like any whorehouse would have to be doing. If they are, they're always talking about their customers. If they're free-lancing, they'll get arrested a lot. If they have pimps, they'll just keep quiet until they get bailed, but all of them know they can always trade some info for a pass.

"Some are junkies, some have managers, some are runaways...

Doesn't matter, not to you. What matters is staying out of traps. "

"So don't—"

"Right," he cut me off to explain the next rule: "Never

in a town where you're going to be working. Not before, not after."

He was quiet for a little bit after that. Then he took a pull on his cigarette, nodded his head like he'd just gotten a message, said: "If things were like they should be, you wouldn't want a working girl, you'd want a girl who works for a living, a grown woman, maybe one with kids of her own. But that's not for our kind. Those good ones, they're looking for a father for those kids. Because the father those kids have, the father who's not around, maybe he just took off. But if not, if he's still close by, that's what catches you up.

Maybe he's jealous, maybe he's a boozer, maybe...It doesn't matter." Another thing that doesn't matter, I thought. There's so many of those.

But I kept quiet.

"You find a girl, she gets interested in you, she's going to ask what you do. You tell her you're writing a book, she's going to want to see it. Tell her you're a photographer, she's going to want to see your cameras. Tell her you're a thief, she's going to ask what you stole. Understand?"

"All right."

"I'm no expert," my father said. "You know the job. I have faith in you.

The rest, it'll come as it does."

He was right about that. It didn't always come good, but never bad enough to throw me off course. I found out women will talk to you even if you don't say anything first. And if you don't mistreat them, you don't even have to lie. You just can't ever stay around, and you can't leave anything behind.

Or stay in touch.

"EVERYTHING IS HERE FOR YOU," the lawyer told me. Abel, his name was. He knew my father, and my father before him. "But the last piece, it's not the same. It doesn't work like that anymore."

"I can't just—"

"No," he cut me short. "When your father...got you, that was a different time. Everything was different. Those...places, they may not be any better now than they were back then, but now they ask a lot more questions. Background checks, all that."

"So what do I do?"

The lawyer was an old man. Looking at him, you might think his eyes were some shade of blue, faded with age. But I'd never seen them any other color. It was like looking into twin pools of dry ice with flat black dots in their centers.

"I can get this one done," he said, drawing on a Meerschaum pipe loaded with medical marijuana. "But you'll need someone else in place—in my place—for when your son goes out on his own."

"Are you—"

"What, dying?" the old lawyer said. "Sure. You too. Everyone is. Only the speed varies. But I wouldn't have another ten years no matter what. And this filthy damn cancer is moving the needle faster."

He took another deep inhale. Said, "You ever hear of re-homing?"

ABEL THE LAWYER BOUGHT A CHILD—JUST past a baby, really. I don't know what that little one expected me to do, but that wasn't what I did. Or, more likely, what I didn't do.

The boy's name on the papers that came along with him was Nathaniel. The lawyer had told me I could make it any name I wanted on the new papers he was going to file. "A clean slate," he told me. But he knew how I'd come to my father's house, so we both knew there was no such thing.

I never asked the boy about his past, whatever he remembered. I waited years before I asked any future questions. When I thought he was old enough, I asked him, "You want to keep the name they gave you?"

"Do I have to?" he asked me, sounding older than his age, like he always had, from the very beginning.

"No, you don't. You get to pick whatever name—whatever first name—you want."

"I like what you call me. "

"Sonny?"

"Yes. That. Or just Son, if you want. That could be a name, couldn't it?" he asked. I never asked him how he knew such things—I already knew he was a lot smarter than I'd ever been at his age. Or maybe even at all.

"It could be," I acknowledged. "But not many would know it for that.

So how about Sonny on the papers, and Son for just between us?" I said, watching his face close for a tell. Kids who are sold or traded don't have any secrets they treasure. But we'd had enough time together for him to know what wasn't going to happen with me, so he'd never learned to pull that mask over his face. His words always matched his tells.

"That would be good," he answered. "Can I have a different birthday, too?"

"Sure, you can pick one, if you want," I told him. "Anybody asks you, you—"

"I was adopted," he finished my sentence. Smoothly, like it was a true account, not something he'd had to memorize. "When I was a baby. You adopted me. You're my father. I don't remember anything else before that. Nothing."

I nodded what I knew he'd take for approval. "You're seven years old, now. Close to that, anyway. So how come you've never been to—"

He was ready for that one, too. "Home-schooled," he answered. "But I'll be going to regular school when I start the third grade."

"You'll be the smartest kid in your class," I told him.

"If you want me to be," he said. Telling me he could play it any way I needed him to.

THE LAWYER DIED when Sonny was nine. We went to the funeral. People around here, that's what they'd expect.

Turned out that Abel left me some money in his will. Another lawyer had been holding that will, but if he hadn't sent me a letter, I never would have known about that. At least that's what that lawyer believed.

"No files," he told me when I first came to his office. "I don't understand that, myself. Abel was a meticulous practitioner, but there wasn't a scrap of paper in any of the cabinets in his office. Just an envelope on his desk. That's where they found his Last Will and Testament, naming me as executor. No family members mentioned. The bequests were to you, the town library, and the high school, for a college scholarship fund. Most of it went to something called the Legislative Drafting Institute for

Child Protection. [Good lawyer] You know anything about that organization?"

"I never heard of it," I told him. Truthfully.

"Me either," he said, like he was confessing something. "So I had to check them out. Do my due diligence."

I just looked at him, keeping my face mild. He sounded...not guilty, exactly, but a little shaky. Like everything was legit, but not quite up to church level.

"What they do is, they write legislation," he said. "For groups who want to make changes in the law. Grassroots groups. People who get together for a cause they believe in."

"Like those people who picketed the abortion clinic over on—"

"Not like them," the lawyer said quickly. "Not like them at all. Abortion, that's an...That's an issue. Something you're either for or against. Like capital punishment or gun control, or the environment...big stuff like that. And big money behind every side. Grassroots, that means what it sounds like. Springs up by itself."

"This legislative thing, that's different how?"

"Well, first of all, there's really no sides. Saying you're against child abuse, that doesn't make you special. Everybody's against child abuse, am I right?"

You're wrong, I thought. Or too ignorant to be a lawyer. But I just adjusted my face so he'd keep talking.

"And there's already laws against child abuse. Plenty of laws. Laws to protect children. But, let's face it, those laws aren't really working."

"How could they?" I asked him. "The government can't put cameras in everybody's house."

"Well...Sure, that's true. And that's the point. Most of those grassroots groups, they know what's wrong, but they don't know how to make it right. And the politicians promise them whatever they want to hear, but that's just words, not laws. So it has to be something specific, you understand?"

I could feel him watching me as he spoke, but I kept looking down at the will he was holding so we wouldn't lock eyes.

"I'm not sure," I said.

"There's an art to writing legislation," he told me, like his office was a classroom and I was one of the students. "You can't write a law that says child abuse is bad; you have to write a law that says what specific conduct is bad, that's an example."

"Uh-huh."

"I spoke with the director. She—the director's a woman, a law professor, in fact—she told me that a well-written piece of legislation accomplishes what it's intended to."

"Don't they all?"

"No. No, they don't. Most laws, they're like Swiss cheese, so many holes in them. To work, they have to be tight. And that's a real skill, writing laws like that."

"Like the birdhouses," I said. "The...what?"

"The birdhouses. The ones my father built. The ones I build now. Anyone can build a birdhouse, but, most of them, birds wouldn't want to live in. All sloppy, big globs of glue around the pegs, bad lines, wobbly perches..."

"Sure," he said, giving me the look that half-smart people think other people are too stupid to understand. "Anyway, what they're working on now is the adoption laws. Some states, the children are just gone once they get adopted."

"Gone?"

"Gone. Vanished, like they disappeared. Nobody keeps track. You could adopt a child and just give that child to someone else. Hand them over like they were dogs, or tropical fish. There's no law against it. And if whoever you gave the child to wanted to loan you some money, say to help you out with some debts you had, something like that, well, nothing illegal about that, either."

"Huh!" I said, as if I was surprised.

"It's what they call a loophole. Some states have laws that other states don't. Like how old a child can be before they get married. If their parents consent, that is."

"So there should be just one law, for all the states?"

"For some laws, the laws that are supposed to protect children, yes. "

"Sounds like you were surprised," I said. "That he left money to them. That organization, I mean."

"We were never that close, Abel and I."

"Abel was my father's lawyer," I said. "After my father passed, he was my lawyer. My friend, too. My father and me, we both trusted him."

"I know," he said, using a lawyer's sincere voice.

"He must have trusted you, too," I said, co-signing his lie with one of my own.

I KNEW the old lawyer with the dry-ice eyes hadn't ever trusted any outsider with the whole truth. And I knew I couldn't find another lawyer to take his place...not on my own. Not another middleman, either. All I could pass along to my son for his mission would be a cache of guns. I didn't have to be a deep thinker to know that wouldn't be enough.

It was as if my father hadn't planned on dying. Or for any of the links in the mission chain to die, either. If you go through life without a retirement plan, all you do is age until you stop aging. All that's left is what you leave.

It didn't so much hit me as come over me, like a wave over a man floating way out in the ocean after a shipwreck. Nothing on the horizon except the next waves, muscling up to roll again. That was the moment I realized that I couldn't teach Sonny what my father had taught me.

Not just killing. That's just getting close enough to shoot, doing that, making sure, and moving away. It's not what happens during all that, it's what happens before that you have to learn. Learn how to do, I mean.

"Some call it an 'adrenalin dump,'" my father had explained. "It's not something you can just wish away, it happens to everyone in certain situations. This...*blast!* inside you: your heart wants to jump out of your chest, you're covered in sweat, you're caught between running away and charging forward...some freeze right between those two, just stand there, can't move at all.

"It doesn't last long. Less than a minute. There's no way to avoid it. Like something knocking on your door that won't go away. So the trick is, you invite it in. Not to fight it. Not to run out that same door you opened. Just let it into your house. Be a little patient and it keeps moving right out the back door.

"You don't freeze, you do the opposite. Well, maybe not the exact opposite. It's like you're facing something solid. Something coming at you that's solid. And you just turn into...vapor. Like you were the air itself. And it just goes right through you and then it's gone."

"I do that before..."

"Just before," my father said. "Maybe you're walking down a street and you know your target's going to be on the next corner. Then. That's when you invite it in, let it pass through you, and it's gone."

HE WAS RIGHT. When we drove up to that bundler's machine shop, I knew what I was going to do. And, like my father said, I pictured that, me doing that. And the *blast!* came. Maybe being ready for it helped. Or maybe it was me calling it up, inviting it in, maybe that's what did the trick. I felt my whole body flush, like it was on fire and freezing at the same time. And then it was gone. And shooting the bundler, that was just a job. A job I was expected to do. From then on, it was always like that.

So killing people, sure, that much I could teach my son. But without the other links in the chain there wouldn't be any use for that one skill. And without a place to come back to when I was gone, how could he keep it going, our work?

I didn't know how long our tribe had been doing what we did, but I knew my father's father hadn't been the first. My father never really talked about it, but I understood our line went back generations. None of us connected by genetics, all of us bound by blood.

Now one line was broken forever. My line of work, that was done. But our bloodline, taking children away from Them, that had to go on.

I didn't know how I was going to make it happen. Just that I had to get that done.

OUR HOUSE WAS BACK a good distance from the road, but we weren't invisible. People came by. Church people, mostly. I guess they figured I'd come home after my father had passed—that's the word they used, never "died"—and I'd pick up where he left off.

Only they were never sure exactly where he left off. We hadn't lived high, but we had a nice house that we kept up well, always a still-in-warranty car, and a work truck, too. We walked around in decent clothes, and didn't owe anyone a dime...not even the bank. Maybe some wondered how anyone could sell enough bird-houses for all that. But none of them ever asked, not straight out.

Oh, I'd heard talk at school, when I was a kid. My father had a pension from the government. Not the mili-tary, something deeper. The American Legion and the VFW had come around, asking him about joining, and they took his answer—"Wouldn't be right. I never wore the uniform"—to mean more than he what he'd said.

"Was your dad a secret agent?" a kid in my ninth-grade class had asked me, once.

"A secret agent? I wish! He was just a traveling sales-man," is what I answered. "My mother used to..." Letting my voice trail off into sadness, like I'd been taught. They all knew my father was a widower. Lost his wife when I was just a little child. That had been in another town, another time, before we'd settled here.

After a while, nobody asked me. Didn't stop them from talking. Writing their own movie, just like my father expected. "When there's blanks, people fill them in," is what he taught me. And that has always proved true.

I SPENT a lot of time thinking about what I knew that I could pass down to Sonny. While I was trying to come up with something of value, time passed. So much time that it got to be where Sonny knew more than I did about most things. He took to school like I never had, and he knew how to look up all kinds of things on the computer he got when I'd asked him what he wanted for his ninth birthday. I'd bought it for him, but he'd picked it out himself.

That computer had seemed expensive to me, but I didn't know what they were supposed to cost. One thing I did know: Sonny didn't want that computer to show it off. It was one of those little ones that just fold up, the kind you could carry around easy. But he never took it outside the house.

And Sonny went out—off the property, I mean—a lot more than I had ever done, too. Not running away or anything like that. Doing things after school. With friends he made for himself. Sometimes I met their parents when I'd go and pick him up. They seemed like nice people, and I tried to be nice to them in return— that was one thing I'd taught Sonny that would always be of help to him, good manners. Sometimes, he'd have his friends come over, but they mostly wanted to run around outside. Or do whatever boys that age did. By themselves, I mean.

WE HAD firearms in the house, but I'd cared more about showing Sonny how to handle them safely than how to actually use them. It's not as if I was ever a marksman, anyway. And Sonny never asked me for a rifle of his own, like a lot of kids around here would have.

Some people in the village—men mostly, but some women, too—they hunted and fished. "Sportsmen," they called themselves. Sonny asked me about that, once. A kind of reverse question, the way he liked to talk.

"How come you never go hunting?" is what he said.

"It...it just doesn't hold much interest for me."

"You don't think people should kill animals? Cara, she's a girl in my class, she won't eat meat. Are you—"

"You know we're not vegetarians, Son. We eat meat. So what you're really asking me isn't if I'm against killing animals, it's whether I'm a hypocrite."

"Someone who says one thing but does another. "

"That's right."

"So, you just don't care for hunting? "

"Or fishing. But we eat fish, too."

"Is that it? "

"Is what it?"

"You don't like killing things for the fun of it."

"Truth is, I don't see the fun in it. But there's other reasons. Some of the folks who hunt deer, they eat venison. And those who raise pigs, they—"

"What about the people who go to Africa and hunt elephants?"

"I don't know if people even eat elephants...although I guess they would if they were hungry enough. But nobody would go that far and spend all that money just for food—it wouldn't make sense."

"I guess not. Those people, the ones who go to Africa to hunt, they take pictures of themselves. With the animals they kill, I mean."

"You see those on your computer?"

"Sometimes," he said, looking directly at me. "I don't like them."

I couldn't tell if he was talking about the pictures or

the people in them, but I didn't say anything more. Didn't react to Sonny changing "hunt" to "kill," either. But I never remembered my father hunting, either, so it made sense to me. Blended in.

SOMETIMES I WONDERED how kids around where we lived dealt with that whole hunting thing. They had the 4-H club stuff, where they'd raise animals to show at fairs. Livestock, really. I don't know if they ever ended up eating them, or keeping them as pets. But if they kept a chicken as a pet, or even just for the eggs, they'd still know people ate chickens.

Those were just passing thoughts. Never stayed with me. So when Sonny started telling me about hummingbirds, I was a little confused at first. But then he explained how those tiny little things would never use any of the birdhouses we sold. "They have to build their own nests," he told me. "Out of all kinds of different stuff, but one thing they always use is spider silk, so the nest can flex as the babies grow. Their nests, they're only about this big"— showing me by making a circle with his thumb and index finger held parallel to the ground— "and the eggs are the size of a navy bean. They have to build them way high off the ground, so nothing can get at them."

I immediately thought of squirrels when he said that, and he cut into my thoughts like he was already inside my mind: "They build on these really flimsy branches. Lighter than twigs, even. An animal couldn't just climb up there—it would have to fly. And...hover, like. The way a helicopter does."

Him knowing all that shouldn't have surprised me. I

remembered a couple of years before, when Sonny told me if we wanted a certain kind of butterfly to be in our yard, we had to plant milkweed. He said "we", but he knew I wouldn't have been thinking about things like that.

Monarch butterflies were what he wanted. When I asked him what was so special about those, he said, "They're poisonous," as if that was a good thing.

He caught the look I gave him. I could tell from his expression that he knew a great deal about those butterflies. Maybe I didn't know about such things, but I knew my own son. "Like Black Widows?" I asked. Those I knew about. My father had explained how I shouldn't ever get near one, showed me how clearly they were marked. But poisonous spiders don't travel far. And they sure couldn't fly.

"Not exactly," Sonny explained. "Monarchs don't bite. They're poisonous because they can kill you if you eat them. Like some plants. That's why they're the colors they are—to warn birds away."

"Black Widows are—"

"What they are is venomous," he cut me off, so excited he never got to hear me tell him about that red hourglass that I knew they carried as a sign of their dangerousness. "They use their poison to kill what they eat. Like a rattlesnake."

"So these Monarchs, their poison is for self-defense?" I asked him.

"I...I never thought of it like that," Sonny said. "But I guess that's true. The milkweed they feed on, when they digest it, it turns into poison inside them. They can't attack you with that—you'd have to eat one to...to be poisoned. But a poisonous snake, it...stabs you, like. I guess maybe that could be self-defense...say if you tried to pick one up in your hand, or even kill it. But a snake's poison, it's a weapon. They need it to get their food. The same way a coyote uses its fangs and claws."

"Is that why you want to have them around?" I asked him. "Because they're poisonous, but they don't use it unless they have to?"

"Well, they can't actually use it. Not like a snake does. A viper makes its own poison, so it can bite again and again. Otherwise, it would starve to death. But the Monarch only gets to be poisonous the one time."

"If it gets eaten?"

"Yes."

"So those colors they have in those pictures you showed me, orange with those black veins and white dots, they're like a skull-and-crossbones?"

"Yes!" Sonny said, delighted with the connection I'd just made. "Like those "No Trespassing!" signs you see on some folks' land."

I let him sit with his thoughts for a while. We could do that, Sonny and me—just be with each other without saying anything. My father was like that with me, only in a different way. My father never said anything that wasn't supposed to teach me something. When I sat like that with Sonny, he wasn't just being with me—he was letting me teach him to be patient. Quiet and patient.

"That can't be why those butterflies are so special," I finally said to him. "A lot of things are poisonous if you eat them. Some mushrooms—"

"They migrate," my son interrupted.

I shook my head. Sonny knew I would never be against anything for no reason, so he knew I was just...confused, maybe. "They come from north of here," he explained, so I knew he was talking about Monarchs, not mushrooms. "Heading all the way down to Mexico. Every year."

"And they come back every—"

"Most of them don't," he said. "Once they get down there, they're...all done. Like it was a job, and they were finished with it. Only a small percentage of them make it back. But they all leave cocoons behind before they go. So there's always new ones. And if we do it right, we'll always have some here."

I got it, then. That was us. What we did, our line. That was us. Vipers who didn't make their own poison.

It wasn't the right time to explain any of that to Sonny, not yet—but I could already tell that when the time came, he'd understand. So I didn't say anything, just took him out and we found some of that weed he wanted. We did the planting, following some instructions he'd looked up. After that, the weed took care of itself. And we had clouds of those Monarchs every year.

———

"I DON'T THINK I've seen any of those hummingbirds around here," I told him that day. I meant on our property itself, but the truth is I never paid much attention to birds, either. Just like my father and me, Sonny and I sold those birdhouses, but we never put any up.

"Oh, we'll have them," Sonny said, absolutely certain. "I got a bunch of fuchsia bushes from Lilly. She's my friend. From school. They have a whole mess of those in her backyard, and she told me I could take some.

"She asked her mother first," he said, catching my look. We don't steal, our people. Not ever. "It's wrong and it's stupid," my father told me, when I was even younger than Sonny. "You always pay for what you want or what you need. And you never do anything that brings bad attention to yourself, okay?" I knew that wasn't really a question, but I nodded to tell him I understood.

SONNY WAS right about those fuchsia bushes. The red-and-purple belled flowers sprung right up, and they didn't need any special care to flourish.

Before long, the hummingbirds came.

The bushes were a good distance from the house, except for one that Sonny planted right next to the big bay window in the kitchen. We could see out that window, but nobody could see in—my father had covered all the back windows with a kaleidoscope mesh, so it looked solid from the outside. By the time I was old enough to ask why he'd done that, I already knew the answer.

There was one of the hummingbirds—a Rufous, Sonny told me it was—that I thought was building a nest, because she always returned to the same branch. Only it wasn't a female at all. "That's the way the males get a mate," Sonny explained, like I was taking a course from him. "They stake out a patch, and then guard it against all the others. If it's a good patch—lots of flowers, plenty of nectar—the females want to get at it. So they can get what they need to make a nest somewhere close by."

I couldn't imagine they taught that stuff in school, not at Sonny's age. It seemed too...specialized. But Sonny was certain about all of it, and I didn't doubt him.

The male only left his post for short times...usually when other hummingbirds got too close, and he'd go airborne to drive them off. "They're all territorial," Sonny told me. "They don't share."

———

IT WAS a few days later when I saw Sonny by the kitchen window. He wasn't saying anything; wasn't making any sound at all. But his eyes were wet, and one cheek was tear-streaked.

I didn't say anything, just moved close to him.

He looked up at me. "He's gone," my son told me. "He just went away. He hasn't come back. It's been three days, and he hasn't come back. "

"Maybe he found—"

"No," he said, sadly sure of his words. "The other hummingbirds, they're still over in the bushes out back. And it's not mating season yet."

A cat, is what I thought, but I didn't say anything, just put my hand on his shoulder. I didn't know what else to do. It felt like I was letting him down by not knowing.

———

"HE'S BACK!" Sonny ran into the living room the next day, all excited. "The bird?"

"It's him! For sure. I recognized the red mark on his throat, like a triangle. And he's on the very same branch. You want to...?"

The bird was there, tilting his head up, swiveling it around like he was watching the sky for invaders.

I could feel Sonny vibrating next to me.

That's when I knew, knew beyond any doubt, that he couldn't be sent out the way I had been. Knew I'd have to find some other way for him to carry it on. I didn't know what that could be, but I knew my own work wouldn't be done until I did.

———

ONE THING SONNY was interested in was cars. He was maybe twelve when he first asked me about getting one. "Someday," is how he put it.

I just waited, knowing there was more to come. "My friend Ross has a paper route," he tossed out. "In town?" I asked, still waiting for the rest.

"Pretty much. He lives there, so I guess it's not so hard—he can do it on his bike. He's saving up so he can buy a car when he turns sixteen."

"Is that what you'd want to do?"

"Yes. Yes, I think I would," Sonny told me, his voice solemn.

"Well, this far out, you'd need a car just to have a paper route."

"Like the man who drops off ours?"

"Just like that."

"That's only three days a week," Sonny said. "I don't see how that man could make much money, doing that. He'd have...expenses and all too, wouldn't he? It's different for Ross. He doesn't need to spend the money he earns—he gives it all to his mother, and she's holding it for him. Like a bank."

"Sounds like a good plan."

"I think it is. So I was wondering...Do you know of any jobs I might get? Not a paper route, but something like that. Part-time. So I could give the money I earn to you, to hold for me."

"To buy a car when you're old enough."

"Yes sir."

I don't know what got Sonny started on that "yes sir, no sir" business—it wasn't anything I'd taught him. But he seemed to like saying it. Saying it sometimes, anyway. So I never remarked on it.

"You figure your friend Ross has a head start on you?"

"I...guess. I mean, I never would have thought of it until he told me. "

"You never would have thought of a paper route? Or of having a car? "

"A paper route," he said, smiling a little bit.

"Tell me something, Son. It's been a long time since I was your age. How do they work this driver's license thing, now?"

"Well, you can get a learner's permit on your birthday," he said, speaking so carefully that I knew he'd given this a lot of thought. "When you turn fifteen, I mean. Then you're eligible to take Driver's Ed at school—first or second semester, depending on if your birthday falls in the summer before school starts. You can take your driving test when the course is over, but you can't actually drive until you're sixteen. And not at night until you're seventeen."

"Driver's Ed? At school, that's where they teach you to drive? "

"Yes sir."

"Everybody has to take it?"

"Oh no, I don't think so. But Ross says, if you do take it, the insurance costs a lot less. For your whole family, on the one policy. That's because the younger you are, the more the insurance companies charge. But if you take Driver's Ed, I guess they figure you'll be safer behind the wheel."

"They don't know how to separate things," I told him.

"Who's 'they'?"

That question brought me up short. For about half a breath, I thought Sonny was asking me the question our whole line knew the answer to, but I'd caught up to what he was actually asking before the breath was done.

"The insurance companies," I answered him. "Cars are like guns—there's knowing how to use them, and then there's what use to make of them. Some kids learn how to use a rifle and they go hunting. Or target shooting. But there'll always be those who bring those same guns to school."

"I know that...happens. I read some of the stories. Do you know why those kids do that? Come to school and just start shooting?"

I was sure I knew why some of them did. I didn't know anything about any individual cases, but I would have bet on being right. "There's no way to know," I said. "Lots of guesses, some probably better than others. But, most of the time, you can't talk to those kids."

"Because they're dead?"

"Some are. The others, what they have to say doesn't really make any sense. Not to other people, anyway. I guess it must have made sense to them."

"It seems to happen a lot. Sometimes. I mean, you don't hear much about it, then one happens, and it starts a rockslide. Some of them even leave...notes, like. Online."

"On computers, you mean?"

"More than that. More public than that. On their blogs. Like a diary, only they want people to read them."

"Suicide notes?"

"More than that," Sonny repeated. "Sometimes, it's year's worth of writing. Sometimes, it's like they know they're going to die. But, sometimes, all they talk about is killing other people, not themselves."

"Are you worried about something like that at your school? "

"No. No, I'm really not. But high school..."

"Protecting yourself, we can talk about that, if you want. "

"Someday, maybe," he said. Meaning "not now."

"Okay. Then let's go back to that head start your friend Ross has on you."

"The paper route?"

"We can't do anything about a paper route. But I can think of some ways you can earn money."

"Like what?"

"We can talk about that later. For now, I know a way you can get your own head start on Ross."

"I don't understand," he said. Not something Sonny said a lot. "How about if you don't wait for Driver's Ed to learn to drive?

Wouldn't that give you a jump on your friend? "

"You mean, after I get my permit, you could—"

"I mean right now," I told him. "Starting right now, anyway."

EVEN AT THAT AGE, Sonny wasn't much smaller than some men. And most women. I'd been tall for my age, too, but I hadn't gotten that from my father any more than Sonny had gotten it from me.

All I had to do was adjust the driver's seat and tilt the steering wheel, and he was good to go.

"There's nothing to hit out here," I told him. "Nothing to worry about. "

"I'm not worried," he assured me.

WHEN HE GOT CONFIDENT ENOUGH, we moved out of the field onto one of the dirt roads that runs through the property. Sonny was good. He always listened, always paid attention, never got too excited.

"You can drive," I told him, after about three months of practicing every day after school. "You know how to make the car do what you want it to do. What you don't have is traffic experience."

"But if we go off the property..."

"We'll have to go at night," I filled in the end of his sentence. I didn't want to have some discussion with him about what the law says. How that doesn't matter. Never matters. Easier to teach him the drills than try to explain why the law lets some drunks to keep on driving after they'd been convicted a dozen times. That difference between the laws as they're written and how they really worked...like the lawyer who thought he was taking Abel's place had been explaining to me.

"Are we going to take the Driver's Ed car?" he asked. He meant the old Subaru I'd brought home one day. Over twenty years old, a couple of hundred thousand miles on the odometer, not much left of the interior. But hardly any rust, and it ran pretty good. Sonny called it the Driver's Ed car because I told him he'd have to learn to drive on a stick shift, so he'd always be able to do that if he had to. And both the regular car and the truck we had were automatics.

He paid attention, listened close, stayed calm. So he learned really easy. "You remember what we went over? What to say?"

"Yes sir. If we get stopped, I'm taking you to the hospital. You were working up in the loft and you fell.

You kept telling me you were okay, but then you passed out. But you woke right up, and I thought it was over. Only you fell down again, and I got scared. Maybe a...stroke or something. So I'm taking you to the hospital. I know I don't have a license. I know I shouldn't be driving. But you're my father, and I didn't think I had a choice."

"Why didn't you just call for an ambulance?"

"I tried!" he said, intensely. "But I couldn't get a signal on the phone. And I didn't have time to see what was wrong with the Wi-Fi. The hospital's only a few—"

"Good," I told him. "Real good. Now what else? For when we're out on the road, what else?"

"Other drivers, they're all dangerous," he answered right up. "Either drunk or not paying attention. Talking on their phones or texting or half asleep. They won't stay in their lane. They go too fast. And some of them are just crazy. Crazy and angry."

"Right. Do we care?"

"No sir, we don't. We give them all the room they want, all the room they need."

"Okay, then. After dinner, when it gets dark, we'll take a test run."

BY THE TIME he was fourteen, Son was as good a driver as he'd ever need to be. We practiced at night, in rain-storms, on icy roads. No speeding—we didn't want to give any excuse to pull us over. That never happened, not once.

In a way, I think Sonny was disappointed that we never got to try out the story about me falling from the loft. But I told him, it's like one of those fire drills—good to practice so you know the steps, but who actually wants the real thing? I'm not sure I convinced him, but I could see he never pushed it while he was behind the wheel, so I guess it made sense to him. Enough sense, anyway.

———

"FIRST RULE, YOU NEVER HAVE A REASON," my father had taught me. "After we do our work, the cops split into teams. They walk two roads looking for clues. One road, they go all scientific: prints, fibers, spatter, DNA. And they check the camera feeds, ask around for live witnesses. While some are doing that, the others look for a motive. 'Who wanted the dead guy dead?' that's the question they ask. The answer can never be you."

I didn't say anything. By then, that was our communication code. If I was silent, that meant I understood what I was being told.

"The job itself, you always make sure. That means you start close, and you finish closer. Guns aren't magic. People get shot and live through it all the time. With us, that can't ever be. This isn't about getting paid. It isn't about building some reputation. It's about not ever meeting the law, or even being known to them. So soon as you drop the target, you walk in and make sure.

That's not going to tell the cops anything. Because it tells them too much." I kept silent, but only because I wasn't ready to ask him anything yet. "That's why you always carry two," he went on. "Or even three, sometimes. You can't ever be sure a gun won't misfire. Any gun, any time. Some guns jam. Some bullets go bad, and the hammer drops on a dud. So you always have a second move ready.

"And you can't be sure someone else won't just show up suddenly. Some civilian who wants to be a hero, some beat cop walking by...no way to be as sure as you always have to be. Dead sure. You can't reload, there's never enough time for that. You can't work with people for backups, so you always carry your own."

I tilted my head just enough to tell him that I didn't understand what he was saying. Not all of it, anyway. He was on my wavelength, had picked it up from before he told me about always carrying at least two.

"Cops, they watch too many movies," my father told me. "This is them, what they always say after they find a body in an alley with three-four holes in it: 'Somebody *really* wanted this one dead.' Because...what? They don't have anything. Entry wounds, sure. Maybe find some of the slugs, too...depends on what caliber was used. So they know...what? That nothing was taken, so it wasn't a robbery?

"Even if that was true—and it's not, some robbers don't ever plan on shooting and, when they do, they panic and run without taking anything—that still leaves a whole bag of possibilities. A hired killer would put extra slugs in, but so would someone who had a deep grudge...or was in a rage, or any other reason you might think of.

"So here's what they actually know: It was either business or personal. And what does that tell them? Nothing. Because when you get down to it, everything is either business or personal.

"What I'm saying is that, sure, somebody really wanted the target dead. Whoever that was, maybe they did it themselves, maybe some of their crew handled it, maybe they contracted it out. So what?

"Why so what? Because none of that points to you.

Even if whoever put out the contract has more rats in his organization than one of those labs where they test drugs, still nothing. One of them might know a call was made. Might even know who the call was made to. But even if the whole outfit is wired up like a Christmas tree, even if it had enough tap warrants on it to wallpaper a palace, it never reaches out far enough to touch you."

I nodded to show him I had it down. Every bit. "Nothing else counts," my father told me.

I NEVER HAD to teach Sonny any of that. But I knew the time would come when I'd have to show him some way to carry on the mission. Because none of us, not a single one of those taken from Them, none of us had a heritage other than what we were taught by those who took us away. Our bloodlines were random, bought with random blood. We wouldn't ever be searching for our roots.

And there was enough money, now. Money and land and buildings.

Even what could pass as a business. Plenty of cover, with no back-trail. Sonny wouldn't ever have to go to work like I had. And my father before me. A long way back. None of us related, all of us connected.

But that didn't mean there was no more work to be done. It would be up to Sonny to start a new line. So when he got old enough to leave, I'd have to show him the last step. Maybe he'd have more than one option, depending on what I could find. But whatever road he picked, he'd have to walk it on his own.

It would be different from that moment on. Because Sonny wouldn't have to wait to learn I was gone. And when he did, it might be the father going away, not the son.

If that became the case, odds were that the going away would be for good.

—————

THERE'S a Post Office in town. Back in my father's time, people used it for all kinds of things, especially packages. So the folks who ran the place had some sense of what was going on with everyone else. It's not like that anymore, but the Post Office is still there. And people still gather. Buy stamps, talk about the weather. If you don't have another place—one of the bars, the poolroom, the Elks, the diner, places where other people know you when you walk in—then it's the Post Office.

"Can't let them think you're a hermit," the man who taught me explained. "If you don't show, people come looking for you."

"Like from the church?"

"Them, sure. But those people, they mean well. Nosy, maybe. A little pushy, sure. But they're not looking for an easy grab."

He waited, but I didn't say anything. So he went on. "I read once that we—all people, I mean, not only our people—started out as hunters and gatherers. The gatherers came first, before we learned how to hunt. But I never saw the distinction. The people who gathered fruit or whatever, they had to hunt around to find the places where that fruit grew, see?

"So everybody's really a hunter, right up to today," he continued. "They hunt different things, but it's usually money they want, for starters. So if certain kinds of people believe there's a hermit living out on some piece of land, they start thinking maybe that hermit's got some money stashed away. Or some old cars he could talk him out of, turn into cash. Maybe antiques.

But it's always something..."

"There's supposed to be a meth lab over to—"

"That wouldn't be a target. The people who run that operation, they've got a lot of guns. Guard dogs. Booby traps. And they're not friendly."

"I know," I told him. "But...Are we friendly?"

"Friendly enough," he said. "We don't fire at folks who come up the road. We don't have those skull-and-crossbones signs up. Nothing wrong with our teeth, either."

I knew he was talking about the meth lab. His way of joking. I didn't laugh. He didn't expect me to.

"Besides, we run a business," he went on. "And we go to town. Pick up our supplies at the Post Office when we can't buy them local. You played Little League—"

"I wasn't any good."

"You were good enough," he said. "Those kids, the ones you thought were so good, they practiced all the time. It was real important to them. Or to their parents, more likely. It was never that important to you."

"You think if I had practiced all the time, I'd have been good?"

"You would have been better," is all he said. When I'd first come to live with him, I'd measured the man by what he didn't do to me. Then by what he didn't make me do. And, finally, by this truth: He never lied to me.

———

AND, true to our line, I never lied to Sonny. But it wasn't until I got a call from his school asking me if they could schedule a time for me to come in for a conference that I saw a deeper parallel. I wasn't sure what they meant by a "conference," but I could tell from the woman's tone that Sonny wasn't in any trouble.

It turned out they wanted him to skip a grade. Maybe even more than one. "He's not really being challenged," the woman—not the same one who'd called, this one was the principal—told me. The guidance counselor—a younger man, with slender build and a serious face—nodded, but I could see he wasn't all in on the idea.

The principal said that Sonny showed great promise. Math and science were "the real frontiers of the future," she added, like that was a deal-closer.

They both seemed a little surprised when I told them I'd talk it over with my son and let them know.

Sonny wasn't interested. In fact, he was against it. "It's a label," he told me. "One you wear all your life. I don't need different classes—I mostly read and study on my own anyway."

That's when it hit me. Little League. I guess I'd wanted to play all right, but it wasn't all that big a deal. All I wanted to do was play—the idea of practicing on my own, that didn't appeal to me at all. Some of the kids, their fathers were always taking them to the batting cages, but I didn't think my father would want to do anything like that.

Still, he'd left it up to me. Even asked me if I wanted him to take me, letting it be my decision.

I didn't lie to Sonny, but I didn't tell him everything at once. He knew that the time could come when I might have to go away for a while. He knew because I'd told him so. And after I left, he'd have to go on with the sort-of mixing with people my father must have done before I'd come and after I'd left.

The day could come when I had to go. Sonny could wait for me, or he could move on. I'd be leaving him with plenty of money. And only the one obligation. I hadn't explained all of that to him yet, but I'd promised to do so when he was old enough. So he knew I would.

SONNY WAS SO proud that he'd learned to drive. I just stayed patient about that, waiting either for him to turn sixteen or for something that might never happen.

He already knew there was another car on the property. In a back shed. Surrounded by the kind of blackberry brambles that make concertina wire feel like silk, with electronic sensors that would flash inside the house if the perimeter got breached. Inside that shed, a Toyota SUV: silverfish gray, full-packed with all the gear we'd need, paperwork too. And enough cash to keep us going for years, if it came to that. I started it up and drove it around back there every couple of weeks, just to keep it flexible. We could be gone in minutes.

It would be better if I drove, but now, Sonny could do that if I was too damaged to handle the job. There was no one to give word if they came for me, so chances were that I could be hurt in whatever happened next.

Or dead.

If that ever happened—as my father had told me it might, to him—and if Sonny wasn't around at the time, he'd been taught everything he had to do next, just as I had been. There weren't a lot of restrictions on that. He could do pretty much whatever he wanted. What he couldn't do was go looking for whoever had come for me. That would have nothing to do with him. Just hired hands. Hired by businessmen doing what they thought they had to do to protect their business.

In our line, there's only one thing we take personal.

The hard part had been when Sonny was a child. A little boy. That was the most dangerous time. Dangerous for me, because I hadn't stopped work all that long ago, so I couldn't be sure there was enough distance between me and the people who paid me.

And dangerous for Sonny, too. Because if I disappeared when he was still a kid, the system would gobble him up. Or try to, anyway. Abel had been poised to step in if they did try. And I'd had complete confidence in the old man. But now it would be up to the new lawyer I'd hired. All he had to do was make sure the foster parents the State found for Sonny were decent people.

They didn't have to be wonderful or anything. Just not one of them.

"That's what Abel was put in charge of," I told the new lawyer. "With me, when I was just a little kid. My father wanted to make sure I would never—"

"I understand," the lawyer said. "Some of these people, they'd try to get control of whatever money there was...left."

"My father wasn't worried about that," I told him, saying it the casual way people state a known fact. "There's a button on that money."

"A button?"

"Yes. If control of that money passes to anyone, anyone at all, that button gets pushed."

"I don't understand," the lawyer I didn't trust said, raising his eyebrows.

"Yes, you do," is all I said to him. "I've been thinking about going back to work. So I may be away for a while. I have some questions about that. Questions I want to run by you sometime. Just let me know when we can talk, and I'll come over and see you."

———

WHEN THE LAWYER I didn't trust called and asked me to stop by whenever it was convenient for me, I told Sonny to stay home from school that day.

"Your job isn't just to listen," I told him. "Although there is that. This lawyer we're going to see, his job is to answer questions we have."

"We?"

"Us. You and me. There could be a...gap in things. "

"A gap?"

"Let's say, for example, I was killed in an accident, okay? You're still a boy. A smart, capable boy, sure. And you could probably take better care of yourself than anyone else could. But the government doesn't let kids live by themselves."

"You mean, I'd have to go back to—"

"You're never going back to that," I told him. A promise truer than any blood.

———

"IN SOME STATES, when the authorities have children they want to put in care, those children would have a lawyer assigned to them. To protect their rights. But, here, that doesn't happen."

"What does 'in care' mean?" Sonny asked the lawyer I didn't trust. I'd told Sonny he could ask whatever he wanted, interrupt whenever he felt the need. And to pay close attention when the contract was sealed, because it wouldn't be in writing.

"Well," the lawyer said, "it could mean—it usually does mean—foster care of some kind. But not necessarily."

"What else is there?" Sonny pressed him.

"There are...institutions," the lawyer said. "There aren't as many foster care options available as there should be. So, occasionally, especially if the child is older, or hard to place—"

Sonny shifted position in his chair. "Hard to place?"

"Children with...problems," the lawyer said. "Challenged in some way. For example—"

"We know what you mean," Sonny said, dropping the temperature of his voice.

"All right," the lawyer went on, as if he hadn't noticed. "Anyway, for older children, if the placement is only going to be short-term, the child could go to the Engle Home."

"The jail?" I asked.

"It's a juvenile detention facility," the lawyer said. Like he was saying "Today is Monday." On a Tuesday.

Sonny and I waited. The silence got heavy. Finally, the lawyer accepted that his answer wasn't going to be enough.

"Older children are much harder to place in foster care. Especially boys. So they keep a few beds in Engle available. But those children are separated from the...others."

"I've driven by the place a lot of times," I said. "They only have one exercise yard. What do they do, give them separate times when they can be outside?"

"I...I don't know," the lawyer said. "A placement is not considered incarceration, so the rules of habeas—"

"You're saying, if something happened to me, Sonny could end up in that place."

"It's not impossible. But there are many other more likely outcomes. "

"A dice-roll?" I asked.

"Oh, I suspect it would be a lot more certain than that. Sonny is, how old now, thirteen?"

"Yes," Sonny answered. Then he went quiet again.

"That's old enough for him to have a say. The court would probably appoint a lawyer to speak for him. Especially if there were to be an estate proceeding involved."

"Probably? But you said, in this state, kids don't get lawyers, didn't you?"

"And what would they need them for?" Sonny added, before the lawyer could react.

The lawyer played with his hands like he used to smoke and wished he still did. Finally, he explained: "Well, say, their parents abused them. Or neglected them. Or...it really doesn't matter: if the State wants to take children from parents, it can't just do it—there has to be a court proceeding."

"So why don't the children get lawyers?" I asked him. "Like I said, in some states, they do. Not in this one. "

"What about the parents?"

"The parents?"

"If the government says kids were abused, don't they have to say who did it? And then prove it? Like any other crime?"

"Oh. Yes. Of course," he said, more comfortable now that he was on familiar ground. "In an abuse or neglect proceeding, the parents are constitutionally guaranteed an attorney. If they don't have the funds to pay, the State appoints one for them. "

"And pays the lawyers?"

"Yes. There's what is called a 'panel.' The lawyers who

serve on that panel are the ones called in when necessary."

"Wouldn't they always be necessary? If the parents have this guarantee, then—"

"Ah. Well, it some cases, the parents have the funds to retain private counsel. The appointments from the panel come only if the accused—the parents—are indigent."

"Like the Public Defender?"

"Exactly like that," he said, approvingly, like I was a slow child who'd finally caught on. "In fact, it's the same panel that they call upon if the Public Defender can't handle a particular case."

"Why would—"

"It could be a conflict of interest," the lawyer said, comfortable now that he was talking about laws instead of people. "More than one defendant in the same case, for example. The Public Defender's Office could only take one of them. If the other defendants were indigent, someone from the panel would step in."

"You're on this panel?" Sonny asked him.

"Why do you ask?" the lawyer picking up on the boy's tone.

"Well...Because you know so much about it, I guess," Sonny said, dropping the aggression level.

The lawyer made a sound like he was satisfied with something. Said, "I've been on the panel for almost twenty years. Started right out of law school."

"What about the other kids in the Engle Home?" Sonny asked.

"The other kids?"

"Well, the ones who steal cars. Or beat someone up. You know, the 'juvenile delinquents,' or whatever they call them there."

"What about them?" the lawyer asked.

"Do they get lawyers?"

"You mean, at their trials? Oh, absolutely. Anyone accused of a crime that could result in them being detained, they have the same constitutional guarantees as anyone else."

"So if a kid beats someone up, he gets a lawyer. Or if that same kid, say, if his parents beat him up, he wouldn't get a lawyer?"

"That's correct," he said, almost smug about it. "Victims don't get lawyers."

"I can see that," I told him. "Sort of. Still, the victims, if they're grown, they get to, I don't know, testify and all. But that's the end of it. The State doesn't get to say where they live. Doesn't put them 'in care' like you said. Seems with so much at stake..."

"I don't disagree with you," the lawyer said, settling into his role. "But the law is the law."

ANOTHER HOUR PASSED, us talking like that. Sonny and I shark-circling around him. Making sure it was safe before we went in.

"That's really good information," I finally said. "But I don't think it would apply to us. To our situation, I mean. Even if I was...gone, for a long time, no one's going to say I ever abused—"

"I'm certainly not saying that, either. And Sonny...That's his name, or just what you call him?"

"That's his name. On all the papers. You know that."

"Sonny it is, then," he said, ignoring my implication that he hadn't read that whole stack of papers that he'd been paid to read. "And he's old enough to speak for himself, now. But that doesn't mean the court would listen to him."

"Because he wouldn't have a lawyer."

"Yes. And because, in the...scenario you outlined, he wouldn't be considered an abused or neglected child, so there'd be no trial. But, depending on the circumstances, he could be regarded as an abandoned child."

If they didn't find my body, I thought to myself. "You mean if I went on a business trip, and I was away too long, didn't stay in contact...something like that?"

"Yes. That's a perfect example. Simply by virtue of you not being around for a long enough period of time, unless some relative were to come forward, that would make your son a ward of the state. And when it comes to placement—"

"Because he wouldn't have a lawyer to say otherwise?

"Yes, that's correct."

"But you, you could be his lawyer, couldn't you?"

He sat quietly for a minute, like he was it thinking over. But I knew he'd been doing that ever since the word "estate" had surfaced.

"I could petition the court to be appointed his lawyer," he finally said. "But there's no state funds to pay for lawyers for children in such cases, so the court might be suspicious."

"Suspicious?"

"Yes. I have a copy of your will, remember? Your son would be heir to a considerable sum. So the court might think I was expecting to be paid out of that money. Do you remember that school shooting in Florida? Parkland? Where all those kids—"

"I do," Sonny said.

The lawyer blinked rapidly a few times. Then he said: "Well, it turns out that the shooter, that young man is coming into an inheritance. A lot of money. So he's not eligible for the Public Defender's Office to represent him. They made a motion to be relieved, and the young man will have to use that money to pay for his own defense."

"Okay..." I said, setting up a blank for him to fill in. "Public Defenders are paid by the State. Private attorneys can charge whatever they want. Whatever the client agrees to, I mean."

"So that big inheritance, it could all be spent on the case?""

"On a case of that magnitude? Certainly."

"And if you represented Sonny—in a case like we've been talking about, here—you could charge whatever you wanted? And get paid by the money in my will?"

"It's not that simple," he said, unable to keep the defensiveness out of his voice. "When you represent a minor, the court sets the fee. A reasonable fee."

"'Reasonable?'"

"Yes. There's some flexibility there, but, still..."

"I see what you mean, now. About them being suspicious," I said. "But if you were just a friend of the family, say you were doing it without asking for any money—"

"That's called pro bono," he said, solemnly. "For the public good. If I made an application to represent Sonny pro bono, I'm quite confident the court would appoint me to that role."

"And you'd make sure whoever they sent him to live with would be..."

"Oh, absolutely."

"And you'd check on him every once in a while?"

"I would," he said, his tone telling me that he knew we were writing a contract with words.

"You'd do that personally? Not just read some social worker's report?"

"Personally," he assured me. "And, of course, Sonny would have my phone number. Home, office, and cell. All my contact information. He's old enough to speak for himself."

"To anyone he wants," I underlined what I was saying. "Not only in court."

"That's right," he said, as if I hadn't just threatened him. But his rapid blinking assured me he knew.

I shifted my posture. Slowly, so he wouldn't think I was reaching for anything bad in my jacket. "How much does that cost?"

"How much does what cost?"

"This pro bono thing."

"Oh. Well, as I explained, it doesn't cost anything. It's...it's like a charitable contribution. In fact, the Bar expects all lawyers to do some pro bono work every year."

I put a heavy manila envelope on his desk, leaving the flap open. Ten thousand, in banded stacks of hundreds. "If I was to...disappear. If Sonny was to be called 'abandoned.' By the State, I mean. Then you could keep him out of Engle. Make sure he went to foster care. And that it was good foster care. Even if I was gone for a long time, I might be back someday. You never know."

The lawyer I didn't trust didn't reach for the money until he said, "I understand."

———

DRIVING BACK from the lawyer's, I thought about how badly I'd handled everything. I'd done the first part right, but I couldn't figure out the next move. And Sonny was growing, in all kinds of ways.

I knew some things. Some my father taught me; some I learned on my own during the years away doing my work. Most of that wouldn't be of any use to Sonny. He wasn't going to be following in my path. He wouldn't need to know how to hit a target who regularly visited the same porno shop, how to avoid the cameras such places used, how to find the dark spots where they'd never put them.

I knew I was done years before I'd stopped working. I only stayed out because that was the contract I'd signed. Not with the employers, with my father. The man who took me from Them. I signed that contract on the only line that matters: our bloodline.

I'd never done anything but the work. Never developed my own contacts or connections. Every single person I worked with had come from my father. Maybe from his father before him. I never asked.

It wasn't a life of killing that had taken those people I'd worked with out, it was the kind of life that runs out on everyone. People get old. Some last longer than others, but it's not a prison you can escape from, it's a sentence you have to serve. A life sentence, for as long as that lasts.

So the lawyer with the dry-ice eyes was gone now, and I wouldn't be able to find another. The lawyer Abel had left me wasn't part of us. I could pay him, I could make sure he understood what would happen if he didn't do what he was paid to do...but I couldn't ever trust him.

The middleman was probably gone by now, too. He'd been winding down hard for a couple of years before I left. I'd never met him, never knew how my father found him. But his voice...You could hear the hiss of the oxygen tank when he was on the phone.

I hadn't been glad to learn my father was gone, but I was tired. I'd really wanted to come in. Stop working. I was good at the work, but I knew time wasn't going to be good to me. I figured that much out. But where I kept getting stuck on was the "What's next?" part. Not for me, not even for Sonny. For the work itself. That couldn't stop.

———

EVEN IF I had wanted to, it was way late to be teaching Sonny the only trade I knew. But I'd been teaching him about the bloodline ever since I got him. Slowly, at first. Same as my father had done with me.

We, all of us, I told Sonny, we were like those gypsies. Moving on, finding a place to camp, moving on again. But not together. We weren't a clan. Our linkage was blood, yes...but not genetic blood. Blood we spilled. We don't know each other. No secret signs, no code words. No one was keeping count—never mind written records —but we know there's many of us. Everywhere. A tribe without a chief. All we have in common is Them.

Sonny wasn't like I'd been. He was warmer inside that I ever was. But he was colder, too, I think, in his own way. When I was little—I don't remember how old I was—I asked my father where I'd come from. He answered me the way he always did: telling me the facts of whatever he was explaining. But there was so much left out. So I waited until I got older until I asked him again.

"You're asking me about biology," my father said. "And I don't know the answers. There was a man—I don't know who he was—and he got your mother, whoever she was, pregnant. I don't know how that came to happen. What happened next is she gave her baby up for adoption. A "private placement," they call it. That means there wasn't any agency involved. No government. So whoever gave birth to you sold her baby. To one of Them. For money. Those people sold that baby again. For money. To more of Them. That's where I found you."

"Did you buy me, too?"

"I paid for you," is what he said.

"So my..." I had been going to say "my real," but I stopped myself. Because I knew the truth. "Real" isn't some bio-accident; it's what you do. I had a real father, the man I was sitting there talking with.

Sonny, he never asked questions like that. He was...I'm not sure how old he was when I got him, not precisely. Almost three, I think. Older than I'd been. Maybe he already knew the people I got him from hadn't been his mother and father. I don't know. I never asked him any questions like that, either.

EVERY DAY, I spent some time struggling with how Sonny could continue the work. And then the day came when our cameras picked up a big white SUV storming up the road toward the house. Later I realized that moment for when our world shifted on its axis.

I knew it couldn't be church people—they never drove that fast, and they never came alone. Wouldn't be tourists, either—the approach road forked so anyone could see the difference between our house and the little cottage we used as a shop, and there was no doubt where the SUV was headed. We'd get the occasional real estate lady seeing if we were interested in selling, and those always came alone, but they never flew up the road. Even cops drove slow when they wanted to ask about something.

"That's Mrs. Tristell's car," Sonny said, looking at the camera screen. "Brenda's mother."

"Brenda, she's a friend of yours?" I asked him.

"From school," he answered. Sometimes he talked the same way my father had—the weight was in what he didn't say.

_____

WE HAD the front door open and were waiting on the porch when the SUV pulled up. A slender woman slammed on the brakes, jumped out of the front seat and fast-walked over to where we were standing.

"That's her mother," Sonny said.

She came toward us, moving with determination, as though she was walking into a dangerous place that held something she needed. Her face was set in a stiff mask, mouth tight, eyes dry. Before I could ask her what she wanted, she started talking, the words coming out like they'd been recorded and she was in playback mode.

"My name is Sara Tristell," she said to me. "My daughter is missing. Brenda, she's just...missing. You know her," she said to Sonny. Not an accusation, just taking note of a presence she hadn't been prepared for. So whatever she wanted, it wasn't anything to do with Sonny, I thought, feeling myself go calmer.

"Would you like to come in? Sit down?" Sonny asked her. Polite; but gentle, not formal.

"Thank you," Sara Tristell said. "The police have my

number," her hand dipped into a shoulder purse and came out with a cell phone. I didn't take that for a "People know where I am" warning—it was self-reassurance, a talisman to show she was doing all the right things.

I stepped aside so Sonny could lead her to wherever he thought best, the kitchen or the living room.

It was the kitchen.

"What happened?" Sonny asked her, holding up a coffee cup by way of asking if she wanted any.

"Happened?" Her voice was pressured but she spaced her words evenly.

Responding, not engaging. "I don't know. Nobody knows. It's Brenda's first year. Of high school I mean. Tenth grade. It used to be middle school was only through—oh!" She interrupted herself, stopped for a second, caught her breath. "She wasn't on the bus when it came to her stop. That's only a couple of blocks from the house. She knew she wasn't to ever take rides home. You know, those older boys, the ones with cars..."

Sonny nodded in understanding, but I wasn't sure they were on the same broadcast band.

Her coffee cup sat in front of her, steam rising. I didn't expect her to drink it, so I didn't fill space with questions about cream or sugar—they were both on the table, anyway.

She took a shallow breath. "It was late, but I knew she had practice." Sonny said nothing. I didn't know if he was following her, but I stayed quiet. Waiting. Certain she'd fill it in.

"She's not ready for cheerleading, not yet," Sara Tristell tumbled out. "But she wanted that so badly that we let her try out for the pep squad. That's the most they let the ninth and tenth graders do. They don't practice every day. And I...I forgot which days it was supposed to be this week, so, when she wasn't on the bus, I guess I thought it was a practice day.

"Miss Debbie—I don't know her last name, 'Miss Debbie' is what the kids call her—she's got this three-row van, so she drives the kids home herself if they practice too late for the last bus. But that's never been later than six. Never."

"You called—" Sonny started to ask.

"I called everyone," she cut him off. "The numbers, they're right in my phone. And Brenda, she has her own phone. That was one of the reasons we let her have it. Ever since she was eleven. So she could call if she ever got stuck someplace where she needed us to come and get her. Or if...You know, if something happened at school. She was the first call I made. When it got to be six."

Sara Tristell took a shallow breath. "Actually, I didn't call her. Not at first. I sent her a text. So I wouldn't embarrass her in front of her friends. 'Helicopter parents,' that's what Brenda calls them. Always checking up on their kids, watching every move they make.

"So I texted her. But she didn't text back. She only did that once before. When she was mad at me for not letting her buy this...'outfit,' I guess you'd call it. No girl her age should be wearing...Oh, that's not important. But when she didn't text me back that one time, we knew it was deliberate, like back-talking, so we took her phone away for a week. She really acted up then, like she was being tortured or something. But her father and I, we believe..."

I sat there, as motionless as I had so many times, shallow-breathing, blending into the background. I didn't know why she'd driven out here to tell me all this—she could have just used that phone she kept talking about.

"That's when I called her," Sara Tristell went on. "But it went to her voicemail. She changes the message every day, it seems like, but it—the message, I mean—it always promises to call back. Only she didn't. My husband got home about half an hour later. I was a little worried about calling the police. I could just imagine how Brenda would take to that, but my husband, he said we had to.

"They were very nice. Came right out to the house. I wouldn't leave, in case Brenda came home. But while we were waiting, I used the land line and I called everybody. Miss Debbie said there'd been no practice that day. I called every number in my book. Every number I had then, I mean. I've got so many more in there now."

As if that was his cue, Sonny slid a phone charger onto the table, held up the plug-in ends so Sara Tristell could see them. She nodded gratefully, and Sonny made the connection for her.

"The police spoke to the bus driver," she said. "He didn't think Brenda got on the bus. It's hard to keep track, he said. And it's not like they have to sign in or anything. But he knew a couple of the kids who got on for sure, and the police spoke to them. By then, I had reached her friend Linda. And Linda was on the bus. She said Brenda didn't get on. And she would know, she said. There's a little group of them, and they always sit together.

"That was Tuesday," she said. "This is Thursday. Forty-eight hours.

You know, like on TV. I can't think of anything more to do. Then I thought to come out here."

"If there's anything we can—" Sonny said.

"It's you I came out to talk to," Sara Tristell said, cutting off Sonny and turning to face me.

"Me?" I asked her, not faking the surprise I felt.

"I didn't know what else to do," she answered me. "I mean, I already did everything I could think to do. Everything anyone suggested, I did that, too. Every question the police asked, I answered. My husband, too. My best friend Connie, she said we could hire a private detective, but that's just..."

"I mean, we're certainly not poor. And for our child, not a question. But a private detective? That's not a real thing, not around here. And dealing with strangers, that wouldn't..."

I shook my head, as if I didn't know where she was headed. "I still don't—"

"You used to...do something for the government, didn't you?" she cut me off. "Maybe while you were away? Like your father did?"

I let my eyes fill with confusion, but I'm not an actor and I don't know if I communicated anything to her.

"Oh, I know," Sara Tristell said. "That's just town-talk. Gossip. About your father, I mean. So when you were gone all that time, people said maybe it was a...mission, or something."

"Like one of those church—" Sonny started to say.

"No," she answered. "Look, I'm sorry. I wish I could explain better. I just have to do...everything. Even if it's crazy. I have to try. Brenda is our only..."

Sonny sat down at the table. He held his tablet in one hand. Tapped it a couple of times. "Brenda had a Facebook page?" he said to Sara Tristell. As if it was a question he already knew the answer to.

"The police already asked us that," she said, as though answering them was the same as answering Sonny.

Everything went quiet for a long minute.

"We had...We have her password. Her father insisted on that when she first wanted to have one of those...pages or whatever they're called. To protect her. The things you read about all the time...But that page, her page, it's...inactive. I mean, there's been nothing on it since..."

"Could I have that password, please?" Sonny asked, very polite.

"It's 'Brenny16,'" she said. "That's Brenny with a two 'n's', and a 'y' at the end."

Sonny tapped his tablet. Moved his head just enough to tell me he'd need some time to do whatever he was about to do.

"Did Brenda ever talk about running away?" I asked. Just an empty question, to buy Sonny some of that time.

"Never!" She spat that out. Fervent. But then she slid back a bit, dropping her tone. "Well, once. But that was the time we'd taken away her phone. She said I was being a..."

"Well, her father told her, if he'd ever talked that way to his mother, his father would have shown him what a leather belt was for."

"Did that—"

"Scare her?" Sara Tristell was quick with her answer. "Brenda? She giggled like he told a joke. Her father and me, we don't believe in that whipping stuff, and Brenda, she knew that. Even when she was little—being a little brat, I mean, you know how they can get—I never so much as spanked her.

"But then she saw how scared she'd made us and she started to cry. Her father, he just melted. But I know that little girl. So I told her, she wasn't getting her phone back no matter how she carried on."

"Did that stop her crying?" I asked.

"No," Sara Tristell said. "I was wrong. When I said I knew that little girl, I mean. Yes, she can twist her father around her little finger, but she wasn't trying to do that, then. So I told her I was sorry. And I hugged her. I guess I was crying, too."

"And she never talked about running away again?"

"Never." Sara Tristell said, like she was swearing an oath.

"Brenda wouldn't go anywhere with a stranger?" I asked her. Another of those questions that really wasn't one.

"Not in a million years," Sara Tristell said. Not trying to convince herself, just stating a fact. "Brenda's...Shy, I guess you'd say. I think that was why she wanted to be a cheerleader so very much. Those girls, why they're nice and all, I'm sure. But at the games, they seem so...bold. Not afraid of anything. I think that's why Brenda wanted to be one. One of them, I mean."

"Did she have a—"

"Boyfriend?" she cut in, barely keeping herself under control. "That was the first thing the police asked, the very first. But, no. No, she didn't. She knows she won't be allowed to car date until she's...older. Sixteen. She's known that for years. And around here, if you don't have a car...well, there's parties. Dances at school, too. She's allowed to go to those, but her father drives her and picks her up. That's the rule.

"He says he feels like a taxi driver when he does that. Because she never talks to him about the...dances, and all. But I told him, that's okay. Because she always talks to me. I'm always awake when they come back. Her father, he goes and watches a ball game or something on

TV. Or works in his office downstairs. Brenda and me, we sit and talk. Every time. So if she...

"Ah, I know," she went on, like she was stopping me from interrupting. "I'm not one of those mothers who thinks she's her daughter's girlfriend. I mean, I know she doesn't tell me everything. But...close to it, I think. One time, she had this crush on...Well, it doesn't matter. That was last year. She asked me so many questions. About...things with boys. So I knew how she...felt, I guess. But nothing came of it. I'm sure of that. He was a senior, after all," she said, as if that settled any question.

Nothing but silence after that, so I finally spoke into it: "What would you have me do?"

"I don't know," she said, reaching over to pat her phone like it was a guard dog she was counting on to protect her home. "But I had to try."

"That's what I can do," I told her.

She looked at me, waiting for the blank to fill in. "Try," I told her. "That's what I can do. Try."

———

SARA TRISTELL DROVE AWAY with our numbers embedded in her lifeline phone. The phone that had been a lifeless lump in her hand all the while she sat there in our kitchen. I had been watching as she waited on it to throb, her heart flexing in her eyes.

When I got back inside, Sonny was still working on his tablet. "She had another Facebook page," my son announced, as if he had discovered something important. "Not the one her mother had the password to. An Instagram account, also. That's all I can find on this thing," he said, holding up the tablet. "I need my computers to get more."

WHEN SONNY SAID "COMPUTERS," he wasn't exaggerating. His room was full of monitors, keyboards, plastic boxes with lights blinking in them, cables running everywhere. He had docking stations, chargers, other stuff I didn't have names for. Whiteboards with numbers and symbols on them, too.

I'd never really taken a close look at any of that stuff. In fact, I almost never went in Sonny's bedroom, or his bathroom, either. A boy needs privacy once he gets to be a certain age. I didn't know what that age was, exactly, but I remember my father saying those words. So once Sonny told me he could clean his own room, I took him at his word...and took his word to mean he was ready for that privacy.

Privacy. I thought about that all the time. I'd tried to talk to Sonny a couple of years ago. About things a man has to know, I mean. I'm not sure how it came to me, but I got the idea that I wasn't telling him anything he didn't already know.

But on the day that Sara Tristell came, I could tell by the way he moved after he mentioned his computers that he wanted me to come with him. Or just expected me to, I couldn't tell which.

Sonny kept his room really neat. Organized and clean, more like a laboratory than a bedroom. I sat on the end of the bed while Sonny worked. I felt like I should be guarding the door or something, but I just waited for him to say something. I can wait a very long time. Sonny knew that.

"IT STARTED OUT AS A CLUB," he finally said. "A club?"

"Yes. All girls. From the same class. Here, look..." On one of the monitors: R/ent Wii Qte?

I didn't know what I was looking at. "What's all that?" I asked him. "Aren't We Cute?" Sonny said, like a translator. "Here..."

Pictures. Young girls, in all kinds of get-ups. Some too old for them...but that made them look even younger, like little girls wearing their mother's clothes, playing dress-up. Others were just regular, jeans and t-shirts, Halloween costumes, mermaids, uniforms like cheerleaders wear.

Most of the photos were of girls posing together. Sometimes in pairs, sometimes more. A few had all of them. Some were individual shots. Not many like that.

Brenda's friends were at that age when telling them they looked older than they were would be something they really liked to hear. That would hold for maybe ten-twelve years, then slide in the other direction.

"That's the club," Sonny said. "That's what they posted. Just pictures, at first. But then they started chatting."

"Talking?"

"Kind of. But not voice, online. The way they posted those pictures, people could comment. Say things. Messages to them, like."

"You can see those? Things people say?"

"Sure. But there's a lot of them. See, it started out like they were taking a poll. 'Aren't we cute?,' that was like them asking the question. And, early on in the string, there's answers. See?"

He tapped some keys and the monitor changed:

=========================

U sho R! 100%!!!
Names! I need names!
The redhead is the princess of the pack! How can I inbox private?

============================

"What's that 'inbox' thing?" I asked him.

"He—or she, you can't tell online—was asking for their individual Facebook pages, so they could DM—Direct Message—get in contact one-on-one."

"Did they answer? Any of them?"

"No. Not really. Just being...flirty, like. 'Wouldn't you like to know!,' stuff like that."

"You said 'started out.'"

"Yes," Sonny said, talking over his shoulder without turning his head. "They started talking—talking back, I mean—as a group. But, later, Brenda went out on her own. She started talking with some of those people herself. Just her."

"By 'talking,' you mean—"

"Online, yes. To do that, she opened that other Facebook page. Her own photograph, but a different name—Thondra Telle. And the profile she made up, it was ... kind of like her, But she...changed stuff."

"Like where she lives?"

"That's not in there at all. But she's a *real* cheerleader, now. On her Thondra Telle page, I mean. A senior she's calling herself, not a tenth grader anymore. But she's slick. Says she skipped two grades in school. So it's like she could be her true age, but smarter. More grown-up, maybe."

"Can you see who she was...talking to? "

"Sure. It's not Snapchat."

"What?"

"The messages, they're not erased."

"But it's her own account, you said."

"Yes. She just made another gmail address: Miss-ThondraTelle17@gmail. So from that, I could have guessed her Facebook password without even breaking in. She just added two years to her real age in the email, so the password would be her new—her fake—birthday. She was already doing that—remember the Brenny16 her mother told us about? She's not really sixteen, so...Anyway, that worked."

"Was she talking to just one person, or...?"

"At first, it was a bunch of them. But they all sounded pretty much the same, what they said."

"How so?"

"They all wanted pictures."

"Didn't she put up all those same pictures? The ones from that first page?"

"She did. The ones of just her, anyway. But they wanted...private pictures, I guess you'd call them. Some of them were pretty gross."

"The pictures?"

"The way they asked for the pictures. Here..." Sonny moved aside so I could see the monitor screen:

=========================

"Could I see that pretty pussy?"
"How about you maybe bend over and flip up that skirt? "
"You could be a model. You have a portfolio?"
"Topless, please!"

======================

I turned away from the screen. "I get it," I told him.

"She didn't even answer those," Sonny said. "But there was one guy.

His name is Ryan. He says he's twenty-two. Just grad-uated from college, started his own business. He's a gamer, and—"

"What?"

"Plays video games. All the time. Hardcore. Not playing for fun—he's a designer. He says, anyway. So he's working on a package. A new game. With some partners. He, this Ryan, he doesn't do code. Or draw. He's a writer. So this 'concept' thing he talks about, that's his part."

"You have his picture?"

"There's a picture," he said, turning his shoulder so I could see the monitor again. Nice-looking young man, standing next to a shiny black piece of metal, flashing a bright-white smile. Blond hair a little on the long side, with a flame streak running through it. Wearing a motorcycle jacket over a white Tee with some ink-blot image on it.

"That doesn't have to be him," Sonny said. "Just like Brenda used a made-up name, people use other people's pictures. Sometimes because they don't think their real picture would work. Get them attention, I mean. Happens all the time," he said, like a cop talking about murders. "There's even a TV show about it. Not a show, actually—more like a documentary, but it happens over and over again. 'Reality TV' is what you'd call it."

"But it's not real?"

"The faking, that's real. I mean, people really do stuff like that. Sometimes it's one person doing it to another, sometimes they do it to a lot of people, sometimes—"

"Why? I mean, why do this? Do they ask for money? "

"Probably. I think some must, it's so easy."

"Easy because...?"

"Because the people they contact want it to be true."

He went back to his keyboards. I went back to waiting.

"RYAN'S A FAKE," Sonny pronounced, an hour later, not a hint of doubt in his voice.

"How can you know?"

"THE PICTURE HE USED, it's really someone else. The guy whose picture it is, he has his own Instagram. And a YouTube channel. He's a BMX rider."

"A what?" I asked, not embarrassed that I didn't know what Sonny meant—when he talked about his...life, that happened all the time.

"Trick bikes." Sonny never got annoyed explaining anything to me; he was a very patient boy, always older than his age. My father to me to him, I thought. A trait. Not in the genes, but still inherited.

"Bicycles, not motorcycles," he went on. "You've seen them—they're like kids' bikes, but built real strong, with those extended pegs coming out of the wheels. You can do all kinds of stunts with them: spin the front wheels when they're off the ground, ride on rails, stuff like that. They have special courses for the big performances. Prizes for the winners. Some of the events are even on television, like the X-Games...but you have to be really good to get that far. Most of the riders, they just do those YouTube performances. Not against other riders, just themselves. Showing off, like. Trying for views. You need those to get sponsors. That's the way—"

"Wait. How can you just steal a picture?"

If it bothered Sonny to be interrupted while he was explaining about those trick bikes, he didn't let it show. "There's nothing to it," he said. "Look." He did something with a big red ball on his desk that was surrounded by buttons, and the photo we were looking at moved off the page. Not the photo itself, it didn't disappear—it was just a copy that was moving. An exact copy. "You could drop that into wherever you want. Click, click, click."

I didn't say anything, but Sonny went on as if I was asking the questions in my mind.

"YouTube's like an Internet TV station. With a zillion channels.

Anyone can put up whatever video they want. Then anyone watching can comment—say something—about the show...whatever show they put on. When anyone looks, it registers, so you can see how many people actually watched. Then, if you get enough views, you could get offers from sponsors."

"Sponsors for...? "

"Products, mostly."

"Products? Like our birdhouses?"

"I guess you...could. But I mean products that get advertised on the Internet. Stuff the people who watch would want to buy. And they could, just by clicking a link. Clothes, mostly. Or gear, like headphones, or...knives. Whatever

"But, really, anything. It depends on what's being showcased on the videos, the people who like that stuff, you could tell what products they'd want."

"So this guy—not Ryan, the one he stole the picture from, the BMX guy—he could be selling bike stuff?"

"He could. It depends on why people are following him, what they're into. They could be people who like the stunts—the crazier the better, that's how it usually works."

Sonny was quiet for a minute. Then he said: "Or maybe they just like him for himself. The BMX guy, I mean. Brice, that's his real name. Brice Mountain."

"Could that name be a fake, too? I mean, it sounds..."

"Sure. It could be. I mean, there's mountain bikes, so it does sound sketchy. But probably not. Not at this level. For him, it's a business. He's looking to get paid. And he rides in competitions, too—I checked. I don't think he'd be a spoof. No," Sonny said, confidently, "that's his real name."

"So Brenda, she wouldn't...no, she wouldn't contact the real guy, the guy who's picture she thinks is Ryan, because she couldn't find the right...channel. Unless she liked these BMX bikes, she wouldn't even know there was that picture out there."

"That's right," Sonny said, like he was proud of me finally catching up. "But wouldn't she find out, eventually? I mean, when they met up?"

"They might never meet up," Sonny said, thoughtfully. "The guy she's been talking to, the one who says his name is Ryan, he could live anywhere. Anywhere in the world, really. They could just talk on the phone. Send texts. Emails. Anything but FaceTime, that would blow the covers off. They'd never see each other IRL."

"IRL?"

"In real life."

"You think that's what he wanted? To just stay on...the Internet, or whatever. Never actually meet her."

"Not him," my son said, an edge showing on his voice. "Here's the last string of messages."

THE MONITOR SCREEN was like one of those ancient stone tablets with writing on it, the ones they find in excavated ruins in deserts, or high in mountains no one has climbed in centuries. And Sonny wasn't just a guide, he was an interpreter, too.

"They made up to meet," he said, reading slowly. Then..."Wait. Not just to meet. To...To be together."

"You mean for sex?" I asked. I wasn't worried about making Sonny nervous. I knew he was old enough to know some things. I didn't know if he'd ever done those things, but I wasn't worried about that, either. My father had never talked to me about girls. Not in specifics, I mean. Not...how to do anything. Or even what to do, or when. My father hadn't taught me about sex, not specifically, but he'd taught me to listen to other people without making a big show of it. So he was confident I'd learn.

Looking at that screen, I knew right then the moment was close. When I had to talk with Sonny. Not about girls, about what we do. Our tribe. Our line. I already knew my son was never going to do what I did, but that alone wouldn't break the line. We weren't all killers, I didn't think...my father, he never said. But no matter what we did to live, we knew what we had to do with our lives. Each of us had to take one from Them.

I was younger than Sonny when I'd done that first job. The bundler. But I'd been practicing way before that. In some way I don't understand, I guess I always knew I'd be doing what my father had done before me.

The same way I guess I knew Sonny wouldn't be.

My father had made his decision. I'd made a different one. We would each send our sons out when the time came.

Send them to the same destination. But on different paths.

"SEX, that would be part of it, I guess," Sonny said, breaking into my thoughts. "But it wasn't some hook-up they were talking about. They wanted to be together like the way people are when they get married. Live together."

"They're just kids."

"Brenda is," Sonny agreed. "We can be sure of that, because we know her in real life. But this Ryan—whoever he really is, there's no way to tell—he says he's grown. Old enough to have a job. His own place. He could take care of her. That's what he said."

"So she's with him?"

"I think so. But we don't know who he is. Or where he is." Or what he is, I thought. I kept that to myself.

SONNY KEPT WORKING. Using his mind like an archeologist with one of those tiny brushes, very deliberate with every move.

"He picked her up," he told me after a while. "The same day she went missing. Right after school."

"No way to tell where they went?"

"There's a way to tell where he said they were going to go. The state line isn't that far, and it's legal to get married there at her age."

"Her actual age?"

"I don't know. I don't think so. But at the age she said she was, sure. Because there's the law, right here," he said, pointing at another monitor. "There's this website that has the age of consent for every state."

"Age of consent to...?"

"Well, the first few I found, it was to have sex. 'Age of consent' meant to have sex and not be against the law.

But I kept looking, and there's ones with the legal ages for getting married, too. Some of the states, there's no age at all."

"There has to be," I said, thinking how could children get married?

How could that be legal? My mind going to what the lawyer I didn't trust had told me about the old lawyer's will. Something about legislation...

"Not if the parents consent," Sonny said, tapping his finger at some of the states on his screen—they gleamed in a bright red color. "Anyway, Ryan looked that up and sent it to her."

"So she was lying. And he was lying."

"She was lying about her age, sure. And he was lying about his picture, definitely. But for all the rest...?"

"Yeah," I said. With nothing to add.

"BEFORE SHE RAN, Brenda never actually met Ryan," I finally broke the silence. "Not in what you said, not in real life. She wouldn't recognize him just from seeing him. So they'd have to be very specific about where they were going to be that day. And it had to be near enough to school for her to walk."

"But not right at school," Sonny came back with. "Or even too close. People would see. They're always watching."

"Which people do you mean?"

"Just...kids. They want to know who's talking to who, who's hanging out with who, who's...you know."

I wasn't sure I did, but I nodded so he'd keep the train moving. "She wouldn't..." Then..."Sure!"

He went back to tapping keys, watching his monitors.

I closed my eyes. Sometimes that helps me think. "His car," I said, after a bit.

"What?"

"His car," I told Sonny. "He could recognize her. From those pictures she put up. Those were actually her, we know that for sure. But his pictures, those were someone else, so we already know he wouldn't look like the ones he put up. And who would know that better than him? So he'd have to give her something to watch for. Some signal, some—"

"A Mustang!" Sonny cut me off. "Here it is. On his page. A new one. White, with blue stripes. All we have to do..."

A picture of the Mustang Sonny was talking about filled one of the monitor screens.

"That's what Brenda would have been looking for," he said. "And, now

...there! In the parking lot behind the library. Not the school library, the big one. You can see it on Google Earth...there. That's all the way downtown. Too far for her to have walked. It would take a couple of hours, at least.

That's too much time. By then, they would have known she'd gone missing."

"That's if she stayed through her last class, right? Did anyone ask...?"

"I don't know," he answered. "Her mother, she never said."

——————

I DIDN'T KNOW how they worked school now, so I asked Sonny a lot of questions: Did they take roll call? How big were the classes? Did the teachers check if any of the desks were empty? Maybe if Brenda had a note from her parents, would they excuse her from afternoon classes? She made a whole new identity, how hard could it be to forge a note like that? Or if she went home sick, would the school call to see how she was doing? If...?

Sonny didn't know any of the answers.

I didn't want to call Brenda's mother. If she knew anything about this Ryan, she would have told us. Told the police, for sure.

"I think I have an idea," I told Sonny. "It might be crazy..."

"Tell me," he said, fingers poised above the keyboard like he was

touching the connection between us.

———————

"U OK?" showed on one of the monitors.

"There!" Sonny said. "You think Brenda will see that?"

"I don't know," I told him. "You said her page is still up, right? The one that everyone knew about, I mean. So it's there, but we don't know if it's actually live." I wasn't so much talking about the page, but I kept any of that out of my voice.

"Oh, she'd still be checking her page," Sonny said, as if stating a fact beyond challenge.

I gave him a look, questioning his confidence.

"It's her...it's her self, in a way," he answered. "She wouldn't, you know, post anything. Necessarily. Not anything new, I mean. But she'd still want to know what was going on. Look, here..." he said, turning the monitor screen.

There were dozens of messages. The oldest ones were all from girls she knew, talking about things girls that age did. Days ago. But not the most recent ones. Those were all some version of the one we just sent. More dramatic, though. Frantic, even...as if they were building momentum.

Sonny seemed to understand without us exchanging a word. If Brenda was checking her messages, she'd recognize everyone who was reaching out to her. All except for us. Except for Sonny, I mean.

"Anyone can send her one of those message things, can't they?" I asked him.

"It's not always that way," he told me. "Some people set theirs up to private, so messaging is only for those they allow. But that's not how Brenda has her page— the one everyone knew about—set up. Hers is set to public, so, sure, anyone could message her. One time, anyway."

"One time?"

"She could still block anyone she wanted, but she couldn't do that in advance for a new person—they'd have to message her first, so she'd even know they existed."

"So we...whoever just asked her if she was okay, I mean...he could be one of those guys who was asking the 'Aren't we cute?' girls for pictures, couldn't he?"

"Sure. But none of those guys would be asking if she was okay. They wouldn't even know there was a...situation. How could they?"

"You have one of those pages, too?"

"Sure," he said, as if I asked him if he had a cell phone. "But I'm not friends with Brenda."

"You mean, not on the Internet."

"Right."

I don't know why it didn't occur to Sonny that any of those people who had asked for pictures of Brenda posing for them might be people she actually knew, but him not thinking that way was comforting, somehow.

———

WE LET the computers sit while we had something to eat in the kitchen. Ham and greens on thick slabs of rye, sweet mustard, carrot sticks and celery stalks on the side. Grape juice, cold.

I can go a long time without food, but I knew Sonny was supposed to have three meals a day. Three good meals. When I had been his age and going to school, my father told me I should eat as little as possible there. "Cafeteria food," he said. "Nothing in that but money for whoever got the supply contract."

I didn't say anything. By then, I knew when more was coming.

"I don't want you to take your lunch with you," he went on, as though he could see my thoughts, "I know how that looks. So just put whatever you want on your tray, but don't put most of it down your belly. We can make it up when you get back home."

AFTER WE ATE, we went back to Sonny's room. He tapped keys and the monitors popped to life.

"Nothing new," he said, the barest trace of sadness in his voice.

"That could mean anything." I told him. Flat. Just the truth, not trying for comfort.

"So it could mean that's she's...not okay?"

"Yes," I said, bluntly, but keeping my voice soft. "It could also mean that she never told any of her friends about this Ryan of hers, and she's afraid that if she told them the truth now, they'd give her up."

"Give her up?"

"I don't mean calling the cops. Just telling her parents that she's all right. But if they ended up questioned by the police, at least one of them would tell whatever she knew, I'm certain of that much."

"So Brenda might really be married and all? Already?"

"Might be? Sure. That's why you sent that message, isn't it?"

"So all we can do is...Wait! What about the car?"

"A white Mustang with blue stripes? That's pretty common, isn't it? There was no license plate in the photo. We don't even know what state it was from. Could even have been a rental."

"But...as soon as she got to the car, she'd see right away that Ryan wasn't the same guy as the photo. So she'd know he—"

"She might already be in the car by then," I cut in, trying to interrupt his chain of reasoning. "And the car could be moving."

What I didn't say: There might have been someone else in the car. In the back seat. I remembered something my father told me. About Them. Most take babies. Or real young children. But some, they want older kids...

"Can you find the real Ryan?" I asked, more to distract Sonny than anything else. "The guy whose picture Ryan used, I mean? That BMX guy? Brice Mountain?"

"We already did, didn't we? That picture-match and all. But I don't see what good that would do us, not now."

"Couldn't we—"

"We found the guy in the picture," Sonny cut me off. "Brenda, she didn't. Because if she had—"

"She'd know the other guy, the guy who picked up her up the day she went missing, she'd know he was a fake. And she would have stopped talking to him way before..." That's what I said, but I was thinking we didn't know how smart Brenda was. Or why she made the choices she did.

Sonny just nodded.

I STAYED PATIENT, inside myself. Trying to work with what Sonny knew, what I knew...what we knew together. When the idea came to me, I thought it over for a while, but I wasn't getting anywhere on my own. So I asked Sonny:

"Can you contact her other page? The fake one she made? "

"Thondra Telle?"

"Yes. That one."

"Let me see...Sure. At least it looks like I can."

"Okay. Can you send her the exact same message you sent to her real page?"

"Sure," he said again.

A few seconds, a few keyboard taps, a click. "It's done." By then, it was way past dinnertime.

A couple of hours later, nothing.

Sonny showed me a little blue plastic box on the night stand next to his bed. "If she answers, this will make sounds. And flash a light. I'll wake up, don't worry."

That's how we left it.

I WAS UP VERY EARLY the next morning. Still dark outside. I made myself a bowl of cereal, waiting for Sonny to get up.

Two things I'm good at: being quiet and being patient.

I was still in the kitchen when Sonny came in. "Nothing," he said, saying everything in that one word.

I sat with him while he had his own breakfast. Same as mine, only he wasn't as quiet putting it together.

No reason for him to be, I thought. I'd never taught him, not as I'd been taught.

"Dad, I want to take a shower. Can we go back to my room? So you can get me if a signal comes in. All right?"

———

"RYAN'S GOING GHOST," Sonny said, about an hour later.

"Going ghost?"

"Well, his page is still up there. But he's not posting. Not public posts, anyway—I can't see his private messages."

"But you could see Brenda's..."

"That's because, with her password and all, I can be Brenda. I could even post to her page if I wanted."

"That wouldn't help us, would it? "

"No."

It's been too long, I was thinking. Time enough to cross a couple of state lines, get to wherever they wanted to be. Or maybe just where...

I watched Sonny work. Time enough to do whatever this Ryan person—him and some others, maybe—time enough to do whatever they wanted to do. Brenda could be...

"Dad," Sonny said. He was pointing at one of the monitors. On the screen: *Who *is* this?*

"WHAT DO I SAY?" Sonny asked me.

Damn! I thought. *My fault. We should have had something all prepared.*

We didn't have time for me to think it through. The best I could come up with was: "You do know her, right? From school? So tell her you're a friend of hers. A friend she didn't even know she had. A friend who cares about her."

"All that?"

"Put it however you think would...get to her. Make her understand, I mean. You're not the law, not going to tell anyone...You're just worried about her, want to be sure she's all right. The important thing, she has to know you're real."

Sonny tapped some keys. "What's my name?" he asked me.

"Maybe just something like 'Senior,'" I told him. "The grade she's supposed to be in."

"I don't think that will work."

"I thought, a senior. At her school, I mean... "

"Because this Ryan guy, he was older than her? "

"I...guess so."

"But she's already with him," Sonny said, not happy with my idea, and not wanting to say so. "Whoever he is. And...I don't know. We don't know it's even Brenda who answered. How would we know if it's Brenda herself who's asking us that question?"

Maybe there is no more Brenda, I thought, keeping that off my face. *Maybe whoever got her into that car is* just buying time. "You want to just say who you really are?" I asked, out loud.

"I guess I could," Sonny said, doubtfully. "I mean, she does know me, kind of, but we're not like good friends or anything. Girls in the same year as you, they usually..."

"You're right," I told him, trying to paint over his worries, coming to a full decision. "No games. If you tell her the truth, no matter what she asks you, you wouldn't have to look anything up to answer her. We wouldn't need to get a story ready, we'd always be ready."

"The truth," Sonny said, like it was something he hadn't considered, but now that he'd thought it over...

"She...or whoever's at the other end of this...she says she's fine. "

"What does that mean?" I asked him.

"I don't know. You want me to...?"

I was frozen inside myself. If we just turned the information we had over to the law, they'd know what to do. Notify the FBI or some big government agency. They could take over from Sonny, maybe track down wherever the messages were coming from.

But then Sonny's name would be on their radar. I couldn't have that. I didn't know how he was going to carry on the line. Not yet, I didn't. But however that played out, being in some federal file might get in his way. In our way. All of ours.

"Would it be safe for her to call?" I asked him.

"Safe?"

"Would she be afraid the call could be traced?"

"She shouldn't be. She probably turned off the locator on her phone when she left. And she could just go to the store and buy a pre-paid—there'd be no way to trace that, especially if she only used it the once."

"Ask her if she'll call. Tell her all you want is to hear her voice."

"There's even a better way," Sonny said.

"FACETIME?" I asked him, a little later.

"I think it's called that because it's all through Face-book," Sonny said, speaking quickly, as if his thoughts were words. "Only that would be Messenger, then. Maybe it's an Apple thing, I'm not sure. But whatever it is, I know she must have the app. Probably on her phone. It doesn't matter–I've got both OS. Linux, too. I'll figure it out–only take a few seconds. Then, when I turn the camera on, she'll see me, and I'll see her."

I nodded a "Go ahead."

"Over there," Sonny said, pointing to the corner nearest the door. "You'll be off-screen," he told me before he started working at the keyboard. "I don't think seeing a grownup would be a good thing for her, now."

For a split-second, I wondered why he didn't warn me about not moving around. But then I knew.

———

THE MONITOR'S screen filled with a girl's face. The same face as in the photograph of Brenda Tristell.

"I know you," the girl said. "Sonny, right? You're in Morning Glory's home room. You always sit in the back. How did you find my page?"

Sonny faced his monitor. "I just figured you'd need another page," he told her.

"Because...?" she prompted, her voice a little edgy but not frightened. "Well, your folks had the password to your first one."

"How did you know that, Sonny? "

"Your mother said."

"My mother? You went over to—"

"No. She came here. To my house. I guess she was going around to all your friends—"

"My girlfriends, I could see her doing that. But you, you and me, we never even—"

"I guess she was just trying everything she could think of."

"She would," Brenda said, a trace of pride in her voice. Then, "Look, I'm not going back. I can't, not right now."

"I'm not trying to make you do anything," Sonny said, sounding...I don't know...not older, exactly...but like he was older than her, anyway. "I was just, you know, worried about you. Nobody knew where you'd gone to. Or even if you were all right."

"Are you going to tell them? "

"Your parents?"

"Yes."

"Not if you don't want me to. But maybe if you—"

"If I even, like, contact them, they're going to make me come back. And I'm not ready. I have some things to figure out, first."

"I could do it," Sonny said. "I could say you contacted me, how would that be?"

"I don't understand."

"Make an account," Sonny told her, his voice calm and deliberate, like he was explaining how to deactivate a bomb, going step-by-step, locking in an understanding on each move before he explained the next one. "You know how to do that. Then just send a message to my page."

"The police could—"

"Go to any store that sells pre-paids," Sonny interrupted. Calmly, as though he'd been ready for her objections. "Send the message from that phone. Then pop the SIM card and smash it. And close down that Facebook account, the one you're going to make. I could screenshot whatever you send me, and show the message to your mother. Even if she shows that to the police, what could they do with it?"

"Oh my God, you sound like one of those terrorists," she said. Her voice bouncing between giggly teasing and giggly nervous.

"It would be just the opposite," Sonny said, gently. "It's your parents who are terrorized, aren't they? Once I tell them—show them—that you're all right...Well, they may be mad, sure. I don't know. But they won't be frightened. Not anymore. That's what matters, right?"

"You make it sound so easy. You don't..."

Sonny didn't say anything. I could only see him in profile, but he leaned forward slightly, as if inviting her to finish whatever she started to say.

I was so proud of him right then, although I couldn't have said exactly why.

"It's complicated," Brenda said.

"Sure," Sonny answered as though he was on her wavelength.

It went quiet for a minute or so. I watched Sonny watch his monitor screen.

"You already know about...Ryan, right?"

"I only know what I don't know," Sonny told her, staying hard on the truth.

"Well, nothing's changed," she said, her voice heavy

on defensive, hovering close to the edge of anger. "He's not...Ryan, okay? I mean, he is, only he doesn't look like...but he's still the same one I've been...talking to, all this time. And we're still going to...you know."

"Get married?" Sonny said, confirming that he did know. "Couldn't you come home and still do that?"

"Come on!" Brenda's voice shifted again. "You know how old I am. How old I really am. It would be years before we could...be together. "Mah—he'd—probably be mad if he knew I was even talking to you like this. Or scared. My parents—my father for sure—I think he'd put the cops on him. I have to think. About all of this. When...when he gets back, I'm not going to say anything. We've got...plans. But not for right now. So there's time. Still time, you understand?"

"He's at work," Sonny said, not making it a question.

"Yes," she answered. "But that's what I mean. If you do what you promised, what you promised before, I mean. So if you tell my parents, that would take off some of the pressure. But only—only—if that's all you tell them."

"I'd do that," Sonny said. "I'd do just what I promised. Not a word more than that. But I can't tell them I got a message from you until I get one, right? I can't say anything about what we're doing now. This video calling, I mean."

"I can do it like you told me," Brenda said, confidently. "I wouldn't have to go out to buy anything—there's everything I need, right here. I can make another page in a minute, and there's already some of those phones. Right here, I mean. Still in the plastic."

"I don't think you should tell—" Sonny started to say.

"Oh, I won't tell him," Brenda interrupted. "Not

anything. Let's see how my parents...act, and all, first. I'll come back. Soon."

"To...?"

"To here," Brenda said. "To you. Like we are now."

"Lock it in," Sonny said, putting his palm flat against the monitor. After a few seconds, Brenda reached out and did the same.

WHEN THE SCREEN FLICKERED, Sonny got up from where he was sitting. "Now we have to wait," he told me, putting his hand out palm-down, thumb holding back the two middle fingers so only the index and the pinky were aimed at me. I inverted my hand, aimed the same at him so the tip of my trigger finger touched his pinky and my pinky touched his index. The secret signal of our family, the one I'd taught him when he was just a little boy—"Just between us.... All of Us."

"NOW WE WAIT," I said to Sonny. "We can take turns—"

"We don't need to actually watch the screen," he told me. "I can link it to my phone."

"We'll be able to see a message when she— "

"No. I don't want to take that chance. "

"Chance on...?"

"On the police. If they were to grab my phone, all they'd find is that it shows when there's action."

"Action?"

"On my computer. Just the one. The one we have the Facebook page on.

But I don't have the app on my phone."

"Sonny, you're—"

"I don't mean to be confusing," he said. Not apologizing, just saying facts. "Most of the kids, they have their Facebook pages on their phones. On the phones themselves. That's where they post. And follow."

My face must have told him "follow" wasn't something I was doing. "Follow other people. People they know. And...celebrities, like.

Famous people. You can get that all on your phone, if you want. Instagram, Twitter..."

"But you don't do that? Any of that?"

"No. This link, it's something I made myself. All it tells me is when there's incoming on any of my computers. I can make a separate link just for the one we use to talk to Brenda."

"But if the police had your phone, they could go right to that same computer, couldn't they?"

"Sure. But they wouldn't know what I was being alerted to. And I can spoof it off. In fact, I already..."

"What?"

"Well, I actually have that all set up. And that computer, it's got a feed to a sports book. So I know every time the line moves on whatever I'm interested in."

My head had been spinning ever since Brenda first said "Mah." What had she started to say and then stopped? "My father"? That didn't seem right, because she said those same words later, without hesitation. And now Sonny was barreling down a different road. "Book?" I asked him. "You mean like in Vegas?"

"Exactly," Sonny said, smiling a little. "I'm a gambler."

"You?"

"Just on baseball," he told me, as if that explained everything. After a few seconds watching my face, he could see it didn't. "Baseball, it's a team sport," my son continued. "But not like basketball or football. Those have teams, and I guess they play together, sort of. But it's not the same. They don't really play together the same way.

"See, every team has stars, but, in baseball, the stars don't depend on the others as much. No one has to throw them a pass, it's like the other team does that...when someone on one team hits the ball, it's someone on the other team that has to catch that ball. Or, even before that, when a pitcher throws, it's only one man who gets a chance to hit the ball."

"So it's more like—"

"It's more predictable," Sonny said. "Not like a video game, not that much. But each—"

"Video games are...predictable?"

"Kind of," he said. Thoughtfully, as if he hadn't considered it before. "The...characters, they can't do things their character can't do. Like fly, say. Some characters have flight powers, others don't. So you can't just move a joystick or push buttons and get a character to fly if that's not programmed in by the designer."

"He, this Ryan, he doesn't do code. Or draw. He's a writer. So it's this 'concept' thing, that's his part." Sonny's words earlier, my thoughts now.

"But in baseball," Sonny went on, "you can't know for sure what any player is capable of. I mean, you know a certain player can't run all that fast, for example. But making a great catch...well, there's players more likely to do that, but it doesn't mean another player couldn't do it once, see? So there's always at least a possibility."

My son is a gambler? That thought fired through my mind, but I let it go just as quick. Maybe there's a gambling gene, like some say there is for addiction, but if Sonny had any such, he couldn't have gotten it from me.

I didn't want to pretend I was following everything Sonny was saying.

That would be lying to him, and I never did that. But I could see if he kept explaining, I'd only get more confused. So I tried to shift him onto a different track.

"Wait," I said. "This...what you did today. With the phones and all...that's not all faked? You set it up in advance?"

"It's not fake," he answered, looking me full in the eyes like he does when he needs me to understand something. "I've had the account for a couple of years now."

"And you actually bet?"

"Not very often. And never a lot."

"What's 'not a lot'?"

"Fifty dollars."

"Uh-huh. And what's 'not often'?"

"That depends," my son said. "If everything's right, that's when I bet. That's the only time I bet. Sometimes, it's a couple of weeks before I make a play. Or even longer. But that's not on a schedule. Like I said, the line has to shift. Once, I made two bets on the same day."

"Is this real money?"

"What do you mean?"

"Well, if you can fake the account..."

"The account's not fake," Sonny said, just this side of offended. "The credit card it's tied to, that's real. You can't bet without money, can you?"

Sure you can is what I thought to myself. The middleman never gave me any information about the work I was to do, but I remembered one time I read in the paper about a man I'd killed two days before. He was famous. Not to me. Not to most people, maybe. But he was a big-time loan shark, with a long record. And he owned a lot of flashy businesses: strip joints, night-clubs...what the paper called the "entertainment industry."

The way they wrote it up, it wasn't even a secret how he made his money. In the movies, someone gets in too deep on a loan, he gets beat up. Sometimes even crippled. But never killed. That would be bad for business—how can you collect a paperless debt from a dead man?

But that's the movies. The same movies where you can knock a man unconscious with a tire iron, and he's okay in a few hours...especially if he's the star. That's what my father taught me when I was still learning. "We use bullets because they work," he said. "And we use more bullets because they don't always work. Some people live through stab wounds, other people die from a paper cut."

I knew this was true. Just as I knew that beating up a man isn't doing science. Once you go a certain distance, it's down to luck. The target could have a heart condition, a broken rib could puncture a lung...there's all kinds of ways those things can go wrong.

No one ever hired me to scare anyone.

I kept all that off my face as Sonny went on, "You use the card to set up an account. With a deposit, I mean. It's like any bank account: you can make deposits—or withdrawals—anytime you want. More like an ATM than a bank, I guess, because they're always open."

"The credit card, that's real, too?"

"Yes. All it takes to get a credit card is money. And you can make that first deposit with a money order. After that, it's all online, so they never see—"

"So you took your own money and you just..."

"I did. Remember when we first talked about a paper route? It was around then."

I didn't want to ask him how much money he'd lost,

so I thought for a minute, framing a neutral question. "Have you had to make a lot of...deposits?" I tried.

"I made three," Sonny said, trying for matter-of-fact, but there was a faint layer of pride coating his voice. "I lost the first one pretty quickly. The second one—they were a hundred each—that one lasted almost two months."

"And the third one?"

"I've still got that in there. I mean, I never had to replace it. "

"Huh," is all I said.

"I only bet when the line's wrong," Sonny said, speaking another language, like we were back to computers. I looked at him so he'd see I wasn't making any judgments; I just didn't understand.

He nodded, like he understood me.

"The line," he said, watching my face. "Say the Dodgers are minus one sixty-five against the Rockies. Because it's a home game for them, the Dodgers, and the Rockies don't hit many homers outside of their own park. But the pitcher—for the Dodgers, I mean—he's a fireballer. A strikeout artist. He throws real hard, so he needs more rest than most. Pitches much better with five days rest than four. And the Dodgers are coming home off a road trip, flying in from New York, so they'll have to adjust to the time-change.

The real line should be closer to minus one twenty-five. So I bet into that gap."

"Fifty dollars?"

"At the most. But that's pretty much the standard, yes."

"You have a...system?"

"I have a formula," Sonny corrected. "A hypothesis I'm testing. There's a lot more that goes into it. And I'm always inside the limits I put on myself. So I do win plays only. I never make prop bets. No parleys, no over/unders, no doubling down to chase."

I let him see he was losing me again. Not showing impatience—Sonny knows I'm never impatient with him —just not able to keep up. He didn't say anything, so I asked: "Prop bet?"

"That's short for 'proposition,'" he explained. "Say, how many strikeouts a certain pitcher is going to have by the sixth inning."

"They take bets on that?"

"They take bets on anything," my son said, as if he was telling me the grocery store carried different brands of soda. "You can even make up your own...proposition...and they'll give you a line on it."

"And they never ask questions? About whether you're old enough to be betting or...?"

"I'm not a person," Sonny explained. "Not to them. I'm an account. Some betting, it can get complicated. But I never go near any of that. I was just giving you a rough idea."

"So all this, it isn't for fun?"

"It's for money," Sonny answered me.

"You said you made three deposits. So that means you still have money on...account?"

"I have three thousand, four hundred and seventy-five dollars," he said, blushing slightly.

"That's...impressive," I told him. The truth.

WHILE WE WERE WAITING, Sonny did all kinds of things on his computers. Too fast for me to follow, but I knew he wasn't showing off, just working at his own speed.

I got up, stretched, moved around a little. Sometimes you can do that on a job, sometimes not. Whenever you can, you do it. The job itself is always over in a few seconds, but you might have to wait a long time to get started, and you want to be full-ready when it's time. A cramp could change the outcome, and the outcome has to be as sure as you can make it.

"Everything's okay for now," he finally said. "My phone will tell me if Brenda's back. So we can go anywhere we want, so long as it's close by."

———

"YOU THINK SHE WILL? Come back? To the computer with you, I mean?"

"I...do think so," Sonny said. "She said she would. There's no reason for her to lie."

"But she's been lying for quite a while now," I pointed out.

"She wasn't lying," Sonny defended her. "She just wasn't telling her parents about this guy. Wasn't telling anyone, I don't think. How could she?"

I didn't know what to say to that, so I stayed quiet. Thinking Sonny hadn't told me about his betting. And how I hadn't seen that as lying. Trying to see some balance point buried inside those different ways of looking at the same thing.

———

I CAN STAY quiet a long time. My father taught me that. He always said waiting is a skill. A piece of patience. "You have to split your mind," is how he explained it to me. "Part of what's going on inside of you is focusing on the target. Not thinking, focusing. Like with a camera viewfinder. Twisting the knobs until the image is sharp. And all the extra stuff is doing. 'Cropping in the camera' is what they call it. Anyone can do that in the darkroom —doing it before you snap the shutter, that's the real skill.

"And that's the job, son," he finished up. "That's always the job. But you don't want to be sitting and staring. People notice things like that."

"The other part, I go over the—"

"No," he cut me off. "What happens after you do the work, that's got to be no-think. Automatic. You don't want to be going over that part in your mind. Doing it, that's all there is. Get it down, get it down right, and you'll just go through the steps without thinking."

I must have looked as if I wasn't understanding, so he said:

"Like when you learned to drive a car. Once you got it down, you never had to think about turning the wheel, or letting out the clutch, or stepping on the brakes. When it's happening, you don't have time to do all that thinking, it just has to...happen. Say you're going to be driving the car to the store in an hour, do you sit and think about how you're going to do that? No. When the time comes, you just drive to the store. Well, the work, that's the same thing. You can't question yourself, or you'll start to question your own answers."

"So what's that other part, then? Before I...before it happens."

"That can be whatever you want. Maybe you're reading a newspaper. Or drawing something in a notebook. It doesn't matter. That's only what people see. What's going on in your mind, that's only for you. All it has to do is let you be calm. This work, you have to be calm. Stay calm, beginning to end.

"This work you're going to do, it's just a job. Some people hate their jobs, some people like them, but most people, the only reason they do their jobs is because they get paid for doing them. They do the job, they go home —or wherever—then they come back the next day and do it again. You just have more time between shifts than they do."

"And...regular people, when they're done working? Done for good, I mean."

"They retire. Just like I did. Just like you're going to do. We—our line—we all have the same retirement plan. That's when we get the next one ready. Like I did you."

"But you're still—"

"No," he stopped me saying what I was going to say, very calm. "No, son. I'm all done working. And you, you're ready."

ONCE I HAD to go inside a house to do my work. There was no choice about that. All I knew was that the target was in a wheelchair—I hadn't been told he never went outside.

I don't like to work indoors. And I guess I could have tried to cancel out of the job because they hadn't told me the part about the target never leaving his house. But I knew I couldn't risk that kind of problem for the middleman. I didn't need any one particular job, but I did need him.

From that time forward, I always asked more questions.

THE TARGET LIVED in a good-sized house. One story, no stairs, so he could be anyplace inside at any time. I know people in wheelchairs can do all kinds of things. Play sports, drive cars, shoot guns...pretty much take care of themselves. But this one, I waited a long time, and he never left the house. I finally accepted that he was never going to.

I'm not a burglar. I don't know how to pick a lock, or cut glass.

Even if I'd been a sniper, the neighborhood wouldn't have given me any good perch. And even at pistol-distances, shooting through glass is tricky...the reflections and all. The target's neighborhood had other problems, too. You could tell it was high-class. And not making that a secret: Architect-designed houses set well back from the street, landscaped lawns, sculpted hedges.

I drove past a couple of times. A quiet block, no thru-traffic. A FedEx truck once. No cars parked in driveways. No kids on bicycles. No dogs watching from behind chain-link.

There's never a time limit on any of my jobs, but I didn't see how this one was going to get any better, no matter how patient I was.

Three blocks over, a small crew of roofers was working. Looked like they were replacing some cedar shakes. Even their nail guns seemed quieter than you'd expect.

I don't like suppressors. Once they're attached, the pistol is harder to carry concealed. But sometimes, there's no choice.

I PARKED the panel van in his driveway, got out and walked to the front door. Dressed in gray overalls, tool belt around my waist, red knit watch cap with some store's logo on my head, pulled down to below my hairline in back.

I rang the bell. Waited. The door opened and a man in wheelchair said "Wha—" as I pulled the little pistol from the tool belt and shot him in the face. He slumped like he'd fallen asleep. I reached in, turned his wheelchair around and pushed him back into the house, kicking the door closed behind me as I crossed the threshold, moving like I was doing something he'd called me over and asked me to do.

Then I shot him twice more: in the back of his head and in his right ear. The little pistol didn't make much noise, even inside.

I kept on pushing his wheelchair, to get away from the door. Even if anyone had a sight line on me they wouldn't see much, but better if they didn't see him slumped.

Then came the patience. If anyone had been watching when I'd first come to his door, I'd need to stay in there for a good half hour, as if I was doing some job he had called me over to do.

I used some of that time to retrace my steps—moving slowly, keeping below the window line. I found the three shell casings lying on the carpet and I picked them up...the first time I'd ever done that since I'd started working.

Then I looked for a corner spot where there wouldn't be any windows, a more comfortable place to wait on the off-chance the target had given out a key—to a housekeeper who might just let themselves in, a girlfriend...anyone.

I finally decided to wait in the same room I'd wheeled him into. His body looked like he was still sitting there; it might distract anyone who walked in just long enough if I had to shoot again.

A computer screen was in that room, with some kind of shield surrounding it, sides and top. When I saw what was on that screen, I could come up with a dozen reasons the people who paid might have wanted that man dead.

———

SONNY'S PHONE made some sound. He got up. I followed him back to his room, took my position off to the side.

"I can't stay long," Brenda said on the screen. "He'll be back soon."

"He'd be mad?"

"Oh, no," she told him, relaxed about saying the words. "He never gets mad. I just don't think...I don't want to say anything yet. I mean, I don't know how I'm going to..."

Sonny let her words trail off.

When nothing followed, he asked her, "Could we do this tomorrow, maybe?"

"Sure, but...I mean, don't you have school? "

"You do, too," Sonny said.

Brenda giggled. "Okay. At...ten, all right?"

"I'll be here," Sonny said. "I feel a flu coming on." She giggled again. Then the screen went blank."

WHEN I GOT BACK from a short drive I'd taken, I sat Sonny down in the kitchen even though it wasn't time to eat. "Maybe she needs a lawyer..." I started with.

"Brenda? A lawyer? Why? It's not her who'd be in trouble, right? It would be this Ryan guy, whoever he is."

"He could be," I told him. "I don't know. I guess it depends on how old he really is. And what they...did."

"So you mean a lawyer for him?"

"No, he's not our problem. For her."

"But she didn't do—"

"She's a runaway," I cut him off. "Her parents could get her locked up for that." That's what the lawyer I'd gone to visit had told me. "Answering a hypothetical" is what he said he was doing, putting some weight behind me telling him that I wasn't asking him about an actual case, just about the law in general. Me raising a teenage boy on my own, it only made sense to be well-informed about some things.

"How?" Sonny said. "How could they do that? It's not like she escaped from prison. It was just—"

"We'll have to ask the lawyer, if it looks like it's going to turn out to be trouble," I said. Thinking, again, that there was so much Sonny didn't know. And what he didn't know, he couldn't be prepared for.

But something else in there, too. Mixed in with all the obligation stuff. I didn't know what to call it. It wasn't sadness, nothing like that. Maybe I was proud that Sonny didn't know all the things I'd learned when I was so much younger than him.

People. Some people. Escaping. So much...So much to our line, so much to carry on. Sonny had proved he could figure out how to do some things, figure that out all on his own. But you can't research a tribe on the Internet when we've walked the same ground for so many years without leaving a single footprint. "It's just something we could offer her," I told Sonny. "Just in case she's worried about it, okay?"

"The same lawyer we went to that one time?" Sonny said, giving me a look I couldn't read.

"Yes."

"Are you sure he'd want to take on a case like that? I mean, if her parents did want to...put her some-place...wouldn't everyone be on their side?"

"I don't know about that last thing," I said. "But taking the case? Yes, that I'm sure about."

———————

I SAT by myself for a long time that night. Thinking about that target in the wheelchair. I knew there was something in that job that could have value. Not some-thing that would help, exactly, but...I just couldn't work it all out. And I had no one to ask.

Sonny always gets up early, but I don't sleep much, so he wasn't surprised to see me in the kitchen when he came in.

"I think I know a way we can find out about this Ryan. Find out some more, I mean." I told him. Saying it like I wasn't sure, just thinking about it.

"How would that help Brenda?"

I was ready for that. At least I hoped I was. "It's not so much about Ryan's...facts. Not what his real name is or where he lives, nothing like that. More about his...char-acter. Whether he's a sincere person."

"You mean, about him and Brenda getting married and all?"

"That's one thing, for sure."

"How could we do that?"

"Maybe the same way Brenda did?"

"I don't understand," Sonny said. But I could see he was already beginning to.

"Everyone in this...situation, they—Ryan and Brenda, they made up those profile things on the Internet for themselves, didn't they? Is there a way we could find out who did that first?"

"The group," he answered promptly. "Brenda and her friends. 'Aren't We Cute?' That had to be before Brenda went out on her own."

"That's logical," I assured him. "But isn't there a way you could find out for certain?"

"I'm pretty sure I could. It could take a little time, depending on how much trouble they went to. Is it that important?"

"I think it could be," I said. "But it's really Ryan's page we care about."

Sonny just watched my face, not even bothering with "Why?" or "How come?"

"I can't do what you can do with those computers and all," I answered his unspoken question. "I don't know anything about things like that. But I do know about some things."

"I know you do," my son said.

I let his words slide over me as if they were a passing breeze, one I couldn't catch in my hands...but knowing the day would come when I'd have to try.

"People range," I told him. "Not just in color, or size, or brain power, or whatever they were born with. Or born to be. The real range is how they act. How they act when they have choices."

"Like bullies," Sonny said, a new register coming into his voice. One I hadn't heard before. "Like the jocks who torture the weak kids at school."

"The ones who don't play sports?" I asked, trying to work around the edges—Sonny didn't play any sport.

"No, it's not that simple. What would sports do without fans? And the fans, they don't play, they watch. And cheer."

"So what is it, then?"

"Just a...weakness thing. I can't explain it. It's easier with the girls. "

"Because they don't care about sports?"

"No, no..." Sonny said, working to keep frustration out of his voice. I wished I knew how to question people, but I knew I was no good at this. I never had any practice with questioning, only with listening.

But I did have patience. And I'm always calm.

"The girls, they're even nastier than the boys," Sonny finally said. "If a girl is fat, or has the wrong clothes, or if she's a...slut, that's a word they use a lot, they all talk about her. Like they're stabbing her with words."

"Don't the teachers—"

"The teachers don't do anything," my son said, as if the question was absurd. "Most of the nasty stuff—for sure the nastiest stuff—that's not in school, it's online. One girl, someone got a picture of her in the locker room. Changing her clothes. They put it on Instagram. Just an account they made that day. Put up the picture and closed the account."

"But if it was closed—"

"It got shared. That picture. Over and over. Once that happens, there's no way to take it down. And people put comments up. Like 'With that gut, she better be pregnant.' Or 'Look at Sally Sow!' Some were much worse than those. Just...evil."

"What finally happened?"

"I don't know," he said. "The girl, she left school. But

they kept sharing that picture of her. Other people did, too. People who don't go to school here. People who don't know the girl."

"Did you see the picture, Sonny?"

"Yes," he said. "You couldn't see her face, just her...She was bending over, like she dropped something. It wasn't anything, really. You couldn't see her face. And they never named the girl. But everyone knew who she was."

"Because...?"

"Because every time she was around, you could hear the girls. Some of them made pig noises. Some of the boys did, too. Anyway, it couldn't have been a secret because whoever took that picture, she had to know."

"The boys, when they bullied someone, they did it like that, too?"

"I think they did. But I don't know for sure. They'd more do stuff like take things from the weak kids. 'Let me hold that' they'd say, and just snatch a kid's iPad, like they wanted to look something up."

"And not give it back?"

"No. What they'd do is just drop it. 'Oops. Sorry about it. I didn't realize you'd left it so greasy.' And the others would all laugh.

"They'd make some kids do their homework for them. Or make them shake hands and put on a bone-crusher until the kid went down his knees and started crying. That's when another of them would get a video. And they'd be sure to post it."

"The school knows—"

"Everyone knows," Sonny said. "They even have a club, like. They all have jackets with Greek letters on them. A fraternity is what they call it, like they were in college. If you want to be a member, you have to go through all kinds of stuff. I don't know what that is, exactly, but the ones who are trying to get in, they have to do what the ones who are already in tell them to do.

And, sometimes, what they tell them to do is take one of the weak kids and throw him in the shower with all his clothes on. Stuff like that."

"How do they decide who the weak kids are?" I asked him.

"I don't know," Sonny told me. "But it's like they wear signs or something."

"They never...? "

"No," is all Sonny said.

I sat there with that for a little while. If Sonny had been one of those kids the...other ones abused like that, I don't know what I would have done.

I didn't like thinking about that. But I didn't have to. The way my son said "No," when I'd asked him, I knew it was true.

I also knew I had to do something with the thread I'd pulled. "That's one way people range," I told my son.

"The weak ones and the ones who push them around?"

"It's not just like that in school," I told him, certain I wasn't telling him anything he didn't know. "But that's where finding out when those pages were started would help us know what to do."

"I don't understand," my son said. And I knew he didn't say that often.

"Let's say it happened the way you reasoned it out," I started. "The girls—Brenda and her friends—they got together and made that page. Just for fun. But they could see—they could all see—that some of the boys who saw their page wanted to...get to know them. In real life, like you said.

"So Brenda, she was...curious about that, maybe?

Anyway, she started her own page, a private page. Maybe to see what would happen, the reaction she'd get just on her own.

"And it would be safe, wouldn't it? I mean, it was all on the computer; she didn't ever have to meet anyone she didn't want to meet. Because that 'Thondra Telle' page she started, it really didn't have any actual information anyone could use. Her picture, that was her, all right. But the page didn't say where she lived, or went to school, or anything that would let someone find her."

"But then she contacted this Ryan guy and..."

"We don't know it happened like that," I told him. "What we know is that Ryan's page was a fake. At least his picture was. So if he had that page up for a while and Brenda found it, that's one thing. That would be what he wanted, wouldn't it? I mean, he knew he wasn't the guy in the picture on that page. That was the BMX guy, not him. So if he met anyone in real life, one look and..."

"So you think maybe Brenda wasn't surprised when she first saw him? That he'd already told her the picture wasn't him? I mean, he could have done that. He might even have sent her his real picture. A DM, an email, maybe even his own Instagram. There's plenty of other ways, too. But that would have scared her, I think. I mean, if he lied about one thing..."

"There's a way that could work," I said to Sonny. "I've been thinking about this for a little while. That's why the order might be important."

"The order of...?"

"Making the pages," I said. "If this Ryan had his page up first, if his page had been up for a while, then he was looking for girls to contact him, isn't that how it would be? With that fake picture and all?"

"Sure. But..."

"It didn't have to be like that," I said, keeping what I was hoping for out of my voice. "What if Ryan saw Brenda's page first? I mean the Thondra Telle page Brenda made? And Ryan didn't have the...confidence to just be himself when he contacted that page? So he made his and then he contacted her."

"If it happened like that, then Brenda would have known everything before she took off with him. That he was looking—"

"Sure."

Sonny was quiet for a few minutes. Then: "But if Ryan's page had been up there for a while, then he was trying to get girls to contact him. Which would..."

I finished his thought. "Make him a different person than if it happened the other way around."

My son slowly nodded. "I can find out," he said.

———————

We were still in the kitchen when Sonny's phone made a sound like a honky-tonk piano. "She's here," he said, getting up to go back to his room.

I watched Brenda on the screen from the same spot I'd used the last time. Invisible to her, just like I was to a target when I was working.

"Hi," is all she said. Not bouncy, but not depressed, either.

"Hello, Brenda," Sonny answered her. The way a grownup talks to a teenager, as if he'd aged some since they last spoke.

Brenda picked up on that, shifting her own voice to move up a level. "I know you're not the cops," she said, hiding a prayer inside a statement. "Not working for them, I mean. You don't lie."

Sonny waited a beat, said: "But...?"

"Well, everybody lies sometimes, don't they?" she said, maybe thinking of herself more than Sonny.

"You mean online?" Sonny asked.

"In real life, too."

"Not everybody," he said. Calmly, as if he was speaking a certain fact.

"I'm not so sure." Feeling for an opening, showing one in the process.

Sonny went to solid ground: "I met your mother," he told her. "She's not lying."

"About wanting me to come back? Sure, I know that."

"And about...about loving you."

"How could you know that?" she asked. A question, not a challenge.

Something Brenda really wanted to know.

"I can't *know* know, not the way you know the answer to a math problem. But—"

"Oh, I forgot. You're like a genius, aren't you?" Brenda cut in, not a trace of sarcasm in her voice.

"Why would you say—"

"Oh, come on, Sonny. Everybody knows. You're in all the advanced classes and everything. Probably have a dozen scholarships stacked up by now."

"Nothing like that," Sonny said, the back of his neck flushing. "I was just saying, about your mother—"

"She does, I know. Love me. My father, too. Maybe him especially. But if he ever got his hands on—"

"We wouldn't have to say anything about where you were," Sonny said, lowering his voice a little. "Or who you were with..." He let the last part slide into silence, maybe waiting for her to answer the "Or what you were doing" question. But Brenda didn't say anything.

Sonny finally spoke into the silence: "The important

thing, the only important thing for now, is we have to find a way to tell them you're okay. If they know they can...hear from you...there's no need for the police anymore. Your folks, they're scared, you understand, right? For all they know..."

"I thought about that," Brenda said, a catch in her voice. "I wouldn't want them to think something happened to me. Something like..."

"I could just tell them," Sonny said, as if he was volunteering for a mission. "Say I got an email from you. Or a phone call. Anything that tells me you're okay, but doesn't say anything about where you are."

"But why would it be you?" Brenda said. A good, clear-minded question. Wherever she was, whatever was going on inside her, she wasn't panicked.

"Why me?"

"Yes, Sonny, why you? They'd expect me to contact one of my friends. "

"I—"

"Oh! I didn't mean you weren't my friend," Brenda cut in, as if not wanting to hurt his feelings. "I meant one of my girlfriends. I don't really have any boy—"

"Did any of them know?" Sonny stopped her from what it felt like was going to be a long speech.

"My girlfriends? About Ryan? Oh, no. If they had, they would have told me not to...do anything. Or made fun of me for...you know."

"We can...negotiate," Sonny said, leaning forward slightly in his chair. "You could come home. For a while, anyway. And if you still wanted to get married when you were—"

"You know about that?"

"Yes," is all Sonny said.

"It's not his fault!" Brenda blurted out, denying what

nobody had said. "He's not...I'm not, like a captive or anything."

"I see that, sure. But just let me tell them you're—"

"How would they know?"

"Know?"

"That you really spoke to me? A message, an email, that could come from anyone."

"I could explain. About real-time and all. They know I know you, so—"

"Is that why my mother came to you? Because she—"

"She said she was trying everything she could think of," Sonny cut her off. Staying inside the truth without going to the full scope.

Brenda went quiet again. Then: "She would do that." Thoughtfully, as if it was a logical step in a puzzle she was trying to solve.

I watched from my position as she looked up toward the ceiling, as if guidance were painted there.

Sonny watched her too.

"Okay," she finally said, making a face I couldn't read.

———

SONNY WAS on his phone to Sara Tristell as I drove toward her house.

By the time we arrived, a police car was parked in front, a plain sedan just behind it. I didn't see any law, but Sara Tristell was on her front porch, a man standing next to her. From the way he positioned himself, he wasn't a cop.

———

BRENDA'S MOTHER ran toward our car before I even had it stopped. The man stayed on the porch, as though he didn't want to scare us away.

"Are you sure—"

"Oh, it was Brenda, all right," Sonny told her. Calm and serious.

Balanced. No doubt in his voice. Back to being older than he was.

"Did she...?" Sara Tristell started to ask. But by then, our car was surrounded: Two men in suits, and another two in uniform. The man on the porch still hadn't moved.

I didn't put my hands on the steering wheel, didn't hold them up to show they were empty. On the drive over, I'd cautioned Sonny not to act like we were being arrested on some TV show—we were neighbors, come there to help.

I just opened the car door, as one of the detectives— standing there with the cops, wearing suits, what else could they be?— stepped back. I didn't look over at Sonny, but I knew he was doing the same. As though this had all been arranged by invitation, we walked toward the man on the porch, Sara Tristell by my side.

"This is—"

"Robert Tristell," the man on the porch interrupted his wife. "Brenda's father."

I waited. "Thank you for coming," he finally said, holding out his hand. We shook.

Robert Tristell—I wondered what his friends called him: Robert wouldn't be what he walked around with, I didn't think—waved his open hand toward the front door.

I just nodded. I wasn't going to walk in to a man's house without him opening the door for me.

Whether he got that or not, I didn't know. Sara Tristell solved it quick: "Can we all go inside? There's more room there. Unless you want to smoke..." gesturing at a couple of armchairs, an old-fashioned wooden stand for the plate-sized bronze glass ashtray between them.

She wasn't asking the cops; she was asking me.

For an answer, I opened the front door and stepped to one side, still holding the knob. "Go ahead, son," I said to Sonny.

———

THE LIVING ROOM took up most of the front of the house. I guessed it had been built that way—the front door was set way over to the right: Asymmetrical, inviting anyone who entered to move to their left.

"You were the one who called?" one of the detectives said, directly to Sonny. He was heavy-set, with flesh-pouched eyes and thick hands, leaning forward but not breaking into Sonny's space.

"Just tell us what—" Robert Tristell cut in. He was standing, arms folded.

"Rob," is all Sara Tristell said. But it was enough.

Brenda's father took a step to the side, put his hands behind his back. "I got a DM from Brenda," Sonny said to the room. "On my Facebook page. She said—"

"DM?" the detective said.

"Sorry," Sonny said. "It means 'direct message.' Like an email. Or a text on your phone. But it comes to your Facebook page. Only it's not a post, it's a message. Private."

"And then she...?"

"All it said was that she's all right. She just wants some time to—"

"How did you know it was her? Brenda. How did you—"

"She asked if we could FaceTime. So we—"

"Face time?" the detective cut in again.

"Could you please ask your questions later?" Sara Tristell said to him, moving closer to her husband.

Everyone was quiet for a long second.

Sonny waited a beat past the silence, then went on: "FaceTime is just an app—an application you can have on your phone or your computer. Or even a tablet, like an iPad. You see the other person and they can see you. While you talk, I mean."

"We have those for training," the other detective said. He was slimmer than his partner. Balding, but he looked younger. Sara Tristell nodded, as if he'd said something profound. She took what the detective said as endorsing her unsaid words: "Get on with it. Get to my child."

"Anyway," Sonny went on, as if he heard her, too, "I could see it was Brenda. I know her. We're friends. And—"

"Friends like...?" the first detective said.

"That's enough," Robert Tristell stopped him, his voice soft and icy. "This...young man, he spoke with our daughter. Our missing daughter. He can tell us what she said. How she looked. My wife asked you, asked you very nicely, if you could just let him tell us what happened. What Brenda told him. What he knows. So just let him do that, all right?"

He said the last sentence like there would be a question mark at the end if you wrote it down, but his voice didn't carry that.

Everyone went quiet for a long second. The two cops in uniform looked restless, like they wanted to do something but didn't know what that should be.

The heavy-set detective wasn't looking at the uniforms, but he must have felt whatever they were giving off. "We've got this, boys. Me and Mel, we'll take it from here." He turned so he was facing me direct: "You don't mind if the officers take a quick look through your car on their way out, do you?"

"I mind," Robert Tristell said, before I could get a word out.

"Sir, I understand—"

"No, you don't," Robert Tristell told the detective. "You didn't find this young man. Or his father. My wife did that last part. She went to their house. She asked them if they could help. And they did that, didn't they?

"That's why they called. That's why they came over. To help. They're not criminals. They're not suspects. They didn't kidnap my daughter. They're not under arrest. You don't have a search warrant for this man's car. You're going to run his plates no matter what I say, but you're not going to treat people who came here to help us like they're suspicious characters. Not on my property, you're not."

"Are you a lawyer, sir?" the heavier detective said, using the cold-polite voice cops go to when they're angry but not in charge.

"No, I'm not," Robert Tristell said, his voice hardening as his wife put her hand on his forearm. "But I know a few."

Back to silence.

It didn't last long.

"We'll just sit here and listen," the heavy-set detective said, hand-signaling to the cops in uniform.

I still hadn't said a word. There was nothing in the car, and the plates would trace right back to me, just as they should. I don't have any real experience with the police. I'm not sure what I would have said if Robert Tristell hadn't stepped in...probably just told them "Okay."

"I know it was Brenda," Sonny said, confidently. "Like I said, we're friends. I know what she looks like, what she sounds like. And she knows me. She knows what classes I'm in at school and all. It was Brenda I was talking to, and it was Brenda who told me she's all right."

"Did she say why she...?"

"She just said she needed time to think. I asked her, think about what, but she just said...things. A lot of things."

Sara Tristell nodded, as if that made sense to her.

"Did she give you any idea where she was?"

"No, sir," Sonny answered Robert Tristell. "You can't see much on the screen when you're FaceTiming. Not unless the person you're speaking to moves their screen around to show you stuff, and Brenda didn't do any of that."

"Did she give you any...hints? Maybe said if she's...?"

"Coming back?" Sonny answered Sara Tristell. "Oh, for sure. She said things like, 'I have to think things through before I come home,' so I know she's—"

Sara Tristell started to cry then. But it wasn't sad crying.

———

SONNY TOLD them the whole story after that. Not the story we knew, the story we had gone over together. It was the truth, but not all of it. The detectives wouldn't be able to catch Sonny in a lie, but we'd put a barrier around what we were going to say, so the only answer

Sonny needed was some version of "No, she didn't say anything like that," or "No, there wasn't any more."

He held up fine, even though they had him go over it a couple of times. I already knew Sonny could tell it backwards, if he had to, but they didn't go that far.

The bald cop shifted his position a little, so he was facing Sonny full-on. "This FaceTime thing you were talking about, is it stored anywhere? Like on your phone, or...?"

"No, it's like Snapchat," Sonny told him, not explaining, as if he expected them to understand.

"You trying to say there's no copy, right?" the heavy-set detective said, leaning forward again.

"There can't be a copy," Sonny told him, as if he was saying "Today is Tuesday." Not arguing, saying there was nothing you could argue about...it just was.

Sara Tristell stood up, like the way you do if company is leaving. I thought we were done, then. Her husband didn't move—he hadn't sat down for the whole time we were there. I rolled my shoulders, signaling I was going to get up—I knew Sonny wouldn't do anything until I did.

Then the heavy-set cop said, "We'll need to pick up your computer so our forensic people can—"

"You can't do that," Sonny stopped him, holding up his hand, palm out like he was a traffic cop.

"Sure we can," the heavy-set cop told him, like he was explaining something simple to a child. "We thought you'd want to cooperate, but if you're going to make things difficult, we can always get that search warrant Mr. Tristell here was talking about."

"No, you can't," Robert Tristell sliced into whatever the cop was going to say.

Everyone went quiet, waiting for whatever was coming next. But nothing was.

"You can't take my computer," Sonny filled the silence. "If the computer isn't there, what's going to happen when Brenda wants to FaceTime with me again?"

"You can do that on your phone," the bald cop said. Meaning he knew more about how that stuff worked that he had let on.

"No, I can't," Sonny said, speaking directly to him. "I don't have that app on my phone. I don't ever do Face-Time with anyone—I never did it at all before this. If Brenda hadn't DM'ed me, I wouldn't even have loaded the app onto my computer."

"So if we took your phone..."

"Then how I would know Brenda wanted to Face-Time? That's how she lets me know. Ping! I can get that no matter where I am—if the signal's good enough, and it isn't always—Brenda will message me, tell me what time to be on my computer, and then we—"

"And that's another reason not to FaceTime on your phone? That the signal's not reliable?"

"Not around here, it's not," Sonny told the bald cop. "But I never thought of that. You're right, it wouldn't be good to use it that way."

"How about this, then?" the heavy-set cop said, trying for a reasonable tone, not quite getting there. "When you get a signal that Brenda wants to do this FaceTime with you, you give us a ring, and we can come over to your house and watch while you talk?"

"No," Robert Tristell said. His voice was flat. Nothing in his tone but finality, like a judge making a ruling. The kind you can't appeal.

The heavy-set cop turned in his chair, looked over his shoulder, like he was waiting for the rest.

Sonny spoke into the silence, like he'd done before. "Nobody can be there," he said. His voice wasn't as flat as Robert Tristell's—he wasn't old enough to put that kind of weight into his words—but he was holding just as solid. "I promised her," he said, as if that settled any argument. "I promised Brenda that when we talk—you know, like I explained—when we talk, it's just her and me. Nobody else in the room, nobody listening, nobody trying to record it. She trusts me. I'm not going against that."

"Your father—"

"He's not allowed, either," Sonny lied with a kind of truth. I've never been on a polygraph, but I knew right then Sonny could have passed one.

"We trust you, too," Robert Tristell said, looking over at his wife. She had been nodding agreement even before he finished speaking. "When Sonny...?" He said, looking at me.

I knew what he was asking me. "That's his given name," I told Robert Tristell. The truth.

He picked it up from there: "When Sonny tells us our daughter is safe, we trust that. And when he says he's working on getting her to come home, we trust that, too."

I knew what he was really saying. He and his wife, they'd made a choice. The only choice that would let them sleep at night while their daughter was missing.

"You just leave this young man alone," Sara Tristell told the cops. "When he has more to tell us, he'll come right over and tell us, won't you, son?"

"Yes, ma'am, I will," Sonny said.

ON THE DRIVE BACK, I couldn't see any cops following, but I figured they'd be close by. Maybe even trying for a warrant if they could convince a judge that Brenda was hiding at our place.

"Do you think they searched the car?" Sonny asked me.

"I'm guessing they opened the doors and looked in, but they didn't tear it up."

"You mean they'd cut into the seat cushions and—"

"No, they wouldn't do that. It's not as if they would be looking for some little thing we'd be hiding."

"Like a thumb drive?"

I knew what those were. Sonny had quite a bunch of them, all different colors—I guess so he could tell them apart without putting labels on them, but I'd never asked. "I can't see where they'd be thinking that," I told him. "Just maybe the glove box or the console—we don't keep those locked, so they'd have no trouble just glancing inside—or under the floor mats. Same for the trunk—that's not locked either."

"So nothing to do with computer stuff?"

"I wouldn't think so," I told my son. "A firearm of some kind, maybe."

"What for?"

"For an edge," I answered, knowing I'd have to say more. "Firearms have serial numbers," I went on, thinking about the ghost guns assembled from assorted parts the bundlers always bragged about holding, and how my son would never need to learn about such things. "So if we had a pistol...or a rifle, or a shotgun, anything like that...they could write down the serial number and check to see if they were registered. To me, I mean."

"What does that have to do with anything? They can't think you...we shot Brenda. That would be—"

"Yes, it would," I finished Sonny's sentence. "But that wouldn't be how they're thinking. It's what I said: them looking to get an edge. Like...an advantage. Something to hold over another person. 'Do you have a license for that weapon, sir?' That's how they'd ask, already knowing the answer. It's a crime to have a gun that's not registered. So maybe, if that was the case with me, they wouldn't need a warrant to come into our home. Because I'd have to let them, understand?"

"Like blackmail?"

"Just like that."

"The police would do that?"

"Not all police. But some of them, sure."

"The fat one?"

"He's not the one to worry about."

"But he was so...aggressive, wasn't he?"

"That's a style."

"I don't understand."

"People have...people have ways of acting around other people.

Sometimes, it's only the one way. But some of them, the trickier ones, they can change how they appear to you. Depending on what they want, and who they want it from. That cop, his style is just like you said: aggressive. He probably doesn't change it, not completely. Just...modifies it, depending on the situation. They know we're not criminals, son. We didn't come there to get anything from the Tristells. We didn't have to come at all, did we? So they knew—"

"They "did" know. But I don't understand what

anyone could want from them. The Tristells, I mean. All they want is—"

"Their daughter back, sure. So if we could make that happen, if we knew where she was, you know what they'd pay for that information?"

"Anything," my son said. Solemnly, as if he had just come to an understanding about the two of us.

"That's right," I co-signed. "But if we were going to do something like that, we wouldn't have come over to their house the way we did."

"Because we knew they'd call the police?"

"Well, we'd know it was a possibility. But we didn't tell them to meet us someplace else. We didn't tell them not to contact the police. I didn't even know you knew the girl—Brenda—I didn't even know her name until her mother came over to our place. It's way too much of a coincidence for us to have been involved in Brenda running away.

"Besides, if it was a kidnapping, something for money, the Tristells would have heard something way before the mother came over to us.

"Someone—if there was a someone—they would have made contact as soon as she went missing."

I took a breath, waiting for Sonny to say something if he wanted to. But he just waited for me to go on.

"Look, son, the police are supposed to be suspicious. That's part of their job. But they can't go around suspecting everyone; they'd never get anything done."

"You said it wasn't the fat one we should be careful of. How come—"

"We have to be careful of everyone," I told Sonny. "You already know that. But it's the bald one who might have a different scenario in mind."

"Like what?"

"Not something crazy. Not like Brenda is hiding in our house, nothing like that. But like maybe you helped her run away. Or maybe you know where she is. Where she is physically. Maybe it was all you and her from the beginning...and maybe now you're getting me to help."

"Help how?"

"Well, wherever she is, she'd need to eat, wouldn't she? And if she's not on our property, she's someplace else. She'd need a roof over her head, and—"

"Wait! Brenda's phone."

"Brenda's phone?"

"Her own phone. That's what they want to look at. And I bet they could."

"If she has it with her, how could...?"

"It doesn't matter where it is. Like you said, where it is physically. All that matters is who the account holder is. Who pays the bill. That's got to be her parents. She's probably on their plan, like I'm on yours. So if they gave the police permission, the police could get the cell service provider to show them the logs. Every call she made before; every call she's making now."

"But she's not using that phone."

"Not to call me, no. But if it's live..."

"Live?"

"Turned on. Active. Then they could maybe tell where it's been. Or even where it is now."

"But if they could do that..."

"They would have done it already," Sonny finished for me. "She doesn't have it with her," he said, his voice carrying dead certainty. "She left it somewhere, probably with the SIM card popped, too."

That was the first moment I realized that Sonny knew more about Ryan than he'd said. That he maybe knew more about all of this.

He trusts me, is what I thought. *He trusts me to trust him.*

"WHAT DO YOU WANT TO DO?" I asked Sonny later that day. We were at the kitchen table, waiting for Brenda to make contact again.

"I don't know," my son told me, so much sadness in his voice that I was taken back to the time when the hummingbirds had gone away. I did what I did then. Did all I could do: just be with him and wait for it to pass. I never had to explain that the hummingbirds would have had their own reasons for not coming back—they wouldn't do it to hurt Sonny. He would have known that.

And he knew it now. Brenda had her own reasons for staying where she was. She didn't do it to hurt her parents, either. Something was pulling her.

Or pushing her. Whatever it was, it was planted deep. And pulsing strong. "What do you...what do you want to happen, then?"

Sonny gave me a look. Not so much as if he didn't understand, but the kind of look he gave me when he thought I knew more than he does. About anything. Using his own patience to ask me to say more.

"It's not so much that you want to do something," I said. "It's that you want something to happen, right?"

"I just want Brenda to come home. To be with her parents. Like it was before."

"Before this Ryan, you're saying?"

"I think so. I'm not sure."

"You don't blame him for her staying away?"

"Maybe...maybe a little. But whatever tricks he pulled

on her, now she knows. I mean, she knows they were tricks, doesn't she?"

"Because she knows he's not who he said he was?"

"She knew that before she got in the car with him— one look would tell her. So whatever happened, it had to have happened fast."

"You mean like someone holding a gun to her head?"

"Not like that. Not like that at all," Sonny said, thoughtfully. "It's more like she...knew all along, maybe. I'm not sure. There's no way to be sure, I don't think. It just feels like she knew all along."

"How could that be?" I asked him. Not challenging, wanting to know how he came to that.

"It wouldn't take a second to see that he wasn't the same Ryan as the BMX guy on those YouTubes. Or even on his own page. Facebook, I mean. This Ryan, he had a private page. A separate page. Who does that?"

Brenda did that, flashed in my mind. *Thondra Telle.*

"And she never even tried to check to see if she was being catfished off that photo?" he said, almost sarcastically. "Never checked out anything at all? It would have been easy enough. And she's smart enough, too. But she never did any of that.

"So you know what I think? I think she had to know. Not who this Ryan was, but who he wasn't. I don't think this was about being with someone who looked a certain way, it was about someone who talked to her a certain way.

That was this guy. What he looked like...whatever he looked like...maybe that wasn't what counted. Not what mattered to her."

I guess anyone could be fooled, is what I was thinking. Not about Brenda, about me. About how much I didn't know about people. I knew there was an Us and a

Them, but I wouldn't know how to tell the two apart from just looking. Not even from talking. I knew about buying guns, but not about buying children. The way it had always worked was we got...middlemen, I guess you'd call them...and they bought the children.

Brenda's parents seemed like all the right things. Nothing like I'd imagined one of Them would be. But then I went to thinking about what my father told me, a long time ago. When he'd explained the mission to me: "They don't wear uniforms, son."

"What they do is—"

"They sell children," my father told me. "Like people sell a used car. Or tropical fish. Or... anything at all. It doesn't matter. When you sell a car to someone, what you want is the money. You don't care how they take care of that car. What they do with it after it's gone, that's not your business. Your business is selling those cars.

"It's like when you buy a gun with no paperwork on either side.

"Whatever you do with that gun, that's of no concern to the seller. You want the gun, he wants the money— that's all there is to it. A transaction."

"But don't little kids get...adopted for real and all? Like you see on TV?"

"Sure. And I guess that could sound like the same thing from a distance. Only it's not. If you adopt a child the right way, there's all kinds of paperwork. And you don't get to make that paperwork, there's an agency that does that. After they check you out. Inspect your home, see if you have a record, a whole lot of stuff. It's a process. Takes quite a while. You can't just walk in with cash and walk out with a baby."

"But...you did, didn't you? Isn't that what you did, to get me?"

"Yes. And the people I bought you from, what they wanted was the cash. They never met me. It all got handled through a bunch of other people."

"Lawyers?"

"There's always some of those around, sure. But it's a whole network that makes it happen. Once you have a baby legally, you own that baby, like the title to a car. You can pass that baby on to anyone you want. A private adoption. Just like those private gun sales. 'Private,' that's just another word for 'no paper.' Some call it 're-homing.' But whatever it's called, the government's not involved. It's never reported, and no one ever comes around to check."

"That's what you did?"

"That is what I did. And that's what you'll do, when the time comes," my father said. Then he added something to that sentence. Just one word: "son."

"It all comes down to one thing," I said to Sonny.

I waited a long minute to see if he was going to ask me anything. Finally, I realized he was waiting for me to finish telling him. So I did. "It's either lies or it's truth," I said.

"What Brenda's been telling us?"

"Yes."

"I don't think she's lying."

"That leaves this Ryan."

"And we know he wasn't telling the truth. About who he was. So maybe..."

I kept quiet, waiting for Sonny to finish his own

thought. Figuring he'd come to the same place I was. But he had another twist.

"Maybe he was lying at first, but he's not lying now?"

"Like baseball and video games?"

"What? I don't—"

"Ryan is either a character or he's a player," I spoke into Sonny's confusion, using his own language to make it clear. "If he's a character, then if he started out lying, he's going to keep lying. Because that's what his character is...programmed to do. But if he's a player—a person, not some video thing—he could start out lying and later start telling the truth."

"You mean if he lied because he thought there was nothing about him so great that girls would want to...contact him and stuff?"

"You said yourself, didn't you? Kids, young people, they do that all the time."

"Sometimes it's just to...see, I guess. Like an experiment, maybe?"

"What Brenda did? With that Thondra Telle disguise."

"Disguise?" he jumped to her defense. "It wasn't a disguise, not really. Not the same as Ryan. That was her picture on that page, wasn't it? Her real picture. She just made herself sound older. A lot of kids do that. Or try to, anyway. Not with the kids that already know them, how could that ever work? But if they were meeting new people..."

"Brenda made that page to meet new people, didn't she?"

"Meet them online," Sonny said, as if that was a point in Brenda's favor. That she hadn't been lying. Not completely, anyway.

"She went past that," I said, gently. "We don't know what they said to each other before she made the decision to run away. Said on the computer, on the phone, too, maybe. But there's no reason for her to be faking anything anymore."

"Because whatever Ryan is, she knows, now?"

"She thinks she does, anyway," I told my son, keeping any judgment out of my voice.

SONNY HAD MADE sure he didn't have his real phone with him when we went to the Tristell's house—there were four phones on our "family plan," but only two of them were ever used, mine and his. The other two were just-in-case, like the SUV we kept in the shed. So I knew there couldn't be a message from Brenda until we got back home. But still I drove the way folks around here always do: a little over the speed limit. Not attracting any attention. Not noticing any, either.

"Nothing," is all Sonny said, when we got inside and he looked at his own phone.

"Doesn't mean anything," I told him. "You said ten o'clock tomorrow, didn't you?"

He just nodded.

"Let's see what happens then," I said. Thinking that bald cop might try to get Sonny alone. And where he'd try would be school. But Sonny wouldn't be there. And that would make the cop do...what?

I thought some more. And the only thing I could come up with was that we couldn't count on the rope staying slack. Whatever we were going to do, Sonny and me, we didn't have too much time to do it.

I TOLD him that early the next morning. "The police aren't going to wait forever, son. The Tristells are keeping them off. Especially the father. I don't know anything about him, but he comes across as a man with friends in this town. Came across that way to the cops, too. Or maybe they already knew. But that'll hold them back only so long."

"Who has the choices?" Sonny asked me.

"I guess everyone does," I told him. "Everyone in this thing, I mean. But when it comes to Brenda and Ryan, we don't know what those choices are."

He looked a question at me. Just raised his eyebrows a bit, and went back to eating his toast.

"Do you think Brenda can leave anytime she wants?" I finally asked him.

"I don't know," he said. "She acts like she could."

"She acts like she could get married, too."

"Or stay away until she's old enough to do that, anyway," he agreed.

"She's smart enough to know that wouldn't work," I said. "And the police, they haven't really made any attempt to find out where she is."

"How could you know that?"

"Because they've got tools they haven't used," I told Sonny. "One thing they have for sure is her picture. There's all kinds of photographs of her they could use, but there's been nothing on the news—"

"Nothing on the Internet, either," he agreed. "Like one of those Amber Alerts. But, sooner or later, her friends are going to start something themselves."

"Because they're so worried?"

"Whatever," Sonny said, his tone telling me that he didn't know the motivations of Brenda's friends. And he wasn't so certain about them, either.

"If her parents asked them not to—"

"That wouldn't stop them all," Sonny said, more certainty in his voice now.

"And Brenda would know that," I said, watching him closely. He just nodded.

"We can't do anything more than we've already done," I told him, thinking about patience as I spoke. "Not until we know more. Let's see how it goes after you talk with her again."

————

TEN ON THE DOT, as if Brenda had set her alarm.

"Hi, Sonny," she said. Her hair was done up differently than I'd see it before. I hadn't been paying that much attention, so I guess what caught my eye was the braids on either side of her head. "Pigtails" we used to call them, when I was in grade school. But once I got to high school, I never saw them on girls again. I didn't know if things were different now. Brenda didn't seem to have on any lipstick either. Whatever she was doing, she wasn't trying to add years to her age.

"Hi, Brenda," Sonny said. I couldn't see his face, but he sounded glad to see her. I couldn't tell if he was putting that on, either.

"I don't know what to do," just popped out of Brenda, like she'd been holding it damped down.

"It's not...it's not so much what you want to do," Sonny said. "It's...it's what you want to happen."

"I don't understand."

"Well, if you know what you want, then we can maybe figure out a way to make it happen, see?"

"I...guess. But I...I guess I don't know. Getting married, I...guess I thought that was what I wanted.

Why I went away, I mean. But it all depends, you know?"

"On your parents?"

"Sort of. I mean, I know they'd never be okay with that, but I don't know what they'd do about not being okay."

"You mean, like with the law?"

"Well, if I was married, then staying with...him wouldn't be a crime, would it?"

I knew—I thought I knew—what she was really asking. But I didn't know if Sonny did.

"I guess if it was a legal marriage, but—"

"But I'm not old enough."

"I'm not a lawyer," Sonny said. "I guess we could look up—"

"I did that," Brenda cut him off. "Even in places where I'd be old enough, I'd still need my parents' consent."

"Well, they're never going to—"

"They wouldn't have to be there to do that. Give consent, I mean. If they signed before a Notary, that would be good enough," she said, sounding very certain.

"Why would they? Why would they do that, I mean."

"I have their signatures," Brenda said, dropping her voice as though she was telling a secret. "Their actual signatures, not a copy. I have notes they sent to school. At different times, I mean. Notes I asked them for, but it turned out the school didn't keep them. I just showed the administration people the notes and they checked it off on the form."

"I—"

"It was never the kind of thing anyone would lie about," Brenda cut Sonny off. "Just permission to change a course, stuff like that. For other things—like the Pep Squad, I remember—the school had to keep parental consent on file. 'For liability' is what they told me. Like that mattered."

"So you could forge—"

"I thought of that," Brenda cut in. Me thinking, she didn't say "we thought of that," but also thinking maybe that didn't mean anything—maybe it was just the way kids talked. "But there's a better way. A much better way. The forms, they're online. All of them. If we had a filled-out marriage license and we took it to a Justice of the Peace, we could probably get it to work."

"And even if it didn't," she went on in the same breath, "what could they do? Call the police? I don't think so. And even if they—"

"That wouldn't work," Sonny chopped in. Flat, straight-out. Not like he was talking down to her, just stating facts. "Even if you got that Justice of the Peace to marry you, it wouldn't be a real marriage. Not one you could go home with."

"We wouldn't have to go home."

"Sure you would," Sonny said. "Sooner or later, you would. No matter how you played it, that's what you'd have to do."

"Why?" Brenda asked, sounding more like a kid than ever.

"If you didn't tell your parents you'd gotten married, they'd start looking for you for real. The police would, too. And if you did tell them, they'd want to meet whoever you married. That's if they believed you. If they didn't think you'd been kidnapped or—"

"That's just silly! You already told them. That I was okay, I mean. Didn't you?"

"I did," Sonny said. "Just like I promised. And it was your father who stopped the police from trying to find you. He believed me. Which really means he believed you. But I could tell he's not going to just wait around forever."

"No, he's not," Brenda said.

"I still think there's a way," Sonny told her.

"What? What way?" Brenda's voice, but pressured now, all the confidence gone.

"You have to call them. You know how to do that. So it couldn't be traced, I mean. The only reason they believed me was I told them that I know you. And you know me. I told them about FaceTiming and all. So they knew I wasn't being tricked. But if they hear your voice, that could make all the difference. The real difference."

"I don't know..."

"Could you think about it?"

"Sure. But..."

"Just for a few hours," Sonny said. "Would you still be able to get back to me this afternoon, say?"

"If it was early enough, I could."

"I'm home all day today," Sonny said. "With the flu, remember?" Brenda giggled a little. Then she cut the connection.

———

WHEN I WAS WORKING, I never followed a target until I was ready to move. The more time you spend around a target, the better the chance something will go wrong, get in the way. And the greater chance other people will see you before you do the work. See you and remember, connect one with the other. The best way to do it is to know where the target's going to be and wait for him.

"Can you find a girl's page?" I asked Sonny.

"Which girl?"

"Any girl. It doesn't matter. All we need is the picture of her."

"To make a page," my son said, instantly on my wavelength. "Yes."

"How old?"

"It doesn't matter how old the girl actually is. Just how old she looks. We want a girl who's still a girl. Your age. Brenda's age. All we want is the picture—we'll make up the rest."

"Sure. That's easy. But what are we going to do with it?"

"Remember how you said Brenda's page was...inactive, or something like that?"

"Yes."

"Is Ryan's?"

"Let me see..."

A few minutes later: "It's not...dead. That's all I can tell. But I can't read his DM's without his password. And he hasn't posted anything new for a couple of weeks."

"So he could be checking it?"

"Sure."

"Do you have to be a 'friend,' or whatever it's called? Do you have to be that to send him one of those messages?"

"I think you're supposed to friend someone first. But I'm not sure exactly how it works."

He tapped a few keys, spun that big red ball, the pointer moving too fast for me to follow.

"It's a public page," he said, nodding to himself, "so I guess anyone

could send him a DM. I just don't know if he'd see it.
"

"Well, that's—"

"That's what we're going to find out, right?"

"YOU LOOK as hot as your car," is what Bella Sweetshop
sent to Ryan's
    page.

    "You think he'll answer?" Sonny asked me.

    "I hope not," is all I said.

"YOU HAVE to learn to do nothing for long blocks of
time," my father told me. A long time ago, it seems now.
"I don't mean just sit there, like you're in solitary
confinement," he explained. "Just not be...active. You can
be around people for only so long before some of them
want to...get close. In different ways. Sometimes, it
might be a woman. You already know how dangerous
that could get to be. And what to do about it. But men
can be like that, too."

    "Men can be...?"

    "Yes, they can. But that's not what I'm talking about,
here. Those kind of men, they won't come too close to
strangers so long as you stay out of their places. Bars,
clubs...they have places just for other men like themselves. You're not going in—"

    "What if a job...?"

    "No bars, no clubs, no...joints, no hangouts. You don't
work indoors if there's any way to avoid it. And you
never work indoors when there's other people around,
period," he said, like he was explaining a rule of life. I
guess it was, at that. "You might have to go in a house,
but that would be...unusual. And only when you're very,
very sure there's no other choice. But those jobs you see
in the movies—a man's taken down inside a nightclub,

shot at his table in a restaurant—that's not real. Or maybe it is, I don't know, not for sure. Some...people, they don't care if they live or die. Some of them, it looks like they want to die. None of that has anything to do with us."

He stopped. Took a breath through his nose. Slow and deep. Held it down for a little bit, then let it just drift out of him. My father never taught me to do that, I just picked it up from watching him. The same way Sonny had picked it up from me. The difference was, Sonny had asked me a lot of questions first, and I'd never done that with my father.

"The best thing is books," he went on, as if he'd never stopped explaining about not being active. "Anything you might be interested in, you can find books about. I figure that helps your cover, too—writers must be readers, don't you think? So you read the books, then you can just leave them when you move on. Never in your room —use a donation box. At one of those shelters they have —for homeless people, or women who are trying to get away from men who beat them—it really doesn't matter. But what you can't do with books is throw them away. Books are valuable. I don't mean they're worth a lot of money, but they're worth something. So anyone sees you throw a book away, they'll pay attention.

"If books don't work for you, there's always radio. Or TV. Radios you can buy a little one, carry in your pocket. TV, that they'll have in almost any place you rent. Hotels, rooming houses, like that. You can rent furnished apartments short-term, too, but some of them run credit checks and you can't be filling out any forms. It's not like they're going to ask for your fingerprints or take a picture, you just don't want anyone back-checking anything, understand?"

I just nodded. One thing my father did was repeat himself a lot. Not like he was...the way people get when they're real old. It was just a habit he had. Once, when I was a real little kid, he told me something he'd told me before, and I told him so. All he said was, "It's worth telling again, son." He didn't get mad or anything. And I never brought it up after that.

"I don't mean you can't go outdoors. You can do anything most other people do. You just can't get close to anyone. Not to anyone who'll miss you when you're not around. That's why I taught you to play pool. And cards. But you know what you can't do..."

"Gamble."

"Right," he said, approvingly. "It's natural for men to be...competitive. You're pretty good with a cue. Better than I ever was, that's for sure. And it's fun to play against someone, isn't it?"

"Yes. Playing alone..."

"That's not really playing," he finished for me. "That's just practicing. You do that to get better, but that's work, not fun. So you can go into a poolroom, play by yourself for a little bit, it's a sure thing someone will ask you if you want to play a game or two. That's okay. In a poolroom, that's okay. Sooner or later, they'll ask you if you want to play for money. Even that's okay, but always small money. And you never walk away with another man's money in your pocket.

"Bars have pool tables, too. Usually those little ones, like for eight-ball. But you're not going in bars. In a poolroom, a man can lose a chunk of money and put it down to the cost of doing business. In a bar, a man can lose a dollar and start a fight over it. Drunks are always dangerous.

"Same for playing cards. You sit down at some little

casino—those places are lousy with cameras, so never in a town where you're going to work—you sit down, play blackjack, you're by yourself. Win or lose, you walk away when it's done. Even poker, you can sit down at a table, walk away when you're done...although it's always better to walk away as if you're bust. But only poker rooms where they have security. You get drunks there, too, but the people who work there, they know how to handle them."

"Stay away from drunks."

"Stay away from drinkers," my father corrected. "You never know when one of them is going to turn out to be a drunk."

"Mostly keep to myself."

"That's the life," my father said. "That's the life until you come back home. And start a new line."

"I know."

"I know you do, son. Just remember to think things through. Jail's not the same as dead. You can't ever be arrested in the middle of a job. Or just after one. You know that. You know why. But if you ever get arrested for...hell, I don't know, something you didn't do, it could even be. Just being in the wrong place when the cops are being silly. If you're not on your way to a job—or coming from one—you're not going to have a gun on you. And you're never going to keep guns wherever you're staying. So you get arrested, you're going to just go along with it. You don't get angry, you don't argue...you just act confused. Because that's what you'll be, and the best act is no act at all.

"That happens, you get arrested like that, your fingerprints aren't going to do anything for the police—they'll just tell them you don't have a record, never been in the army, don't have a pistol permit. That's most people.

Your ID, it'll be whatever it is. But it won't trace to anyone they want.

"They should just kick you loose after that, but, some small towns, they don't like to admit they made a mistake right off, so you might sit in jail for a little bit before they let you go.

"Or they might even charge you with some nonsense. That happens, you don't have any money for a lawyer, just take whatever Public Defender they give you. Whoever that is, they're going to tell you to plead guilty —it's just some petty charge, and you could go home right away.

"But you never do that. Tell that lawyer you're not pleading guilty to anything. You know what happens then?"

"I have a trial?"

"No. There won't be any trial. You might have to stay in jail a while—but, eventually, they'll drop the charges."

"All right."

"That's only in a small town," my father said. "In a city, you plead not guilty, even if you don't have a dime, they'll cut you loose, tell you to come back at the next court date."

"And I just leave?"

"You leave the building, sure. But you don't leave town. You come back on whatever date they set. You might have to do that a couple of times, but they see you're actually going to show up for a trial, that's when the charges get dropped."

"All right," I said. Again.

"That kind of thing, it could happen to anyone. And it's no big deal, not by itself. But if that happens, if that ever happens, then they will have a set of fingerprints. They're not supposed to keep them if they don't keep you. I mean, if you're not convicted of anything. But they'll absolutely keep those prints. You know what that means."

"I'm done."

"You're done," my father said, nodding. "You come back, and we'll figure out what the next step is. But once the police have your prints, you're done working."

I knew what "figure out the next step" would turn out to be. My father would go back out himself again, and I'd have to take over moving the line forward a lot earlier than I expected. There were a lot of reasons I didn't want that, but most of them came down to me being afraid I wouldn't be ready.

And that's one thing I learned from my father, above all else—you always have to be ready.

———

"WE NEED DEADLINES," I told Sonny when I came back inside. "We have to be ready for that."

"Deadlines?"

"Things can't just...go on," I told him. "We bought some time—some time for Brenda—when we told her parents that you were in touch with her. So they know she's safe. Or they believe it, anyway."

"You don't believe it?" my son asked me.

"I don't know what to believe," I told him, honestly. "She doesn't sound like she's afraid. Or even anxious. But that doesn't mean..."

"It doesn't mean she's safe."

"No."

"Because we don't know anything about Ryan."

"We don't even know if she knows anything about Ryan," I said, putting it out there.

"So this deadline..."

"With a deadline, we buy some more time. But we can't buy that much more without Brenda's parents doing something. The police are thinking the way we're thinking."

"But we don't think she was kidnapped or anything."

"They don't either," I told Sonny. "They think she went willingly. But they don't know if she's...staying willingly."

"But she said—"

"You listened to her," I interrupted Sonny. "They didn't. You're her...age and all. Her friend, that's what you both said. But that doesn't mean you're a good judge of—"

"I know her better than—"

"I don't doubt that," I told him. "But the cops could. Doubt that, I mean. In their minds, Brenda could be...I don't know...drugged or something. Or sitting there with Ryan in the background—like I was when you were talking to her—and he's holding a gun on her or something."

"There's no way."

"There's always a way for the police to believe...well, anything at all, son. Remember, as far as they know, it was Brenda who contacted you, not the other way around. The police don't know her. So whatever they know, they know from her parents. And they don't know you, not even a little."

"So if we had a deadline, they'd leave things alone until...until it was up?"

"I...think so. It's worth a try, anyway."

"So we ask Brenda—"

"First, we ask her parents," I interrupted. "After we hear what Brenda has to say, later."

———

It was about one-thirty when Brenda called. I didn't know what time zone she was calling from, but it somehow felt like it was the same as ours.

"It's me!" she announced herself, as though she was some kind of pop-up surprise.

"Hi, Brenda," is all Sonny said.

"Is something wrong?" she asked, switching moods in an eye-blink.

"Not with me," Sonny said, leaving a door open.

"Not with me, either," she came back with, not smiling anymore.

"I wish I could be sure of that."

"What does that mean, Sonny?"

"I guess I'm...reflecting. Your folks, they're really scared. I told them you were all right, but nothing about this makes sense to them. Why you'd run away like you did. Why you didn't leave them a note or anything. Why you..."

"What could I have told them?" Brenda stopped Sonny in his tracks. "What could I tell them? How could I make sense to them when I don't even know..."

"Maybe if you could just...I don't know...be by yourself for a while? Think things through without..."

"Without what? Ryan, you mean? I've got plenty of time to do that. Every day. Ryan goes to work, like I told you. He's not here until it gets...until way into the afternoon. Sometimes, even later than that. I've got more time to myself than I ever had in my life."

"So what do you do? With the time, I mean," Sonny said. Making me think about what my father told me about being by yourself, how to fill that time. Fill it without taking risks.

"Do you ever talk it over with...him?" Sonny asked, when Brenda didn't say anything.

"There's nothing to talk over," she said. Not sad. Or even resigned. Like she was just saying something very obvious. Maybe getting a little tired of saying it.

"You're going to get married?"

"I...guess so. That was the plan. From the beginning."

"Brenda, you wouldn't have to change that plan to...change other things, would you? I mean, couldn't you just put it on hold? It would only be a couple of—"

"What, years? Look, I lied to him, Sonny. He thought I was almost eighteen. Old enough to get married no matter what anyone said. But now, now he knows."

"Because you told him?"

"Ah, I didn't have to tell him. I think from the moment he saw me—in real life, I mean, not a picture—he knew."

Thoughts bang-burst inside me: *And you, Brenda ... what did you know?*

From the moment you saw him, what did you know? Whatever his age, you knew he wasn't the young man in those pictures. Knew that right away. Or did you know that all along?"

"But he still—"

"We were in it by then. Him and me. Together."

"He wasn't mad? When you told him your real—"

"Not a bit. But he said—he said after I told him the whole truth, even my real name—that we couldn't...do anything. You know what I mean."

"I'm...not sure. He didn't send you home or anything, so..."

"Not that," Brenda said, sounding like girls her age do sometimes. Superior, maybe...I don't know the right word for it. "Like...in bed."

"Oh. Because you're underage?"

"It's not that. I mean, he didn't say anything about that. But he knew I was a...that I'd never...you know. I mean, he did know that, all along. I told him way before we got together. Together like we are now, I mean. That was hard. To tell him, I mean. I didn't know if he'd think it was weird, being a senior in high school and still a virgin. But when I told him, he said that was such a righteous thing for me to be. That's the word he used, 'righteous.' Like I was a girl who made her own decisions. Not a girl who just went along with...crowds, and all.

"And now, now he wants to keep it that way. Keep me pure. That's another of his words, 'pure.' I really like the way he says things. Keep me pure until we're married. He asked me if I thought he was weird. For him being old-fashioned and all. Isn't that like...a perfect fit? Here I was worried about how he'd—"

"But you said he wasn't what you...expected either, right?"

"I said he didn't look like what I expected, that's all," Brenda answered, in a *Don't you try and trick me!* kind of voice.

"I know," Sonny said, soothingly. "I just meant, everything else."

"Everything else is the same as he said," Brenda responded, her tone just short of proud. "Every single thing. The same car. The job, everything. He's not some faker living with his mother or something. He's got his own place. And he can take care of me, just like we planned. You can go to school online, you know. So nothing's stopping me."

"Just how old you are."

"Just how old I am," she echoed. "And everything that goes along with that."

"Your mom and dad."

"Exactly. You're an only child, too, so you know how it is. Imagine how your father would act if you just...ran off."

"I have," Sonny said. I was still feeling the shock when he went on: "Imagined it, I'm saying. That's why we have to make a...deadline, or something."

"Deadline for what?"

"For this. For all this. If I told your folks you needed some more time—not much more, say a week, maybe?— I think they'd hold off."

"Hold off what?"

"Mostly, I was thinking the police. I mean, I've talked with you, but who am I? Just some kid you know from school. Your folks believed me, I'm not saying they didn't. But I don't think the cops did."

"They don't think you and me—"

"Oh, I'm sure they think you and me talked. But they don't know if I was in on this from the beginning. They wanted to come and search the house—our house, where my dad and I live—but your father wouldn't let them."

"My father? You mean your father, don't you?"

"No. Yours. He believed me. He believed we talked, just like I said. Your mother believed me, too. But it was your father who made them back off."

"Wow." Softly, as if deeply impressed, not a trace of sarcasm in the word.

"Yes. Only I don't think that's going to keep going on. If they—the police, I mean—if they really go all out, put your picture up everywhere, find images of Ryan's car...If they do everything they can do, they'll find you."

"But if we're married..."

"You're not going to be married, Brenda. Not for real. Like we talked about. Anything you can fake up, they could get undone. But that's not even the big thing."

"What is, then?"

"Your parents. They're scared. Your father hides it pretty good. Your mother not so much. But they're really scared. If we can't give them something, something to count on, they're not going to be able to keep the cops from...Well, doing whatever they do when a kid goes missing."

"I'm not a kid!"

"Stop it, Brenda," Sonny said, very calmly, but with a lot of strength. "You know what I meant."

Everything went quiet for a long minute, but I could still see Brenda's face on the monitor so I knew she hadn't disconnected.

"That deadline," she finally said. "That's what we have to do?"

"Yes. Let me tell them you need a few days. To think things over. I won't say anything about Ryan. Or where you are. Just that you're safe. And you need a little time to think before you come home. Would that be okay?"

"I don't know."

"I have to tell them something, Brenda. And if what I tell them turns out to be a lie, then they're done trusting me."

"And you could get in trouble, too," she said, a fine edge sharpening on the edge of her speech.

"I...guess," Sonny told her, like he hadn't thought about that. I guessed he probably hadn't. "I'm just saying things can't stay like they are. You know they can't, too."

"I should...oh, it doesn't matter. Go ahead and tell them, Sonny." The screen made some sound and then it went blank.

SONNY SAT STARING at the empty screen for a couple of minutes. Then he clicked off the monitor and turned his chair so he was facing me.

"What do you think she's going to do?" he asked.

"That depends," I told him.

"On...?"

"If she talks it over with this Ryan, he'll know she's been in touch with...someone from her life. Maybe even with you, specifically. And if he knows that, he'll probably figure you've told her parents.

"From there, he could think they'd call the law. So he might want to just shut down everything and run. That wouldn't be so bad...unless he convinced Brenda to go with him."

"Do you think she'll do that? Talk it over with this Ryan, I mean."

"I don't," I said, thinking it over as I spoke. Seeing a movie playing in my head. One of those old-style home movies, where you can hear the sound of the projector reels moving as they play on the stand-up screen. The movie was a little girl blowing bubbles through one of those round things on the end of a plastic stick. Seeing her not wanting those bubbles to burst. Seeing her figuring out that, sooner or later, they all did. "But it doesn't matter," I said to Sonny. "What we've got to do now is tell her parents about the deadline. The one Brenda just agreed to."

He reached for his phone. "Do you want me to—"

"We're not going to call them," I told my son.

"WHY ARE WE WAITING?" Sonny asked me, later that afternoon. "Wouldn't it be better—?"

"We can't only tell Mrs. Tristell. We have to tell her husband, too."

"Wouldn't she just—"

"It's not the same, hearing something second-hand. If we go over there without calling, like we plan to, we cut down on the chances the police will be around. They don't have the manpower to be sitting out there watching us around the clock, and they don't have a tracker on our car."

"How can we be sure about the tracker?" Sonny asked. "You don't have..."

He didn't finish the sentence, but I knew he was saying: I don't have that kind of knowledge. Sonny might have, himself...but I'd never asked him. So I reasoned it through, the way I did when I was working. Only, this time, I did it out loud: "I don't think they go around carrying those things the way they do pistols, son. I'm pretty sure they'd have to get a warrant to put one on someone's car, and we know for sure they haven't been close enough to attach anything after we left the Tristell house. No one's been on our property since, no one at all. And there's something else."

Sonny didn't say anything, but from the way he looked at me, I could tell he wanted me to keep going.

"The police only knew about us coming over there that time because Robert Tristell told them. So, sure, that would have given them time to grab one of those track-ers. But even if they had one, I can't see them using it."

"Because Mr. Tristell wouldn't—"

"That's part of it," I said, not surprised that Sonny had picked up on a...power coming off that man. "But, also, it just wouldn't add up. If we knew where Brenda was, there'd be no reason to go over there at all. Knowing how anxious Mrs. Tristell was, wouldn't we just have called and told her?

"And it's not like they're the FBI working a kidnapping, not with what you told them about Brenda herself being the one who contacted you. And there hasn't even been a single word about a ransom. No, the only ones who could be putting pressure on the police to be watching us now would be Brenda's parents...and I don't see that happening, not with the way her father was acting."

"Couldn't we call now, and say we were going to be coming by later?"

"I don't see how the law could have a tracker on us, but a tap on their phone? Maybe. And we only have Mrs. Tristell's number, not her husband's. He works, I'm sure. For all I know, she does, too—Brenda's old enough so she could have a part-time job, at least."

"I guess she could," Sonny said. "Brenda's an only child..."

He didn't add "like me" to what he said, but I could feel it. Not some sense of sadness, more like they were members of the same club. "Even if she had a job, she wouldn't go to it while this was happening," he said, absolute certainty in his voice. "Sure, a cell phone goes anywhere, but...What if Brenda just came home? Just walked in the door? No," he said, dead-certain, "her mother wouldn't leave that house, not now. Not for anything."

"I don't think so either," I agreed. "I don't know what her husband does, but it doesn't seem like he could just drop whatever that is and go off. Not without telling people why, anyway. And he doesn't seem like a man who'd want to do that."

"Because..."

"Because he'd know how people talk."

"But Mrs. Tristell's already gone around everywhere and—"

"She has," I acknowledged. "But we don't know who she's told, and it's for sure not been made public—there's not a word of it anywhere. Since we have to tell them both at the same time, I wouldn't want to go over there until around whenever her father came home from work. If things were like they were before Brenda ran off, I mean. When they'd all be home, together."

"Dad," Sonny said, me thinking how he only called me that when he was truly serious about something, "what if we get them to give Brenda a week, and she just uses that time to get further away? And she never contacts me again?"

"I don't know," I said. "I don't know that there'd be anything we could do. But we have to play this like that's not going to happen. Right now, we're only holding two cards. One is Brenda being in contact with you. The other is Mr. And Mrs. Tristell taking your word about that.

"Those are both trust cards. The way you break trust is to tell lies. Brenda told you she needed a week. You're going to tell her parents that. Tell them the truth. You already told Brenda you were going to do just that. So you told her the truth, too. If she runs, that'll be bad. But you won't have lied."

"So her parents would still trust me, maybe?"

"Brenda would, too," I reminded him. "Even if she runs, she could still contact you later."

"I hadn't thought of that," Sonny said.

That was the opening I'd been waiting for. "Tell me something, son. Remember when you were just talking to Brenda? You said, 'I won't say anything about Ryan. Or where you are.' Remember that?"

"Yes," my son said, giving me a look. I wasn't sure, but I think he was surprised that I could repeat what he'd said word-for-word; he knew I hadn't written anything down.

"She didn't say anything to that," I told him. "Didn't brush it off. Like when she said 'I'm not a kid!' That tone of voice."

"You mean, like correcting me?"

"Like that, yes. But that tone, it was just a reflex, I think. Something a girl her age has to say a lot. A girl, fourteen-fifteen years old like Brenda, she's not a grown woman. But she's not a little girl, either."

"That's not only for girls," my son said.

"I'm sure that's right," I agreed. "It just seems like it's a trickier road to walk for girls. But I don't know. I never was a girl. Never had any, either."

That got a smile out of him. Not a kid's grin, a man's twist of the lips, no teeth showing. "You think she wasn't listening? Wasn't paying attention when I said that? Or..."

"Or she thinks you know something about where she is. Not the address or anything. Not even the town. But...the area, maybe? She may not think you're as...sophisticated?...as she is, but she knows you're smart. Not just from how you found her, how you got word to her, but from school. She said as much."

"It could be," Sonny said, thoughtfully. "One thing about kids—people my age, I mean—they have this awesome respect for technology, but they don't understand it. They think posting something on a Facebook page is 'coding'; they think using someone else's password is 'hacking'...So, sure, she could think I've got some magic locator thing going, that maybe I've got a rough idea about where she is."

"But you don't," I said, like I was just saying it, but it really was a question. And Sonny knew it.

"I thought of trying some social engineering, but I didn't want to risk it."

"Social—"

"It's just tricking people out of information. You take some information you do know, like someone's email address, or their date of birth...it doesn't matter. Then you use that information to leverage some more. Out of someone else. That's really how most hacking works. One piece of information leads to another, and eventually you're inside a whole system. Then you re-direct a path, so information that should have gone to someone inside an organization goes to you, instead."

"What good does all that do?"

"If the information is, say, a bank account number, you can 'tell' a computer to move money from that account into one you control. Then you bounce it around, maybe even buy bitcoin with it—"

"You're losing me, son."

"It doesn't matter," he assured me. "I was just saying that I didn't even start that game. I didn't ask Brenda something like, 'Is it raining over there today, too?' Just a little probe, to narrow things down before I went in deeper."

"Have you ever done anything like that?"

"I haven't," he said. "But I know there are attacks like that on the gambling websites all the time. Because of all the money they handle. So I was curious about how those work."

He can carry on our line, I thought to myself. He can carry on our line maybe better than any of us ever have. But he'll have to do my kind of work to get that done.

"I HAVE to leave Brenda a message, first," Sonny said, just as we were getting ready to drive over to the Tristell place.

I looked at him, maybe a little surprise on my face.

"Just to let her know I'll be out of reach for a couple of hours," he explained. "In case she tries to...visit. I don't expect her—not while Ryan's around, and she said he always comes home after work. Only I don't know what he does—what he really does, no matter what he told her —so I don't know if he works regular hours. So if he calls and says he's going to be late, maybe Brenda would want to talk or something while she's alone."

"And you wouldn't want her to..."

"I wouldn't want her to think I wasn't here for no reason. That she wasn't important enough for me to be here for her."

"Being considerate," I said, not making it a question.

"Brenda has to know who to trust," Sonny said, gently reminding me of what I'd told him earlier.

"YOU'RE GOING to have to do most of the talking," I told him on the way over. "Remember, all your conversations with Brenda, I wasn't there."

"I remember."

"It's okay that you told me everything. That's what they'd expect. But they'd still want to hear it first-hand."

"I know."

As we drove through the countryside, I paid more attention to the places we passed that I usually did. Fact is, I didn't leave the property all that much. I wasn't a recluse or anything, but I wasn't one of those people who go shopping every day, either. I usually stocked up on whatever I figured we'd need for, I don't know, two-three weeks at a time, and I'd run over in the truck and fill it up. Plenty of people around here do that; it wasn't behavior that would draw notice.

But this was later in the day than when I made those shopping runs. Starting to darken out already. The stores were still open, but some of the other places seemed to just be coming to life. I knew there was plenty of off-to-the-side stuff going on where we lived. I guess there is everywhere, if you know where to look. The people who paid me over the years, they had to get their money from such things. They might have changed with the times—different technology and all—but it would always be the same products: gambling, prostitution, hijacking, drugs, money-lending, extortion...whatever brought in an income.

There was no reason to think our town was different from any other. It just never mattered to me. Not when I was working, not now. But as we passed different places, I gave a little thought to what might have been going on behind all those doors, all those windows, all those fences.

And then I let all that pass right on through my mind without sticking.

My father had taught me that—not letting things stick to you, distracting you from the job.

You can't let thoughts like that stay with you. Bother you. Take up space in your mind. So you never try to guess why someone had been marked down. Most of the time, there wasn't anything you could even make a guess from. Who knows why a man who climbs telephone poles to fix whatever's wrong up there has to die? Or why a man with ten pounds of gold around his neck and gold emblems on his car is on the spot? I never thought about any of that, only about doing the job right. And then nothing, not until the next one.

I wasn't always successful at doing that. Once, the target was a teacher.

At a private school. One of those schools where the kids live there. I was pretty sure he didn't live there himself, because the spot I was going to use was the parking lot. That lot was only for the teachers. And people who visited, I guess. The kids in that school were too young to have cars.

I don't know how the people who paid for the work knew this teacher would be coming back to the school at night. Not every night, is what I was told. But at least two-three times a week, for sure.

The parking lot wasn't guarded in any way. It only had room for a few dozen cars, and it wasn't full, even in the daytime. At night, almost empty.

Never completely empty, though. Some cars always came after dark. I figured those were the cleaning crew, the same way a couple of vehicles that always parked in the daytime belonged to the groundskeepers.

I learned a long time ago you can't tell occupations by cars. Some people with really high-up jobs—supervisors, even bosses—they might drive old clunkers, while some janitors drove fancy new ones. But in that lot, it was easy to tell. The teachers all parked in the same section, and the workers parked way over to the side farthest from the school, as if they were segregated by lines I couldn't see. There weren't any names on the parking slots, but

everyone seemed to know where their personal
spot was.

At night, the teachers' area was empty. I guess the
people who watched over the kids at night had their own
parking lot, somewhere else. Or maybe they lived
there, too.

I never knew any of those movie tricks. It wasn't like
the time I'd done the work on the guy in the wheelchair;
that had been a closed-in space where nobody was going
to stop me and ask questions. I knew I couldn't disguise
myself as part of a maintenance crew. And I couldn't put
on camouflage and hide on the grounds like some magic
ninja.

Maybe the people who hired me could have planted a
little camera in the entrance to the lot so they'd know
when the target drove in. But I never communicated
with the people who paid the money. Not during the job,
not at all, not ever.

The entrance road to the school was a long, winding
driveway, probably a good quarter mile from the main
road to the parking lot. From there, much less than half
that to walk over to the first building.

The information I'd been given included his car. A
little white one, one of those that doesn't look like a
convertible, but the top disappears when you push the
right button. I was glad of that—the car, I mean—
because the description of the target could have fit a
million people.

All I did was drive into the lot at night. I knew the
target would get there around ten and leave before
midnight—that's the information the middleman had
given me. I didn't know what a teacher could be doing
there at those hours, but I didn't want to take him until
he was finished. If others were expecting him inside, I

didn't want them to get nervous and come outside looking for him if he was late.

The first night, I drove in a little after ten. The place where the target parked was empty, so I just turned around and left.

I wasn't worried about the school having its own cameras. There weren't any visible in the daytime, and it didn't seem like a place that would have invested in an infra-red setup. Anyway, when I worked, I always expected to be seen. Sometimes even to be seen actually doing the work. Just not identified.

The real trick was not to get stopped by accident. I couldn't work without guns, and if some cop decided I looked wrong, I'd have to make a decision on the spot: take whatever they had for carrying unregistered weapons, do whatever time that cost, and be done working forever...or kill the cop and abort the job.

That decision would only kick in if I was stopped before I did the work.

If it was just afterwards, there was no decision to be made.

Getting stopped was always a stronger possibility if I was in a car.

Especially in a place where you wouldn't expect to see a lot of cars...like a private school at night. But the information was that the school didn't have its own security force walking the grounds, and I'd been told the cops didn't have the parking lot on their radar for a make-out spot.

So, finally, I decided that the lot itself was the safest place to wait. I only had to risk an hour or so. That risk wasn't complicated. I'm not one of those smooth ones who could talk his way past a cop with some story I made up on the spot, and I wasn't any great driver to be outrunning a police radio even if I could get out of the lot first. There was only one risk I could cut down some, and I did that: The guns were in a little black tote bag, sitting behind a bush a few yards away. If a cop did show, if he did decide to search me or the car, he wouldn't come up with anything. I had a digital camera I'd bought sitting on the front seat, so either the cop would buy my story about photographing the moon from that spot or he wouldn't.

If he didn't, there was still no reason to hold me—they'd check my license, ask me a couple of questions, and tell me to get lost. But the job wouldn't get done. Not done by me, I mean. So when it did—and it would—maybe the cop would put something together. But I'd be gone by then. And finished with working just the same as if he'd arrested me.

For a flash—not even a second, just some tiny fragment of time—I thought maybe it would be nice if that happened. Being done. I'd go home and tell my father what had happened, and he'd understand. We'd have to find a new way to continue the line, but...

Then the little white car drove into the lot. Parked in its usual spot. A man got out. His hands were empty. I watched him walk toward the school. He wasn't in a hurry, but he wasn't sauntering. Moved like a man sure of where he was going.

I waited a few minutes, then got out and retrieved the tote bag. I put it in the car I was driving, then started it up and moved until I was only a few spots away from the little white car, a couple of rows back.

I threaded the suppressor into the barrel. In an open setting like that parking lot, sound would carry a long distance.

In the movies, I would have waited in the back of his

car. But all cramped up like I'd have to be to do that, it wouldn't work. Anyway, this wasn't the movies, and one of the rules is you never trap yourself.

What I did was crank back my driver's seat, put on a dark gray ball cap, draw the bill down, and angle my head so that only my eyes were above the dashboard. It was comfortable like that, and any casual observer would only see another empty car.

When I saw the entrance door to the school fill with a man's image, I slid out of my car, leaving the door open and the key in the ignition. No light went on—the owner's manual had told me where the fuses were.

The target walked to his car as I was crossing the lot. I had to take the first shot at a longer distance than I wanted, so I hit him someplace in the midsection. The pistol didn't make much noise. He didn't make any as he dropped.

I leaned over him, like I was trying to help. "I'm sorr —" he said, as I put another two rounds into his face. At least that's what I think he was saying.

I didn't see any police at all.

Of all the jobs I did, that was the only one where I ever wondered what the target had done, why it was needed for him to be dead. I don't know why that was. Or why I sometimes still think about that.

———

THERE WERE lights in the windows at the Tristell house. A light on the porch, too.

I rang the bell. Some kind of chimes on a scale.

Sara Tristell opened the door. Said "Oh!" and stepped aside like she'd been expecting us.

By the time she was in the living room and fully

turned around to face us, her husband came in through another door.

"I heard from—" Sonny started to say, but Robert Tristell made a "sit down" motion with his hands, standing there like he was waiting to see if we did what he wanted.

We took seats on one of those little couches. There was a big leather chair that I figured for the husband's. And he did sit there, but on the separate footrest, hands on his knees. He never took his eyes off us, but his wife seemed to know she was supposed to sit, too. Her chair was high-backed, embroidered in a blue-and-white weave, no footrest.

Robert Tristell nodded at Sonny.

"We heard from Brenda," Sonny started over. He waited a beat, saw no one was going to stop him again. "She sounds okay. Good, even. But...well, not confused, really, just...undecided, maybe?"

Neither of the Tristells said anything. Sara Tristell shifted her position slightly, leaning forward as if to catch every word. Her husband sat like he was carved from stone.

"What she wants is a week," Sonny told them. "She said she has to make up her mind. About a lot of things."

"Did she tell you what things?" Robert Tristell asked. Nothing in his voice at all—he could have been asking directions to the nearest gas station.

"She's not alone," Sonny said, surprising me. "She's with someone. Someone she met online. He's not who she thought he was, but—"

"She's not being held?" Robert Tristell interrupted.

"I don't think so," Sonny told him. "It sure doesn't sound like it."

"But this person she's with, he's not—"

"He's not the person in the picture she had. The picture that was online.

On his Facebook page," Sonny answered. "But everything else about him—whatever that is, Brenda didn't say, specifically—that is him. I'm not sure what that means, not exactly, but I'm pretty sure it means he didn't trick her. About his...personality. Or how he feels about her, maybe?"

"What are you saying?" Sara Tristell said, her voice like a mouse under a blanket. Or maybe a snake looking for a mouse, I couldn't be sure.

"She's not being held against her will," Robert Tristell said, not turning his head toward her, eyes not leaving Sonny...who nodded agreement.

"So the reason she needs a week is to decide if she wants to run away with this...guy. To stay with him?"

"I think so," Sonny answered Robert Tristell. "That's what it sounds like to me. But I think she...I think she wants to come back. Come back home. Only she's afraid."

"Of?" Robert Tristell still hadn't changed his tone.

"Of what you'll do," Sonny told him. "Not to her," he added, nodding his head a little for emphasis.

"You tell her—"

"I already did," Sonny cut him off.

"Told her what?" Sara Tristell demanded.

"That I wouldn't do anything to this...guy, whoever he is," Robert Tristell answered for Sonny. "If Brenda's with him of her own free will, he's in the clear. Not just from me, from anyone else. You tell her that?"

"I did," Sonny said, like he was taking an oath. "I told her I'd met you. I could tell all you wanted was to have her back. Home, I mean. This guy she's with—"

"You know his name?" Robert Tristell asked, not raising his voice.

"I don't," Sonny told him. "I know the name that was on his Facebook page. Ryan, that's the name he used. And that's the name Brenda calls him. But I don't know that's his real name. It might not be."

"If you had to guess...?"

"I'd guess it's just a name," Sonny told him. "And only a first name. Maybe he made that up, too. Maybe Brenda knows another name for him. But she calls him Ryan when we're talking. Her and me, I mean. So maybe that is his name. I just can't say for sure."

"This Facebook page of his...?"

"I looked at it," Sonny told him. "It's gone inactive. Like it was shut down. But it's not removed."

"You don't think it would do any good to trace it?"

"I don't see how—"

"The phone number!" Sara Tristell jumped in. "When Brenda wanted to make a page, one of her own, I mean, she had to give them—Facebook—she had to give them a phone number. And they called. To verify it was a real number."

"Did they ever call again?" Robert Tristell asked his wife.

"Again? Why would they...?"

To make sure that number wasn't a one-time burner cell, I thought, *or even a motel room*, hoping Sonny wouldn't say that...thinking Robert Tristell already knew it, although I couldn't say why.

"It doesn't matter," he said to his wife. And right then I was sure he did know. "We're going to do what Brenda wants. There'd be no reason for her to contact Sonny if she didn't want us to know she was all right. And that we're not going to do anything wild. Not now, and not when she comes home. She's just...confused. But she's a smart girl. She'll figure out what she has to do."

He kept his eyes on Sonny. "You haven't spoken to him, right? Not to this...Ryan person?"

"No," Sonny said. "Brenda only calls when he's at work."

"At work?" Sara Tristell said. "He's old enough to have a—"

"Any kid can have a job," Robert Tristell said to his wife, as if he was wiping images from her mind. "That doesn't mean anything."

"I think if he was much older, she wouldn't have gone with him," Sonny said. "I can't tell you why I think that, it just doesn't...it doesn't feel that way. Because you're right, sir—Brenda is smart. It's just that there's a lot for her to figure out, now."

"Thank you for bringing your son over," Robert Tristell said to me. "We'll give it a week, as agreed."

That sounded strange to me, like he was talking about a contract to buy a house or something, but I kept that to myself.

"You haven't gone to the police with any of this?" he tossed out as we got to our feet.

"No," I told him. "The way I see it, this is between you and your daughter. My son got chosen for his role. Chosen by Brenda. After it all happened," I added, even though I didn't think Robert Tristell was a man to miss such things.

"We're not going to either," he said as he stood up and extended his hand for me to shake. Speaking more to his wife than either of us. He extended his hand to Sonny, too. That made me proud of my son, although I couldn't have said exactly why.

As soon as we were about a mile down the road, Sonny turned to me. "I don't think we should wait a week," is all he said.

"Because..." I tried to lead him, but he wasn't going any farther.

Things were already too speeded up for a man like me, a man used to planning everything out down to the last card being turned over. Not so much success or failure, not even prison or freedom. Maybe not even life or death.

Past all that. Down to rooted bedrock: the continuation of our line.

I wasn't used to speed, only to waiting for speed. Waiting weeks, days, hours, minutes...all for the few seconds of my work. I didn't know how to handle the way Brenda had connected with Sonny. Telling him so much, so quickly. Like there were no walls, nothing between them but trust. Where did that come from? Come from so all-of-a-sudden? In my world, the only ones you trusted were the ones you knew over a long time. Knew what they said, what they did, how much you could count on them.

Back in my day...I thought to myself. But then I pulled up short.

Understanding for the first time. I'd never had a day. I'd been purpose-built. I don't mean like a robot or some mindless bomb. I knew my father had truly loved me. I knew I was his true son, part of a long line. But I'd been raised to continue that line. That would always come first.

And now, for the first time, I wondered if I was being true myself. I'd done the work, sure. But, now, all I could think about, all I could plan for, everything I was doing was to protect Sonny. So I tried again:

"Why do you think we shouldn't wait the week?" I asked him.

"I guess I...I guess I don't really know," my son finally said. "It feels like, like betting on baseball, maybe. I can do all the math, but all I can work with is what I know. Only what I know.

"When you bet, all that 'insider' stuff, how can you trust it? One source—on the Internet, I'm saying; I don't actually know any of these people—one source will say a player has a hamstring pull, but he's going to start anyway. He'll still be able to hit just as good, probably, but he won't be able to run as fast, for fear of a big injury.

"If that's true, it could shift things a little bit, move the line. But if it's not true, if it's just a plant, whoever planted it, he's trying to change the betting pattern. Whichever way the money's going, he's going the other way. So there's information, always plenty of information. Only you don't know how good it is."

"So you ignore it all?"

"That's where you end up," my son said, as though he were a little disappointed in himself. "It should be trackable, shouldn't it? If there's this one source—some expert, some insider, someone who supposedly has his ears open in the clubhouse—then you could keep track of everything he says. The same way you keep track of anyone who sells his picks. Then—"

"Wait. People sell what to bet on?"

"Sure. You have to subscribe to their service, first. Then you get the day's best plays, the longshots most likely to hit, the—"

"Those are the ones you could track? Like you just said?"

"Sure. But you'd have to subscribe to do that. That costs money. And you'd be paying for years before you could make a reliability guess. And even then, that'd only be for one of those sources, and there are—"

"A 'reliability guess' is how often they're right?"

"Yes," Sonny said, sounding pleased that I was following him—I guess I wasn't always able to do that. "Validity—whether one pick is right one time—that doesn't mean a thing in gambling. The longest shot could come in, otherwise there'd be no gambling at all. Reliability, that means how often they're right.

"In science, reliability, that would mean more like truly reliable. Something you can count on. Like if you mix isopropyl and peroxide, you get an explosive. Every time you do that—if you do it correctly—you get the same result. But in gambling, it just means more correct than not. Better than fifty-fifty, that would make you reliable in gambling."

"It doesn't seem very reliable to me."

"Well, you have to have controls," Sonny said, more interested in explaining this than he'd been in explaining why he didn't want to wait the week. "Like...okay, take a roulette wheel. Half is red, half is black. But if some insider told you one particular wheel was actually showing fifty-five percent red, and you always bet on red, if you played long enough, you be guaranteed to come out ahead."

"But don't those wheels all have—"

"Zeroes on them? Sure. That's why it's not actually a fifty-fifty bet. That's the house edge. But when you bet on baseball, there's no house. Not one that cares about the odds, anyway. The house on that kind of betting, it takes a little piece of every bet to bet. The cost of playing."

"Why isn't that the same as the zero on the roulette wheel?"

"It is," Sonny said, very soberly, like it was something he'd been thinking about. "The service—the people you place your bets with—it doesn't care if you win or you lose. It makes its money by setting the line. Like when they give points in a football game."

"Points are only in football?"

"No, they're in most sports where you can score points. Especially a lot of points, like in basketball."

"In baseball, you score runs."

"Sure. But I don't think people are comfortable betting on the number of runs unless it's in a bundle."

"What?"

"A bundle. Like the total number of runs. That's the over-under. Say the line is seven runs. If the two teams score more than seven runs and you have the over, you win. If they score fewer—"

"What if they score exactly seven runs? "

"Then nobody wins."

"You get your money back."

"No," my son said. "You don't. That's the zero on the wheel." I gave him a look he translated easily.

"Roulette," Sonny explained. "You could cover the whole spread, one to thirty-six, red and black...and still lose if the ball lands on zero."

"Could you bet the zero?" I asked him.

"Sure. But on American wheels, there's a double zero, too. There's always a house edge."

I DIDN'T SPEED on the drive back, but I made the best time I could, knowing Brenda could have called while we were gone.

It only took Sonny a couple of seconds to scan his phone. Nothing from Brenda.

"Want something to eat?" I asked him.

Sonny nodded. I'd taught him that: When you're working, the work is the only schedule you have—nothing else intrudes. You eat when you can, you sleep when you can...because you'd don't know when your next chance will come.

"I'll wake up if my phone signals," my son said later, as he went to bed.

I already knew that was how Sonny had it set up, so I guess he was just reassuring me he was on the job.

THE SIGNAL DIDN'T COME until mid-morning the next day.

As near as I could tell, Brenda looked the same on the monitor as she had before, but I noticed she'd changed her top—now it was a bright red pullover with a high neck—and her hair was pulled back off her face, plus a heavier dose of lipstick. If all that was supposed to make her look older, it wasn't working. Not to my eyes, anyway.

"Did you get the chance to—"

"I did," Sonny assured her. "Just like I promised."

I hadn't tried to give him any advice about dealing with Brenda—I wasn't even sure I spoke the same language they did—but I'd always taught him that when you promise somebody something—anything at all—it's good to remind them when you've kept that promise.

That's how reputations are built. Most folks say, "I'll try my best," or "I'll see if I can." Those aren't promises. When you say you'll do something, you have to do it.

Life-and-death simple, that was. Like the work I'd done. And my father before me. Work I now knew for sure Sonny would never be doing.

But the rules don't change just because the work does.

——————

"WHAT DID THEY SAY?" Brenda asked. She didn't sound anxious about it, but I'd watched her take a deep breath just before she asked.

"They said 'okay,'" Sonny told her. "They said—"

"Who said? My mother or—"

"Both. They were on the same side, all the way."

"The same side?"

"Your side."

"Oh. I wasn't sure my mother would. You'd think she'd just go along with my dad. Not me, you, I mean. You'd think. If you just met them. If you didn't really know them, that's what they...look like to people. What did they say, exactly?"

"They said they'd give you—give all of this—the week you said you wanted. They know you're making up your mind. And they're...confident, I guess. Confident that, once you think it all over, you'll go back home."

"They're not going to try and trace me?"

"How could they do that?" Sonny asked her. "I'm sure they tried everything before they even—"

"Before you reached out to me? Found me, I guess I should say."

"Yes. Only I didn't tell them that," Sonny said, very measured. "I told

them that it was you who contacted me. I didn't want them to think they could do the same thing I did."

"Or the police could."

"Yes."

"But now that they know...About the week and all..."

"If you mean the police, they don't," Sonny filled in the gap, knowing it was really a question. "When I went over to your house, the police weren't there. And your folks said they weren't going to say anything to them. Your father, he even said Ryan is safe, too."

"Safe?"

"From...the police, I guess. From the law. Your father said, so long as you were with Ryan of your own free will, he—Ryan I mean—he had nothing to worry about."

"But even if my parents don't say anything to the police, wouldn't they still have a lot of questions when I came back? The police, I mean."

"I...guess so. But you wouldn't have to answer them, would you?"

"I wouldn't," Brenda said, chin up in a teenage-determined face. "I never would. But I don't know if they could...put surveillance on me, or something. Keep a watch out for Ryan."

"I don't know," Sonny said. "But I could ask my father."

"Your father? Does he know—"

"He knows what I told your folks," Sonny said, putting a little patience on top of his words. "Because he was right there with me. He drove me over. Both times. So he knows everything I said."

"Oh. I guess that makes sense. But why would you ask him anything?"

"Not about you," Sonny said. "About Ryan."

"Ryan?"

"Sure. My father has a lawyer. For his business and all. He could ask the lawyer what kind of trouble Ryan could be in. For helping you run away, maybe, I don't know."

"My father knows a lot of lawyers," Brenda said. I flashed on Robert Tristell saying something like that himself. To the police. "But I see what you mean. He'd make sure nothing would happen to me. He'd never let anyone...anyway, I don't think it's a crime to run away like I did. Kids—I mean people our age—they do that all the time, don't they? There's all kinds of shows about them on TV."

"Those shows are about missing kids," Sonny said. "Sure, maybe they ran away in the beginning, but it's where they ended up that those TV shows are about. Those kids, their parents don't even know if they're alive. It's a whole different story from...from yours."

"Ryan's older than me," Brenda suddenly said, like she was revealing a big secret.

"Older than you are in real life? Or older than you said you were?"

"Both. He's...he's a grown man."

"You mean, like over twenty-one or something?"

"Yes," Brenda said quickly. "So maybe he would be in trouble, I don't know. Your father would ask his lawyer?"

"Sure. I know he would."

"How do you know?"

"Because I know him," Sonny said, absolutely certain. "If I asked him to, he would."

"Just like that?"

"Just like that."

"I already told you we haven't...done anything."

"I wasn't even thinking about...that," Sonny assured her. "I...like I said, I'm not a lawyer. I don't know anything about this kind of thing. You're right. What you said. About kids running away all the time. I don't think they ever get in trouble for that. But, maybe, helping them do it...especially if you're much older..."

"Ryan's not that much older. Not than he thought I was, I mean."

"Okay. Do you want me to ask my father or not?"

"Yes, please." She was quiet for a few seconds, then: "I'm sorry, Sonny.

I know you're trying to help. I didn't mean to sound like a spoiled brat."

"You sound just like...well, like anyone in...this kind of situation.

I'm sure—I'm absolutely sure—that things will be fine when you come home."

"I couldn't ask him, Sonny."

"Ask Ryan, you mean? Ask him to bring you home?"

"Yes. Like you said, maybe he could get in trouble."

"Well, my father's lawyer could check into that. I know my father will—"

"What if he doesn't want to?"

"Brenda, I just said—"

"Not the lawyer. Ryan. What if he doesn't want to come...with me?"

"But if he doesn't come with you, if he doesn't meet your parents, how

could you—"

"You already said we couldn't get married, didn't you? I mean, even if my folks...liked him and all, I'm not old enough."

"Not to get married, no. But if Ryan lived close by,

you could maybe...I don't know, go out on dates and stuff..."

"He wouldn't want to do that," Brenda said, as if she had already talked it over with Ryan. "He has a job here. And his own place. And...friends, I guess. Although I haven't met any of them, not yet. He has a car, too. So if the police had the license number, then..."

"Okay. Well, maybe if you came back alone first...?"

"It's not that easy, Sonny," she said, something floating inside her voice, but I didn't know what to call it. Or what it meant.

"Why not? You can't be that far away. We could come and get you. Not to Ryan's house, if you didn't want. But to—"

"Who's we, Sonny? You and your father?"

"Sure."

I guessed Brenda's being quiet for a minute made Sonny think she was going the wrong way. "It could even be just me, if you wanted," he told her.

"Just you? But you'd have to drive and—"

"I can drive," Sonny said, surprising me. "I'm a good driver."

"You don't have a license. Not a real one, anyway," Brenda said, as if she were his older sister, telling him not to act stupid.

"That doesn't matter," he said, not arguing, just telling her what the truth was. "I know how to drive. I've driven plenty of times. And I could take one of our cars. Not steal it or anything" he put in quickly, as if he knew what Brenda was thinking. "My father, I know he'd let me."

"Your father sounds like he'd let you do...anything, right? But if you got stopped, then you'd be the one in trouble."

"Not any real trouble. Driving without a license, kids

get caught doing that all the time. It's not like it's some big crime or anything."

"Well, if we got caught doing that, you bringing me home, I mean, the police would probably think we ran away together," she said, a little chuckle bubbling under her voice.

"I..."

"Oh, Sonny. I can see you blushing, even on the screen. I was only joking. They wouldn't think that. You're just a kid."

"So are you," my son said, a little heat in his voice.

"Girls mature much faster than boys, didn't you know that?

Sonny didn't say anything. After a few seconds, Brenda said, "Well...I still have to think. There's a lot to think about."

"That's okay."

"I can only do things in the daytime."

"That's okay, too."

"You're going to miss more school," Brenda half-teasing, half-testing. "Well, like you said, I'm pretty smart," Sonny assured her. "I can do all my homework online until I get over this flu."

"You are smart," Brenda said, flashing a real smile.

———

"WE COULD DO THAT, couldn't we?" Sonny asked me, as soon as the connection broke.

"Go and get Brenda? Sure," I told him. "Do you think that's what will happen?"

"That's up to her, isn't it?"

"Maybe," Sonny said.

I waited for him to say more, but he didn't.

"You're sure they haven't had...relations?" the lawyer asked. When I'd called and asked to see him, all I'd said was that it was important. And that I'd be glad to pay him for his time.

"I know that's what she said," I told him. "And if she's not pregnant, if she doesn't have...something she could catch from...another person, how could they tell?"

"They could take her to a doctor," the lawyer said, raising his eyebrows, like he was the one asking the questions.

"That wouldn't prove anything," I said, including Sonny in my answer without looking at him. "Not about anyone in particular. Not about Ryan, anyway. Besides, I can't see them doing that."

"You know them that well?"

"The mother and father? I think I do," I told the lawyer. Remembering what my father said to me, a long time ago: "You can tell more about a man under pressure in ten minutes than you might be able to tell from watching that same man during ten years of peace."

I didn't think my father had ever been in a war—he never talked much about his life before he went out to do our work. Same as I came to do. But, thinking back, it always seemed as if he had learned a lot more than I ever had from doing that work.

"Even if they had, it would only be Ry—the guy who'd be in trouble, isn't that true?" Sonny asked, before the lawyer could respond.

"That's correct," he answered. "As I explained, running away, that isn't a crime in and of itself. The girl's parents would have to get her declared a 'person in need of supervision' for the authorities to...have any access."

"What does that mean, access? To have her...put someplace?"

"To even so much as question her," the lawyer told Sonny. "Now I'm talking about different authorities, you understand. There's Child Protective Services—those are the ones the parents would have to make a complaint to. They, the agency, they couldn't go anywhere near this unless there was an actual complaint by the parents.

"Now the police, that's a different thing altogether. They can question anyone if that person is being questioned as a witness. But they wouldn't do that without her parents present. And witnesses don't have to cooperate."

"I thought—" Sonny started to say.

"Forget TV shows," the lawyer dismissed whatever Sonny was thinking. "Witnesses, actual witnesses, not people who might be involved in the crime themselves, they don't have to say anything if they don't want to."

"So what if she wouldn't talk to them?" my son asked. I was proud of him for remembering we weren't to use any names in front of the lawyer.

"Then she might need a lawyer. She was...at the very least, staying with the individual the police would be interested in," the lawyer said. "But I can't imagine this coming to anything like that."

"I think she may be...concerned about this young man," I said. "I think if she was really certain nothing was going to happen to him, she'd be more willing to come home."

"Well, you could certainly promise her that much," the lawyer said.

I wasn't sure Sonny took the true meaning of what that lawyer was saying, although I was damn sure I did. So I said: "But, just in case the law might want to charge him with something, you could represent him, couldn't you?"

"If that's what he wanted," the lawyer said. "But I couldn't even say I was his attorney unless there was an agreement between us first. Between this young man and myself, you see?"

"I do," I assured him. "And you wouldn't have to meet him to have that agreement, would you?"

"I would not," the lawyer said, on solid ground, now. Ground he was sure of, anyway. "A client could call me from jail, for example. Maybe someone else in the holding cells gave him my business card, who knows? But I could certainly come to an agreement for me to represent...whoever...based on a telephone conversation."

"How would he pay you over the phone?" Sonny asked.

The lawyer gave Sonny a look. A lot of things in that look, but I was sure I saw some respect mixed in there.

"That depends," he answered, speaking directly to Sonny for the first time since we'd come into his office. "Some people have credit cards. Some have a bank account. Some have family or friends. Depending on the time of day—and the seriousness of the charge—I could send an associate down to the jail and obtain the necessary signatures."

"Are there—"

"That's not an inclusive list," the lawyer went on. "There's almost always the matter of bail, so it could be the bondsman who makes the first contact. Or if the...person who had been arrested puts up bail themselves, I could take an assignment of all or part."

"But if someone puts up bail, don't they get out of jail?"

"If they can make the bail, certainly. A bail bond is

usually ten percent of the total. So if bail were ten thousand, the bond would be a thousand. The bondsman keeps that money, no matter how the case turns out. But if the bail is put up in cash, or if property is put up as collateral, there doesn't have to be a bondsman involved. That's what I would take an assignment on."

"So the money would go to you, not the person who put up the bail?"

"That's generally correct," the lawyer said, a dusting of caution over his

words. "It doesn't always work out to exact numbers. If bail were ten thousand, and it were put up in cash, and my fee were ten thousand, then, when bail was exonerated—"

"What does—"

"It just means 'returned,' the lawyer explained. "If the defendant is later convicted, or say he pleads guilty, then bail is exonerated. If there's a trial and the defendant is acquitted, bail is exonerated. Or if the charges are dropped, same thing."

"And the court is holding the money until then?"

"That's correct."

"So it's even better than a promise to pay," Sonny said.

"You'd make an excellent attorney," the lawyer said.

Sonny didn't look flattered, but he said "Thank you, sir," very politely.

―――――――

ON THE DRIVE BACK, I was thinking about patience. How I'd been taught to understand patience as a tool of the trade. Something of value that I'd never want to operate without. Not just a skill to be learned, something planted deeper than that. A part of me that nothing could take away.

But patience has to play inside pressure. If there's only a few days left on the clock, your patience can't last beyond that or it's no good to you at all.

I'd been patient. But the clock was running. Sonny and Brenda, they'd agreed on a week. But they weren't the only ones on that schedule. Brenda's father was keeping them off for now, but the police were waiting, too.

————

ALL THOSE BOOKS I read over the years, all those discarded paperbacks, they hadn't taught me anything I could use now. Fact or fiction, it didn't matter. Just like the movies, true or false didn't make a difference to the audience we had—that wasn't why they were watching.

What I knew was what I didn't know. I don't know how many men I've killed, but I do know I never tracked one of them down myself. Every time I worked, I was told where to find the target. After that, it was up to me. But I never had more than the information I was given. I didn't know how to get any of that information. I didn't know what those spy books called "tradecraft." I didn't know how to follow a man; I didn't know how to check if I'm being followed. I didn't know people with access to information.

I didn't have a network. Contacts. Informants. Nothing like that.

Until this all happened, I considered myself a useful man. A man with a purpose. Part of a long chain of purpose. I'd done everything I was supposed to do. Listened to my father. Learned from him. Took over when it was my time. Came back home. Took one of Us from Them.

But I'd broken the chain I'd been linked to. I hadn't taught Sonny as I'd been taught. I hadn't told him what he needed to know to do the work I'd done. I'd kept telling myself there was time. Telling myself I was being patient. And the clock ran past my patience even as I watched the hands move.

So I was behind the wheel. Taking us home. All the while thinking I was more a passenger than a driver. Thinking about what was valuable, and what wasn't.

How, this time, things were backwards: I knew how to kill Ryan, but not how to find him.

SONNY and I were both patient, then...but we went about it differently. I don't know what Sonny was doing back in his room, but I guessed he wasn't placing bets.

Me, I was waiting for it to get dark.

"SHE DIDN'T CALL," Sonny said, after afternoon turned into evening. "No message, nothing."

"That doesn't necessarily mean—"

"It could mean she's already taken off, couldn't it?"

"It could," I acknowledged, thinking it could just as easily be a dozen different things, none of them good.

"Do you think she's in trouble?"

"You mean, what the lawyer said about—"

"It doesn't matter what he said," Sonny cut me off. "He doesn't care about Brenda. Not like we do."

"Okay..." I said, dragging it out to see if Sonny was

going to add anything. He didn't, so I went ahead: "Do I think she's in trouble because of Ryan? Because Ryan could be...up to something?"

"Yes," is all he said. Then he went quiet again.

"He's good at lying," I told my son. "But Brenda already knows that. From everything she said—said to you, I mean—she's at peace with whatever lies she knows about."

Sonny jumped on that like a terrier after a rat: "There could be a lot of lies she doesn't know about, couldn't there?"

"Yes," I straight-answered my son.

"I've been trying to find out more about him," Sonny said. "But he hasn't left footprints. Just that profile. The Facebook page. The Instagram. It's not enough. But I've been working on something. An idea I had."

"To find out who he is?"

"Sort of. It's more a way to get a picture of him. A real picture, not another one of that BMX guy."

"Do you think you could do that?"

"Oh, I can do it," Sonny assured me. "It's just a question of whether Brenda would want me to."

I sat with that for a moment. Then I told my son what I knew to be true: "Sometimes, when there's only two people talking, there's a...space between the things that get said. An empty space—"

"Like a vacuum?"

"I guess so," I went on, although I wasn't sure exactly what he meant. "It's like, one person is waiting on the other, but that other person's waiting, too, okay? Maybe one person wants to answer a question, but he isn't sure what the question is. Not exactly, anyway. So he waits. But the other person, he's sure. So he figures—"

"It's me waiting on you, Dad," Sonny said, instantly shifting my focus.

Thinking on how he only calls me that when he's dead serious about something. So I just went ahead:

"We can't be certain what Brenda would want us to do without her telling us outright," I told him. "And she hasn't said. But if we so much as ask..."

Sonny nodded. On the same wavelength as me, I thought.

"So it's that...vacuum thing," I went on. "We think Brenda knows everything about this Ryan. Knows everything now, I mean. Because she knows what he really looks like, that's one example. But if there's more to know, more she doesn't know..."

"Sometimes, people don't want to know things," my son said, sounding like a grown man.

"That's true," I agreed. "But it's a question of...responsibility. And once we put ourselves in this..."

"It's our responsibility to protect her, isn't it?"

"It is," I told him, flat. Thinking of my father telling me things.

Thinking of how sure and certain he was when he was explaining about our tribe. Our debt. Our path. I'd had so many questions, then. If he'd wavered, if he hadn't been so dead-sure and dead-calm about it, I might have had more. "If there's something wrong with this Ryan—I don't mean him lying, I mean something much worse—we have to do whatever we can to find out."

"Brenda just wants to be happy," Sonny said. He was quiet for a bit after that, but I matched his quiet with my own until he spoke again. "But if she's not safe, how could she stay happy? So if we don't try...everything, it would be like we let her down."

"That's right, son," is all I said.

SONNY WENT to work after that. I left him alone. It wasn't that I thought me being there would bother him; it was just that there was nothing I could do to help.

At least that's what I told myself. But, deep inside, I knew I'd need some things. Might need some things, anyway. I didn't want to leave Sonny alone long enough to get those things. And I didn't know what that bald-headed cop was doing with his time, either.

"I HAVE TO WAIT, NOW," Sonny told me a couple of hours later. "But I did find something. Do you know what Brenda's middle name is?"

"Her middle name? You mean, her real name, not the one she made up?"

"Yes. The name on her birth certificate."

"No, I don't."

"It's 'Starr,'" Sonny said. "Spelled with two r's, not one."

I must have looked puzzled, because Sonny said: "'Brenda Starr, Reporter' was the name of a comic strip. About a woman reporter. It started before World War Two, but it got really popular after the war was over, especially during the Fifties. It was ahead of its time, because it was drawn by a woman, Dalia Messick...although they changed her name to 'Dale' so people would think it was written by a man."

"She was a reporter? In those comics, I mean."

"More like an investigative reporter. She had all kinds of adventures."

"Why do you think Brenda's parents named her after her?"

"I don't know," Sonny said. "But the woman herself, Dalia Messick, she had a child. And she named that child 'Starr.' Spelled that same way."

"Huh!"

"It doesn't show on her school records," Sonny went on. "Those just say 'Brenda S. Tristell,' or sometimes just 'Brenda Tristell.' The 'Starr' is only on her birth certificate."

I didn't ask him how he'd found all that out. By then, we were standing more equal, Sonny and me. He'd always accepted that I knew things, and now I was accepting that he knew things, too.

IT WAS WELL past dark when Sonny came into what people around here call a "sitting room." It was the first option off the hallway that led back to the kitchen. Not formal, like a living room where invited guests might sit. Not a place for food, either—no table, just a couple of relaxing chairs and a little couch made out of a futon slung over a wood frame. Any stranger invited in would be offered something—coffee, lemonade, depending on the season—but that was just good manners. Expected manners.

We never used that room much—it was just the way the house had been built. Same for the living room. If there was anything serious, you'd go to the kitchen to talk. But the sitting room had the best view of the driveway leading up to the house.

I didn't have the lights on—I was just watching. Thinking of how often I'd done that. But my hands were empty. We had firearms in the house. A couple of shot-guns, and what folks around here would call a deer rifle. Not really weapons, just tools.

A thought flashed—that's all those pistols had been for me: tools. And I wasn't working now.

Except that it felt as if I was. And as if I didn't have the right tools for the job.

"Ryan's no good," is all Sonny said.

———

I FOLLOWED him back to his room.

"This is the page I made," Sonny said, pointing at his largest monitor.

Bella Sweetshop ("Because calories are my mortal enemy!") was an almost pretty young girl in a white T-shirt with "Riiipe" graffiti-sprayed across the front and a short blue plaid pleated skirt. She was a redhead with very pale skin, big blue eyes. A light sprinkling of freckles made her hair look natural. She was slightly bent forward, hands on her knees, mock-pouting. Looked like she'd come into puberty with quite a bit of baby fat still on her.

"Bella says she's sixteen," Sonny told me, like he was reading my thoughts. "These girls always add a couple of years. The way Brenda did, when she was being 'Thondra Telle.'"

"You just took that picture—the one of...Bella, I mean —you just took that from another page?"

"Sort of. I mean, I did take it from another page, yes. Three pages, actually. And then I altered the image. To make her look younger. And a little...chubbier. It wasn't that hard. And I didn't feel right about just...using some actual girl's picture."

"So if the police...even if the police had this same page, they couldn't match the photo to any other one?"

"That's right," Sonny said. He seemed pleased that I'd listened when he'd explained how you could put any picture you take off the Internet into some search thing and see if there was a match anyplace. "But it wasn't the police I was thinking of, it was Ryan himself. That's what he did. With that BMX rider. So if he knew how to do that, the first thing he'd do..."

"Sure," is all I said, to let Sonny know I was still with him.

"Bella got messages so fast I couldn't believe it. Like people were out there just watching for...for whatever she's supposed to be."

"Sixteen?"

"That can't be it," Sonny said. "There's too many. It had to be her profile."

I looked. It didn't seem so unusual to me. Bella liked horses and cats. She didn't have a horse, but she really, really wanted one someday. She did have a cat. A black one named Midnight. Bella hated school. She wasn't going to college, so what did she need high school for? She hated "body shamers" too, whatever they were. She didn't like working out, but she knew she had to "make my body match my face" if she was going to "grow up and be a sugar baby" for the right guy. Or good enough to pose on Instagram—she wasn't ready for that yet, but she would be. "Promise you!"

There were a bunch of pictures, but none of them showed her face too closely. Bella in a padded snowsuit with a hood, Bella in a witch's outfit holding up a "Trick or Treat" sign, a photograph of a pair of stiletto heels, black with red soles, with "This is what I need!" scrawled across the front in a rounded immature handwriting...looked like the same as the writing across the front of her T-shirt.

"Those got a lot of people to contact her?"

Sonny clicked something and a monitor to his right lit up. A series of messages covered the screen. Some were from other girls. Some encouraging:

==========================

Don't put yourself through hell working out. You've got plenty of time.
You'll lose the weight *naturally*. Check out my page, you'll see!
You have to learn to love yourself. Don't listen to those hags!

==========================

Some were nasty, telling her she couldn't ever lose enough pounds to not be fat, no matter what she did. One even said the only way she could "make weight" would be to cut off her ugly head.

Sonny kept scrolling. More girls. Some coming off sweet and supportive. "I was there, too. DM me and we can talk about this." Plenty of the girls told her she was pretty. Some came on stronger: "Are you bi-curious? Even a little? 'Cause I am, too."

Boys wrote, too. She was cute, she sounded so sweet, a girl pretty as her didn't need school...

Asking for private pictures, that was a common thread.

Not just boys. Some were grown men—not just from their photos, from their speech. Calling her a cute little brat, saying she looked like she could use a good spanking, they had a present for her if she was as sexy in person as she looked in her pictures...

Pages and pages, dozens of messages, but they all sounded like some versions of the same three or four.

And then there was Ryan.

Ryan was different. Telling her she had beautiful eyes, sure...but that wasn't what was important...it was what those eyes were saying...and he knew what she was really saying.

School, that was important, too, he wrote. Because it was obvious to him that she was just playing dumb—just playing a game. The truth of her came out when she'd said what she wanted out of life. He could tell what she wanted was to live in a house with lots of land. Where she could have her horse. And a car, too. He could tell she liked fast cars. A convertible, so that her flaming hair could flow out behind her as she drove.

Brenda ignored everyone but Ryan. She messaged him right away.

========================

You say looks aren't important, but you're a doll, so that's easy for you to say.

> *You really believe that's what counts in life?*

Well, no...but that's what most people seem to think. I'm not most people. And you're not, either.

========================

"THERE'S A LOT OF THAT," Sonny said. "They're just private messaging, now, nothing public."

"Did Ryan ask her for pictures?"

"He didn't," Sonny told me. "But she sent some, anyway." I didn't say anything.

"They're...innocent," he said. "Some of her just...doing regular things. But things he told her to do. Like there's a few of her reading. Looking at books, anyway."

"He send any pictures to her?"

"Yes. Similar. But there's a few of these..." Sonny clicked his trackball holder and a picture of a car popped up. A white Mustang, with blue racing stripes.

"That's the one we needed, to make sure."

"Still no license plate."

"No. He's very careful." I stayed quiet.

"Bella loves that car," my son said, his voice soft and cold.

BY THEN, I knew what had to be done, but I wasn't confident about it. I knew what Ryan was. Or what he was involved in, anyway. I knew that from the man in the wheelchair I'd killed years ago. From what had been on his computer's screen.

Knowing that didn't make it easier.

I thought about why that would be. Maybe because it was the first time I'd thought about killing a man. I'd never done that before.

It wasn't like I knew Ryan. I didn't even know what he really looked like, or where I could find him. There was nobody paying to make him dead. But that didn't make it feel...personal, or anything. I didn't have any feelings about him. Not even about Brenda, although I guess I should have.

Just about Sonny. It was as if Sonny's heart was

beating inside me, only at a distance, so I had to really listen to hear it, really concentrate if I wanted to feel it.

Sonny wouldn't see things the way I always had. When I was working, I killed people for money. We needed the money to continue our line. Nothing else mattered. Not who those people were, not what they might have done before they died, not what they might have done if they hadn't. I didn't know them any more than those men who went to the outdoor rifle range knew the paper targets they shredded.

Sonny wouldn't see things the way I had, because I hadn't taught him what I'd been taught.

But I knew something about Sonny that he didn't even know about himself. He was one of Us. Taken from one of Them.

And then I remembered something my father told me, a long time ago. It was a little while after I'd killed my first man, the gun bundler. "They don't just take babies, son," he said. "They'd even take a boy your age if they could."

"To sell? Like they do the babies?"

"To use," my father said. Then he went very quiet, the way he got sometimes.

I just stayed with him while he was quiet. He never asked me to do that, but somehow I knew it was what he wanted. To just...be with him.

When finally he turned to face me, I knew I could ask him anything. So I did.

"Couldn't we just kill them? We know how to find them, so..."

"No, son. There's far too many. And it's not as though they were all in the same place, like an enemy country we could drop bombs on. We don't know who they are, or where they live. We don't know what they look like, only that they don't all look alike. They don't wear uniforms, or carry marks on their skin. And there's no map with dots on them, like they'd had on TV to show where the virus had spread, remember?"

"So how do we know who they are? How do any of us find any of them? How can we take—"

"The only way we find them is by what they do," my father said. "When they make it known they have babies for...And, even then, we can't kill them. We pay them. And we take one of us from them every time we do."

"But—"

"We can't do it, son," my father interrupted, as if he knew what I had been about to say. "If we started killing one of them every time there was a...transaction, soon they'd be like the gun bundlers are now. Word would get out that they were at risk, and they'd be a lot more careful about what they do. Take way more precautions. Make it a lot harder for one of us to find them.

"The way things are now, it's really easy. They have nothing to fear, so they're right out in the open. Like looking in the paper if you want to buy a used car. That part of our mission, it's really easy. All we need is the money, the money for each...time."

"One at a time. It doesn't seem like enough."

"That's because you're still young," my father said. "From where you stand, you can't see progress. If you don't look behind you every so often, you can't see things ahead of you. Things change over time. A long time. I won't live to see the end of the road. Neither will you. Neither will your son. Nor his son. But we're not the only ones doing the work; we're just the only ones doing the work our way."

"Okay," is all I said. I believed that when I said it. I

believed it still. Each of us did our piece, in lots of different ways.

If I could see Brenda as one of us, if I could see Ryan as one of them, it...wouldn't do me any good. Because Ryan wouldn't sell her to us. We're not the buyers he'd be expecting.

Sure, Ryan going after Bella Sweetshop made him a bundler, and killing the bundlers had been part of our work, me and my father's. But guns are things. Disposable things. Brenda, she was a person.

A person to us, anyway. To Sonny. And me, I guess. Surely to her parents. Someone they loved. Wanted to protect.

But, to Ryan, a disposable thing. That's when I knew what to do. What I didn't know was how to do it.

I closed my eyes. Not to sleep, to see better.

"It's good we don't have a lot of time," I told Sonny, an hour later.

"Why?"

"Because this Ryan, he doesn't have room for two girls in his house."

"You think—"

"Did you understand what I meant when I said Ryan didn't have room for two girls, son?"

"I'm...not sure. I know they—girls—they get jealous, don't they? It would be like he—Ryan—was cheating on Brenda, wouldn't it? So, really, he's dumping her for Bella Sweetshop. Is that right?"

"Not like you mean," I told him.

Sonny was quiet for a little bit. Then he said: "You mean, he doesn't want Brenda for a girlfriend anymore?

He doesn't want to marry her...if he ever really did. But if he just tells her to go home or whatever, she'll know where he lives. And that could get him in trouble."

"That's not it," I said, not sure how I should put what I knew to be true.

Sonny was smart—smarter than I ever was at his age—but this was a different kind of smart he needed to be. I never had to be that good with words, not to get by, not to do my work. I wasn't...close...with anyone after I left home. But I was with Sonny. And I was out of choices. "I know when you said this Ryan wanted to 'dump' Brenda you meant something like...like not want her for a girl-friend. That happens with"—I almost said 'kids' but I pulled back in time—"people your age all the time, doesn't it?"

"I...guess. It's the kind of thing you hear about at school. Who dumped who."

"This is different," I told my son. "Ryan, he's like one of those homeless guys you see around town. The ones with the big plastic bags of cans and bottles they pick up. You know what they do with that stuff?"

"Take it to the recycling center."

"Why?"

"They cash it in."

"Yes. That's what Ryan's going to do with Brenda."

"What? How could he just—"

"Sonny, here it is, okay? I know about things. Not about the things you know about—computers and gambling on baseball and that math you do. Me, I know about other things. Things I learned about in the work I did. Before you came. Before I went and got you."

"Okay..."

"I bought you, son," I told him. "I bought you for money."

AND I KEPT on telling him, then. I told him in a few hours everything my father had taken years and years to tell me. And I answered every question he had.

"What do we do now?" he finally asked me.

"It's what you do, son," I answered him. "No matter what Brenda says tomorrow, it's up to you. It's up to you to get her to tell us where she is. If we have that, we can do something."

"You mean you're going to—"

"If it comes to that," I told my son. "It might not. I don't know. That's not the...job. This isn't a job at all."

"I think it is," Sonny said, his voice carrying weight. "Even if we get Brenda to come with us, this Ryan, he's going to keep...making these girls think he's going to...marry them and all, isn't he?"

"Yes, he is."

"Let's see what Brenda says tomorrow," is all Sonny said.

_____

"HI!" Brenda greeted him the next morning, bright and bouncy. "Brenda," Sonny replied. Gravely, like he'd aged ten years overnight.

And maybe he had—neither of us had slept. Sonny hadn't asked as many questions as I'd expected, but it had taken me longer than I'd expected to tell him everything I'd waited too long to say.

"What's the matter, Sonny?" Brenda asked, picking up on it right away.

"What did you decide?" Sonny responded. "Decide?"

"Are you going to let us bring you home? So you can explain everything to your folks?"

"You said I had—"

"You don't," Sonny cut her off. "Not anymore."

"Sonny, why? You said—"

"Things have changed," Sonny interrupted, his voice flatter.

"What's—"

"It comes down to trust, now," Sonny told her. "You trust me...about some things. You trust your parents...about some things. And you trust Ryan...about some things, too."

"So I have to make a choice, you're saying?" Brenda asked him. She sounded older than she was a few minutes ago, too, as if she was reaching toward wherever Sonny was standing.

"You already knew that," Sonny said. "But this is something different. Something new."

"What, Sonny? You're...scaring me."

"We have to...change the odds," Sonny told her.

"I don't—"

"It's like a gamble, isn't it? If you come back home, that's a gamble. Maybe your parents will do everything they promised. And Ryan will be safe, just like you were maybe worried about. He might even come and meet your parents, and you'll be...engaged, like. Just waiting till you're old enough to get married. Maybe, maybe. Any 'maybe,' that's a gamble, right?"

"I guess it is. But I believe...I guess I believe...everyone. Everyone you just named, I believe."

"You can't," Sonny told her. Bluntly, leaving no room for argument.

"Sonny, stop it! I don't understand what you're saying."

"If you tell Ryan you decided to come home, tell him you'll wait for him, all of that, what if he says no? What if he says no, he's not bringing you back? No, he's not going to meet your folks. No, he's not going to stay there and wait for you.

"What if Ryan says you have to run with him? Then what? You can believe everyone if you want to, Brenda. But you can't do what everyone wants you to do."

"I..."

"So it is a gamble, isn't it?" Sonny said, closing in. "You have to put your money on one choice or another. And that's what I'm trying to explain, okay, Brenda? That I want to change the odds. I have something to show you. Something that would change those odds. I promise it would."

"Well, then...show it to me, can't you?"

"Not this way," he told her. "Because the FaceTime won't—"

"Oh, I could show you on the screen easy enough," Sonny said. "But I won't do that. I don't know what you'll do when I show you. So I have to be there when I do it."

"Be...where?"

"It doesn't matter exactly where. I could show you on my phone. Even on yours, if you wanted. But I have to be with you when I do. Not over some WiFi connection, standing right there with you."

"Why?" she demanded.

"Because you'll...get upset," Sonny said, running out of vocabulary for what he had to get across. "I'll meet you anywhere you say. I'll show you what I...found out.

"And I'll bring money, too," he added. "Twenty-two thousand, four hundred and fifty-some dollars. My whole college fund. If you want to run away after I show you, you can have the money. To help you and Ryan set yourselves up, wherever you go."

"I don't see how—"

"I only need maybe half an hour," Sonny said. "Even less, if you say so. You can pick the place. You don't even have to tell me in advance, if you don't want. Just tell me the direction to drive in, and text me while I'm on my way."

"I do trust you, Sonny. It's not that. And I could go out. In the daytime, I mean. I could go out right now, if I wanted. But I'm not exactly sure where I am."

"Then *go* out," Sonny said, his voice just short of challenging. "Go out and look around. I don't know if you're in a town, or out in the country, but it doesn't matter. All you need is some...marker. Some place I could find myself. Maybe, even...can you look out the window?"

"Well, sure. It's not like I'm a prisoner or something, Sonny. Only... "

"What?"

"It's...well, it's not a cellar, exactly. It's what people call a 'daylight basement,' you know what that is?"

"Like on the same level as the street?"

"Yes! That's it, exactly. I never heard of a 'daylight basement' before. Ryan told me that's what this is. The whole apartment, I mean. You come in straight through the garage."

"So when you look outside, what do you see?"

"Not much. There's some houses. And a huge field, it looks like. With some woods behind. I can see the trees. So it's not downtown anyplace. But it's not way out in the sticks, either."

"Okay. Did you ever go upstairs?"

"Sure. Ryan took me. It's like...empty. I mean, there's furniture there and all, but there's no people. Ryan says the house is for sale, and the top floors have to be kept clean and new-looking so the real estate people can show the house. It's going on the market in a couple of weeks. That's what I was going to tell you. Before, I mean. Remember when we were talking about a time limit? To make up my mind? Well, the way it turns out, there's another one. Another time limit. Because once the place goes on the market, Ryan and I can't stay here, either. He says we have to leave this place just like the upstairs. All neat and clean, like no one's been here for quite a while."

I could feel Sonny desperately wanted to look over at me. I was proud of how he held himself in check.

"Brenda, now I have to show you what I found."

"It's a long drive, Sonny. You're only fourteen."

"Fifteen," Sonny corrected her. "My birthday was last week. "

"Okay, fifteen. You still don't have a driver's license."

"I don't look fifteen, do I?" Sonny said, as if no reasonable person could argue with him. "And no cop's going to stop me if I stay inside the speed limit."

"And you promise, you promise you won't tell anyone? Even if I still decide to go away with Ryan?"

"I swear," Sonny said, tapping his heart. "Just hit me back later today and tell me where to come. I'll leave...well, I'll leave whenever I have to. So I can see you tomorrow. Tomorrow morning. Way before Ryan would be coming back."

Everything went quiet. I could see Brenda biting her lip, Sonny in profile watching the monitor screen.

"I'll do it," Brenda finally said.

The screen flickered, then went blank.

IT WAS mid-afternoon when Brenda reached out for Sonny. Late enough in the day so I knew she was calling from the same time zone.

"I'll look at it, Sonny," she said. "I'll look at whatever you have. But no—"

"Promises," Sonny finished for her. "Do you want me to come to the house? Where you're staying, I mean."

"No. I don't think so. I'm going to walk across the field—the one I can see from the window. When I get to the other side, wherever that is, I'll go into the woods and wait right there. I'm going to wait for you, Sonny. You can show me. Then I'll either come with you...or I'll just walk back."

She didn't say "walk back home," I thought, listening without moving.

As I'd had to do so many times in the life I once believed I had left behind. But the longer Sonny was in my new life, the less certain I'd grown of that.

I snapped back to attention when I heard my son ask Brenda: "Can you take one of the burners with you? So we can stay in contact in case I have trouble finding you?"

"Sure. There's boxes of them here. If I decide to...come back. Come back here, I mean...he wouldn't even notice one was missing. I'll take the whole thing. The plastic wrapping and all," she trailed off. Leaving the door open.

"I'll be there, Brenda," Sonny told her. "I'll be there for you, whatever you decide.

———

SONNY PULLED up a map on one of his monitors. Driving directions, too. Even some views of the house Brenda was staying in. "I'm positive that's the one," he said. "But the daylight basement must be covered by those trees; I can't find a view of it."

The house on his screen was two hundred and twenty-seven miles from our place.

"I've got to get a couple of things done," I told Sonny. "I'll be back way before we have to leave."

"You want me to come with you?"

"No, I think it's better if you stay here. Just in case Brenda calls back. In case anything changes."

"What about Bella Sweetshop?" he asked. "What if Ryan...?"

"Just keep him going," I said, leaving it in his hands.

———

IT WAS STILL LIGHT out when I pulled into the Tristell's driveway. If there were any police around, I couldn't see them.

Sara Tristell answered the door. Stepped back a little when she saw me, a fearful look on her face.

I stepped inside as if I'd been invited. Walked myself into their living room and sat.

"What...what's going on?"

"I need to speak to your husband," I told her. "It's really important. "

"He won't be home for—"

"I understand," I said. "But I thought maybe you could call him."

I watched her face closely. And then took a gamble of my own. "I need to talk to him as soon as possible, Mrs. Tristell."

"Sara," she said, her manners on auto-pilot.

"I need to talk to him as soon as possible, Sara," I said

again, not changing my tone, keeping the urgency out of it. "I don't know where the police are in all this. But if they're listening to his phone and they hear me asking to meet with him, they might...interfere."

"You're going to get Brenda?"

"I thought your husband might have a private number," I said, sliding past her question. "A number he gave you. You alone. A just-in-case number. Maybe on a cell phone? Or just a way of telling him to call you?"

She nodded. Slowly, as if taking in what I was saying bit by bit.

Then she got to her feet. "It might be better if you put your car in the garage," she said. "There's plenty of room in there. We can open one slot at a time, or all of them at once, depending on what we want."

———

Sara Tristell sat across from me while we were waiting. She asked me if I wanted anything...maybe some coffee? I told her thanks, but I didn't need anything. *Not from you,* I thought. Then I canceled that thought, suddenly realizing that she must have known more than I'd believed she did.

I didn't know what she'd told her husband, but it didn't matter. Either I was right about him or I wasn't. If I was wrong—and I'd never be able to say why I thought I wasn't, not in words that would make any sense—he wouldn't be coming back alone.

I settled into waiting. Sara Tristell did the same. It wasn't long before we heard a garage door slide open. She got up and left the room. In less than a minute, Robert Tristell took her place. He didn't offer to shake hands. Didn't greet me at all.

"This is what I can tell you," I said to him, keeping my voice level. "I don't know who Brenda is with—"

"That boy?"

"Not a boy," I said. "A man. A young man. But he's not a young man who's interested in marrying your daughter. He's not her boyfriend, although that's how Brenda regards him."

"So he's...what?"

"All this time she's been there, he's never even touched her," is all I said.

Robert Tristell went well south of quiet. He didn't move, didn't change expression.

"I don't know much about him," I went on. "And even what I think I know I could be wrong about. But I also think I know where they are. And, tomorrow, tomorrow some time, I hope to get your daughter away from him. And bring her back to you."

"Hope?"

"I'm going to do my best."

"And you need...?"

"A couple of pistols," I said, turning my cards face up. "Three would be better."

"I could get you some—"

"This is something I have to do myself."

He went back to his quiet. Finally he said: "I know."

———————

WHILE HE WAS GONE, I thought about what Robert Tristell meant with "I know." Very different from "I understand."

I didn't come up with anything.

Sara Tristell never came back to the living room.

It was quiet in there. I went over the plans I'd made. I

knew I could do the part I'd laid out for myself. I knew Sonny could do his job, too. It was Brenda I didn't know about.

It was well into darkness outside when I heard a garage door open again.

ROBERT TRISTELL HAD one of those soft carry-on bags that fit under a seat on an airplane. He was wearing deerskin driving gloves.

"A Colt Woodsman," he said, removing a long-barreled semi-auto from the bag. "Takes twenty-two long rifles, soft points. With this attached, it won't make more than a puff, even indoors," he went on, holding up a suppressor.

He put them both on the rug next to his chair.

"A Glock Nine," he said next. "Full magazine, nothing chambered. All hand-loads. Don't worry about the casings on either of those—they don't have stories to tell."

He put that one on the rug, too.

"A Ruger Three Fifty-Seven," he said, carefully placing a big, deep-blued revolver with a ventilated rib running over the barrel next to the other two. "Loaded with hardballs. Go through anything."

He looked over at me as if he was waiting for a sign. I didn't give him one, but he seemed satisfied.

"Used or not, you can leave them all wherever you want," he said. "They're as cold as the Arctic."

I nodded, waiting to see if there was more.

"If something goes wrong before...if anyone gets to ask, you bought them at a gun show. Years ago. Here's a list of them over the past few years," he said, dropping a piece of paper on the carpet. "Just pick any date that you could have been there. Pick a date—a day, too, once you settle. Doesn't have to be all that specific...say, some Sunday in May a couple of years ago."

I didn't even nod. Just sat there, waiting for the rest.

"So if you get stopped before...before you finish, the worst you're looking at is possession-of-unregistered. That happens, make a call. I'll give you a number to put in your phone. Your registered phone, not a burner.

That number's a lawyer. He'll answer no matter what time it is. And have you bonded out in an hour, wherever you are."

He re-packed the airline bag as I put on the gloves I'd brought with me.

Nothing special: plain black leather, thin. I picked up the bag with my left hand. He held out his right. We locked in the deal we'd never put into words.

SONNY PULLED the emergency SUV out of the shed while I checked all the gear. We moved out just past midnight. I'd budgeted six hours for the drive, leaving a considerable margin for things like a bad tire or the need to use another route because of an accident ahead.

It was mostly highway. Past farmland, mills, truck stops...broken up with bright billboards flashing promises like lottery tickets and casinos.

We were dressed for the outdoors. I had my father's old photography equipment stored in the back. In plain view. If anyone should ask why I was using such dated equipment, I'd explain that digital was a lifeless format—nothing could compete with the depth real emulsion film provided.

And if more questions came, we had been driving at those hours hoping to catch first light where we were headed, but I'd booked us for the three days in case we needed it: Thursday to drive, unpack, scout some good spots; Friday to work on Sonny's independent studies project—the one he'd cleared with his teacher while he'd been home with the flu. We had all Saturday to finish up and drive back home.

Photographing redtail hawks sky-dancing during the mating season was a tricky business. Sonny could explain more about that than any cop would ever want to know—he'd spent an hour working on his computer to get the details just right.

The pistols were in an aluminum compartment built into the back seat cushion. The kind of search the police do when they work up an excuse after a speeding ticket wouldn't ever turn them up. And no K-9 is trained to alert on plain clean metal—what would be the point if they had to sniff out drugs inside cars?

I had a complete set of ID in the Toyota, behind a false wall at the back of the glove box, but it didn't seem as though we'd need it. When I'd called around to the motels in the area, one of them said they couldn't take reservations.

"This is a court, not one of those concrete things," the woman on the phone said, proudly. "We have nine cabins, and it's first-come basis. Right now, we have three openings, but I can't make any promises."

"Do you take—"

"No American Express," the woman said, as if guessing what I was about to say. "And none of those phone things, either."

"That sounds fine," I told her. "It will be me and my two children. We're going to—"

"Hunt," the woman said, just short of impolitely bored. "There's plenty of birds around here this time of year. That's why folks come. If your kids are old enough to hunt, they'll need licenses, too."

"All right," I agreed, knowing she was telling me they sold those licenses. And that they'd take cash for the cabin.

———

SONNY HAD PRINTED out maps and driving directions, and he had those on the car's GPS, too. I had studied the images of the house where Brenda was staying, but I paid the most attention to where she and Sonny were supposed to meet—a small clearing in the area just past the expanse of flat land, less than a quarter mile off the road that ran past. That road was two-lane blacktop, with plenty of shoulder to pull over if you had a problem or just wanted to...walk around in the woods or whatever people did when it got dark.

We had lots of time to talk during the drive, and we'd used most of it with me answering Sonny's questions.

I only had one for him: "You told Brenda you'd just turned fifteen..."

"I just...I just felt like I had," he told me. "Remember, a long time ago, when you told me I could pick my own birthday?"

"I do."

"Well, I don't know, that was just an arbitrary number, wasn't it?"

"I guess it was. I mean, I could never really be sure, and you can't go by what any of...them say, but I could tell pretty close, even as small as you were, then."

Sonny didn't say anything.

"I don't mean small in size," I filled in the silence. "It was my way of saying you...you weren't a baby, exactly, but you were...I don't know, two, maybe? You knew words, but you didn't say anything until we were a good ways away from where I...found you.

"So I just took a guess, and that's the way the papers got made out. Now your birthday, that's another thing, entirely. I said you could pick for yourself because that's what was going to be just between us. You understand?"

"I do," he said. I thought he sounded like me when he said that. "I guess I thought maybe Brenda would feel...calmer, maybe. If she thought I was older. More..."

"Capable?"

"I think so. Most people don't know how capable we are. "

"Who's 'we' in that? You mean kids—people—people your age?"

"You can say 'kids,'" Sonny said, half-smiling. "It's just the way people talk. It doesn't mean anything. You can't be...capable unless you learn to be, isn't that true? So to the people who teach you to be capable, it's like you always stay a kid. To them, I mean."

"I didn't teach you to be capable, son. All that computer stuff. And the gambling. The grades you get in school. And...I guess I really didn't teach you much of anything, all the things you know."

"You taught me I could do all that," my son said. "You gave me room. Not like 'room-and-board' room, room like...space. A safe space. I'm not saying I even knew you were teaching me. I didn't know much about what you did. I didn't really know anything about it, not really. Not until all this happened."

"I didn't know how to tell you. It was like I kept missing my chance. And you kept growing."

"If you'd told me before, I know what I would have said. I would have said it didn't matter. What you did, I mean. You're my father. My real father."

"Would have said?" I wondered out loud, picking up on his tone.

"The last few hours. When we talked. What you told me. Now I know it does matter. What you did. It matters more than anything. But I don't think I can do it, Dad. I don't think I can—"

"I know you can," I cut him off. "Not what I did. I guess I've always known that, from the time you were a little boy. But that can't be the only way. Not the only way to carry on the line. It just can't."

"I know. What you said before, how you explained it to me...there's no one left to...do the things those other people who worked with you did."

"No middleman," I said, making it clear. "And no Abel. Mostly Abel. Without him, I couldn't even tell you where to start."

"I wouldn't—"

"I know. But you're smart. A lot smarter than I ever was. You can figure out a way. If you wanted to," I ended, realizing right then that I might be ending our line.

"I do want to," my son said. "Not because I have to, but...well, I do have to, don't I?"

I didn't have any words, so I just nodded.

I'D BEEN RIGHT about the motel court. They sold hunting licenses. Fishing licenses, too. No guns for sale, but they had stacks of boxed shotgun ammunition, right next to the energy drink machine.

The woman at the desk looked tired. Probably close

to the end of her shift, I thought...although she seemed more like an owner than a worker. She wrote down the name I gave her, took cash for a three-day stay, gave me a receipt that had the cabin number on it. One key, on a ring attached to a placard big enough to serve as a coaster for a beer mug.

"Park right in front of your door," the woman told me. If she was surprised I hadn't brought my children in with me or that we didn't need licenses, she didn't show it.

THE CABIN WAS PRETTY small by house standards, but it was huge compared to a motel setup. The front room had a couch and two chairs, a worn blue rug, and a TV with a cable box on top with one of those triangular pieces of cardboard telling you what was available on pay-for-view. There was a bedroom with a pair of beds, a kitchenette with a refrigerator and a microwave, and a bathroom with a stall shower.

"Where you have to meet Brenda, that's only a few minutes from here," I said. "Want to catch a couple of hours of sleep?"

"I'm not sleepy," Sonny said. And he didn't look it. Didn't look wired, either. Just ready to do what we'd come to do.

"Then let's both take a look at where we have to work," I said.

WE FOUND a good place to park. I carried the camera bag. Sonny hefted the tripod. It was three hundred and forty of my paces to where the woods opened onto the clearing.

"It's a good spot," Sonny said. "There's clear sky overhead. If the redtails show up, we'll be in a perfect position for me to get what I need for my project."

I didn't say anything, still looking around. The pistols were in the car—I hadn't ever touched them with my bare hands.

Finally, I found a good spot where I could wait. I pointed it out to Sonny. "It's too far away for me to hear whatever you'll be saying, you and Brenda. But it's close enough for me to cover the whole space. So if anyone but Brenda shows up..."

"If that happens, what should I do?"

"See that tree? The one lying on the ground? It's a monster. Probably fell over from age. Been there a long time. If you sit there, facing me, facing where we're standing now, you'll be looking at whoever comes from your right, through that opening. See it?"

"Yes."

"So be sitting on that tree like you're at a table in a restaurant, waiting for her to join you. If she shows by herself, you know what to do. It'll be your play after that —you know what we want to accomplish; you've got your own plan for that.

"So listen carefully, now, son: If anyone but Brenda comes through that opening, you move to your left, understand? Fast! Roll to your left and get flat on the ground. Then just wait. Whatever happens, it won't be long.

"If I'm still here when it's over, come to me. If I'm not, keep going to your left and circle around to the car. You've got your own keys. Just get in and drive home.

Don't go back to the cabin. Just get in and drive. Not too fast. You know how to do it."

I couldn't see Sonny, but I could feel him nodding his understanding. "When you get home, put the car back in the shed. Go in the house and wait. If I don't get there by Monday, just go to school, like usual. The police will come by, sooner or later. Depends on what happens with Brenda. What you tell the police is the truth. I took off Wednesday night. After that, all you know is that you haven't seen me since."

"Dad..."

"I don't expect things to go like that," I told my son. "But if they do, you can find your own way."

"My way home?"

"Your own way in life," I told him. "When Robert Tristell comes by the house—and he will, sooner or later —you tell him the truth. The whole truth. Whatever that truth turns out to be, that's what you tell him. He'll help you after that. But no matter what he does to help you, you still find your own way. Understand?"

I looked back at Sonny. His eyes were wet, but his voice was steady. "I do," is all he said.

———————

BACK IN THE CABIN, I didn't want to go over the plan with Sonny again. He might take it as a lack of faith, and I didn't want to take a chance on unsettling him. And I knew he was comfortable with silence.

About an hour to go.

Sonny spoke up: "Remember when you said you'd be able to see us, but not hear what we're saying?"

"Yes," is all I said.

"I'm pretty sure I've got a way to fix that. I'll have my arms crossed over my chest, like this." Sonny sat on the bed, facing me. The way he crossed his arms, each hand was in the opposite pocket of his field jacket. [not sure I can visualize that] "When I see Brenda, I'll tap a button on my phone. That will call you. My phone will be on speaker, and we'll set yours to vibrate. You tap the button to answer. But, first, you plug this in. It's the connector to the earpiece. You'll be able to hear pretty well, I think. Me, for sure. Brenda, it will depend on how close she is to me, or how loud she talks."

"Do you want to test it first?" I asked.

"Good idea," he said, smiling almost indulgently, like he was the one teaching, and he was pleased I'd caught on.

IF SONNY WAS upset watching as I threaded the silencer into the Colt, he didn't show it. We left the car where we had before and walked for a bit before we split up. I found my spot and lay down flat. In a couple of minutes, Sonny came around and took up his position on the log.

We were about twenty minutes early, but Sonny was barely settled when a girl walked into the clearing. She was shorter than I had expected—I couldn't say why I had any expectations at all, but I'd thought she'd be closer to Sonny's height. Wearing a long off-white coat with two red stripes across the front, one of those hats that droops over one eye. It matched the coat, even down to the stripes.

Sonny stood up, gestured with his hand for Brenda to sit down. She sat a little distance from him, as if she was keeping her options open.

My phone vibrated. I tapped the button. Brenda's voice came through clearly.

"Hi, Sonny," she said. "Hi, Brenda."

"I'm a little nervous."

"There's nothing to be nervous about," Sonny told her. "We had a deal, you and me. And I'll keep up my end."

"I...I know. But I can't...I can't just..."

"I promised to show you something," Sonny said. "So let me do that. Then, whatever you decide..."

Brenda shifted position, turning more directly to Sonny. But she didn't make a sound.

Sonny reached into an inside pocket of his field jacket and took out a tablet.

"It's all on here," he said. "This is a page to look at first."

I eye-swept the clearing. If anyone else was out there, they were better than I was.

"Who is this?" Brenda asked, looking at the tablet.

"I don't know her real name," Sonny said. "On the page, she's 'Bella Sweetshop.'"

"What a name!"

"It's because she thinks she's fat, I guess."

"She is a little bit of a chubbo," Brenda said, a little bubble of a smile in her voice.

"Okay," Sonny said. "Now look at this."

"That's...that's Ryan's picture. Not...not real Ryan, but it's the picture he used when he—"

"It's the picture he always uses," Sonny told her. "This is him. On a new page he made. See? He doesn't look like that in real life. But this is his car for real, isn't it?"

Brenda didn't answer. Her head moved a little, but I couldn't tell if she was nodding in agreement.

"See what he's doing, Brenda? Doing with this page he made?"

The whole clearing went quiet for a little bit, as if the whole forest was waiting for her to answer.

"Are you saying he—"

"They're talking, Brenda," Sonny said. "To each other, talking. Here's a message string I grabbed."

Silence again as Brenda tapped the tablet with her forefinger a couple of times.

"He's the same," she finally said. "The same as he was with me."

"There's more," Sonny told her. "Here..."

I knew the message string Sonny was showing her. It was the one he'd constructed himself, a mirror of messages between Ryan and Brenda. On the tablet, Ryan was going to meet Bella. They were going to go away. Be together.

"This is a trick," Brenda said. "It's a trick to make me..."

"It's no trick, Brenda," Sonny said. "This is what he does. Ryan, or whatever his real name is. He—"

"Martin. That's his real name, Martin."

"Maybe."

"No, it is," Brenda said earnestly. "He's got all his ID. He showed me himself. He's twenty-four. All grown. He has a job and—"

"His job is getting girls," Sonny said, his voice heavier with the extra it was carrying.

"But what could he do with...girls? He can't marry more than one—"

"He's not marrying anyone, Brenda. He gets girls, young girls, to come

and stay with him. But they're not waiting to get married; they're waiting to get...taken away."

"Sonny, that can't be true. You don't know him. He's a real...gentleman, I think my father would call him. He's never even...tried anything. He said we had to wait until we were married. He wanted me to be pure. He always said that. Pure."

"It's not Ryan—Martin—whoever he is, it's not him that you had to be pure for. Understand?"

"I don't..."

Sonny didn't say anything. Brenda put her face in her hands.

Sonny stood up. Put a hand on her shoulder, as gently as if he was capturing a butterfly.

When she stood up, I could see her face was tear-streaked, but she still hadn't made a sound.

Sonny held out his hand. They walked away, together.

————

"THIS IS MY FATHER," Sonny said, as he and Brenda climbed into the back seat.

I didn't say a word on the drive back to the cabin. I left the two of them there and went back to where I'd parked before.

I found the same spot, but it wouldn't work. Too far away.

I circled around so I was in position behind the big log. With the balaclava and gloves matching the mottled green of my jacket and pants, I was a blot in the forest.

Then I waited.

————

I DON'T KNOW what Sonny was saying to Brenda. But I knew what was happening, provided everything worked like we'd rehearsed. Brenda would be lying down, probably already sleepy from what Sonny put in the big glass of apple juice with lots of ice—her favorite—that she had been sipping. And Sonny would be on her phone, texting to the number she had for Ryan.

Remembering to first tap the red button Ryan told her to use only in an emergency.

====================

I'm sorry, M. I'm so sorry.

           Sorry? For what?

I ran away. Not with you. Not like we said. Just now, I ran away.

           Where?

Not far. I was going to go home, but I couldn't. I guess I knew I couldn't, but I wanted to...I don't know.

           What are you saying?

I was *going* to go. But I only got as far as the woods.

           What woods?

Just across the big field. On the other side where the road runs. I was going to hitch a ride. But I couldn't.

           You couldn't get a ride?

I didn't *try*, M. There's a clearing. In the woods, just a little ways from the road that goes past. There's a big log there. That's where I hurt myself. So I sat down to think. But I couldn't think, I was so scared.

>   *Scared of what?*

Of losing you. I want to come back. But I thought you'd be mad.

>   *I'm not mad, B. I could never be mad at you.*

I knew it! Say it, M. I need to hear you say it now.

>   *I love you.*

I love you too.

>   *Just come home. I'll meet you and we'll—*

I can't! That's how I hurt myself. I twisted my ankle over a stupid tree root. When I try and walk, I just fall over again. It really hurts. When I try and stand up. I think I broke something.

> *It's probably just a sprained ankle, honey. We'll put ice on it. And I've got some pain pills for you too. Don't worry. I'll come and get you. I'm close by. Just be calm. I'll be right there.*

You promise?

>   *Of course! Just stay there. I know where it is. I'll find you.*

Hurry, okay?

On my way.

I HEARD the menacing sound some cars make from their exhaust pipes. But it wasn't coming from the road; it was behind me. Closing in. Branches cracked. The car was coming, slowly. I shifted position, moving back to put myself deeper into cover.

A car poked its nose into the edge of the clearing. A white Mustang with blue racing stripes. A man got out, leaving the engine running. He moved toward the back of the fallen tree. "Brenda?" he called out.

He was a pudgy young man in a white shirt over black slacks with a white stripe running down the seams. His black sneakers had a white band running all around them, matching the soles. He had a round face, longish dark hair, eyes invisible behind yellow-lensed glasses.

I stepped out of the woods and shot him in the chest. The pistol hardly made a sound, but it did spook some birds into taking off.

He grabbed where his heart was, made some grunting noise as I closed the distance, shooting him twice more in the chest. He fell down. I stood over him and put two more rounds into his head.

Then I walked to his car, turned off the ignition, and threw the key ring as far as I could. I removed the suppressor and put it and the pistol in the console between the front seats.

I walked back to my car, the Glock now in my hand.

I LEFT the two unused pistols in the first gas station bathroom we ran across on the drive back. Then I took off my gloves and washed my hands. I didn't wipe down any of the surfaces—most of those places had cameras scattered all around, and I didn't want to do anything I couldn't account for if it came to that.

For a few seconds, I thought about the pistols I'd left all around the country. In dumpsters, alleys, pickup truck beds...I guessed they'd all been found. Some of them even turned in, maybe.

Brenda came around pretty quick. She and Sonny stayed in the back seat as I drove. I couldn't hear a lot of what they were saying to each other, but I could tell by the tone and volume that she was calm.

When we got within twenty miles of home, I called Robert Tristell. He was there with his wife when we dropped Brenda at their house.

———

SONNY SPENT Friday night working on his computers. "Scrubbing," he called it. My job was Brenda's phone. I took it apart as much as I could, then I put the pieces into a heavy steel bowl and went to work on it with a sledgehammer that I held upside down, pounding it like a mortar and pestle.

Then I added some sulfuric acid I kept in the workshop for etching the metal plates that I attached to some of the birdhouses I sold. When I finished, it was just a pool of dark liquid.

ON MONDAY, Sonny went back to school.

SUMMER SNUCK UP ON US. Other things, too, not just the season. I didn't see as much of Sonny as I usually did. He was out a lot. Doing things. I guess at his age he could think of a lot of things to do.

Sometimes I wondered about Brenda, but I never asked if Sonny spoke to her. I was glad she was back with her parents, but, mostly, I was grateful that Sonny hadn't had to be around when I killed Ryan. Or Martin. Or whatever his real name was.

Sonny had never asked me about that part. But he had other questions. Questions I didn't have answers for. Who was Ryan collecting girls for? How many others were there like Ryan? Who was in charge of all that? What did I think they'd do when Ryan turned up dead?

"That wasn't our job," is all I had to offer. "But who knows what the police will find when they go through his computer. And his phone. And anything else they come across."

"But...what you told me. About...us. Those people, the ones Ryan must have been working for, that's Them, aren't they? All of those people, them?"

"I guess that's true," is all I had.

"I wish we could put them all in the same place," my son said. "Like inside Dodger Stadium."

I knew what he was going to say next, so I stopped him. "That wouldn't be anywhere near big enough to hold them all, son."

He didn't say anything for a good while. Then he looked up: "We—I mean all of us, we—we know how to find them, don't we? Like you said, they always show us where they are. But even if we could find them all, we couldn't just shoot them, not one at a time."

"No." It was all I had.

"That doesn't mean there isn't another way," Sonny said.

Maybe that will be your way, I thought. But I didn't say anything.

IT WAS a hot day in August when a call came in from a number I didn't recognize. "I owe you," Robert Tristell's voice said.

"No, you don't," I answered him.

"An explanation," he said, as if I hadn't spoken.

THAT NIGHT, I left Sonny working on what he called his "playoff prediction matrix" and drove over to the Tristell house.

Sara Tristell brought me a tall glass of lemonade, heavily iced, with a sprig of mint. Then she sat down on their couch across from me.

"Why did you think I could get you what you need-ed?" Robert Tristell asked.

I flicked my eyes to the side, raised my eyebrows.

"We're not talking in code here," he answered my unspoken question. "Not between us. Sara knows everything. She always has. But, still, you don't have to be specific if it makes you uncomfortable. This house is swept every day. Physical and electronic. Audio is blocked and jammed. There's more, too. All just a business precaution, nothing to do with you, understand?"

I nodded. Carefully and deliberately. To each of them

individually. "You're really here to listen," Robert Tristell said. "I'm the one who owes, not you."

————

I STILL DIDN'T SAY anything.

"So?" he spoke into the silence. That's when I knew he was still waiting for an answer to his question.

"It was just a guess, that you could get me what I needed," I told him. "From the way you handled yourself with the police. That thing about you know some lawyers. So casual, like it was just part of your life.

"This town, it's like any other town. Things go on here. Business things. None of my business. But I know someone has to run those businesses. "

"Just a guess, is that right?" Robert Tristell said. Not quite dead-on skeptical, but floating around its edges.

"A guess, plus the time pressure," I told him. "There wasn't time enough for me to...get everything I needed to do what I had to do. I didn't know if I was right. About your business, I mean. Like I said, not my business. But even if I was wrong about what I...guessed, one thing I was confident of: You had money. And that's all it would take to get me what I needed as quick as I needed it. Money."

"Logical," Robert Tristell said. Made me think of the way Sonny talked sometimes.

"And I knew you'd do anything for your—"

"It wasn't an accident that I came to your house that day," Sara Tristell said, like she was a scalpel cutting into the tissue of the polite dance her husband and I were doing.

I tried to keep my face flat as I turned to face her, but it was Robert Tristell who spoke next.

"You had to go away for a while," he said. "Before you came back. And inherited the business from your father."

I felt a banging inside my chest. But I said nothing.

"I did the same thing," he went on. "Not exactly the same as you, but for the same people. How do you think I knew you wouldn't need extra ammo for any of the tools I gave you?"

Why didn't I? I asked myself. Thinking how it had never occurred to me to even so much as wonder about that.

"Only, when I came back, I inherited a different business than you did," Robert Tristell said. "We came back about the same time, but we went different ways after that."

A shockwave hit me. Not because of what I thought Robert Tristell was saying. I knew there were more like me—I just never expected to meet one.

But that wasn't the shock. The shock was Sara Tristell. She wasn't just his wife. She was his partner.

I knew we could kill. I knew it from my father. I knew it from my own life. And I knew the equation: We take one of us from one of them. One at a time.

Taking one of us from one of them, that took something from us.

Money, that's what it took. A lot of money. I didn't necessarily think we were all assassins. There were a lot of ways to get a lot of money. I knew we were a lot of different things, in a lot of different places.

I didn't know we could mate.

———

"YOU WANT to know how I came to know. How I came to know...you, right?" Robert Tristell asked. "Remember what you said before. About how you marked me telling the police that I knew some lawyers myself? I wasn't lying about that. I know a lot of lawyers. In my business, they're a necessity. But one of the lawyers I know, used to know, you knew him, too.

"Abel," he said into my silence. "It was my father who brought me to him. He was my father's lawyer first."

I shook my head.

"I get it," Robert Tristell said, very softly. "You're thinking, why would Abel tell me about you, but never you about me."

I nodded, still not speaking.

"It was a safety play," he went on. "A just-in-case. Like I said, we both came back. And took over the businesses that had been left to us. Abel wanted to make sure I'd be...available. In case anything came up where you needed me. Only that's not the way it worked out."

"Just in case?" is all I said.

"What you do, what you did, it was always possible that the law could come around someday. If that happens, there's a lot of...outcomes, depending on what you do next. You might need a top lawyer. Some money. Some help with ID. Or to just disappear. But, if you did that last thing, well...well, you really couldn't, could you? Not once..."

He didn't have to say Sonny's name for me to fill in that blank.

"In my safe deposit box, there's a set of guardianship papers. The ones you signed. So Sonny would be raised by us."

"I never—"

"Yes, you did," he said. "It's your signature, notarized by Abel himself. You signed a lot of papers in his office over the years.

"That was in case something happened," he went on. "Something where I had to help. Say by getting you lawyers—real lawyers, not like the one you used to wind up your father's estate; he's a low-level hack. Lawyers for doing things in court. Or, better, for fixing things so they didn't have to go that route.

"If it went like that, there'd be no need for those guardianship papers. You'd be out from under whatever it was. You'd be with Sonny. Until he was grown, anyway. But if you had to go, that's when those papers would matter. Even if it was a car accident, or a heart attack, or anything like that, same thing. We couldn't leave Sonny for the authorities," he said, just a touch of contempt over that last word.

I just shook my head, thinking *Abel*.

"Abel," Robert Tristell said aloud. "Your father trusted him. So did mine. Because he was one of us."

I was still on "us" when Sara Tristell spoke up. "If Robert ever had to...leave, I would be the one raising Brenda. But you, you don't have anyone. No partner to do that for Sonny. So if you did...have to leave, then those papers would come out. But only then."

I stood to go. Thinking Sonny was close to where he could raise himself if...

Sara Tristell cut into my thoughts. Cut in so deep it was as if we were sharing the same space. "If you had to leave. For any reason, it doesn't matter, then Sonny should be with his own people. Raised with his sister.

Don't you think that's right? That Sonny would be best, his best, if he was cared for by us?"

"I do," is all I could get out. I left the "now" unspoken.

I stood up, shook hands with the Tristells, not saying a word. Then I drove home to my son.

IF YOU LIKED THIS, YOU MAY LIKE DOHERTY'S WAR AND AGAINST THE ROPES: TWO CHARLIE DOHERTY PULP THRILLERS

BY TERRENCE MCCAULEY

AWARD-WINNING AUTHOR TERRENCE MCCAULEY WHIPS UP A FAST-PACED PULP THRILLER REMINISCENT OF THE CLASSIC GANGSTER MOVIES OF OLD.

1918 –As a corrupt patrolman in New York City, Charlie Doherty had the ward bosses of Tammany Hall and other political cronies to watch his back. But in the hell-storm that became known as the Battle of Belleau Wood, only his rifle and his training keep him alive.

A world at war. A lone marine fighting to survive.

Fast-forward to 1925 where pugilistic prowess is discussed anywhere and everywhere. On the tough streets of New York City, boxer Terry Quinn is on the rise. The heavyweight title is within his grasp but the gangsters pulling the strings in the fight racket have other ideas and will do whatever it takes to get Quinn in line.

Hard answers to hard questions drive a story that isn't going where you think it is and make for one heck of a ride you don't want to miss.

AVAILABLE NOW

ABOUT THE AUTHOR

Andrew Vachss was a federal investigator (USPHS), a social-services caseworker, a labor organizer, and directed a maximum-security institution for "aggressive-violent" youth. He was a lawyer in private practice, and he represented children and youth exclusively. His articles and essays have appeared in Parade, Antaeus, Esquire, Playboy, the New York Times, MSNBC, the New York Daily News, Newsday, the ABA Journal, and the Journal of Psychohistory, along with numerous other forums. He is the author of more than thirty novels and three collections of short stories, which have earned him such international awards as the Grand Prix de Littéra-ture Policiére (France), the Falcon Award from the Maltese Falcon Society of Japan, the Deutschen Krimi Preis (Germany) and the Raymond Chandler Award (Italy), as well as song lyrics, graphic novels, essays, and a "Children's Book for Adults."

CPSIA information can be obtained
at www.ICGtesting.com
Printed in the USA
LVHW040618250122
709219LV00004B/124

9 781639 772414